FIONA PARTRIDGE is an award-winning Holistic Therapist and Teacher.

Having always been a bookworm, you'll tend to find her nose deep in a good book, or possibly fast asleep with a book on her face!

Originally from the majestic Forest of Dean, Fiona now lives in Worcestershire with her husband, daughter and their two cats.

The Colour of Marriage is Fiona's debut novel. Why not pop over and say hello at www.fionapartridge.co.uk and tell her what you think?

The
Colour
of
Marriage

FIONA
PARTRIDGE

SilverWood

Published in 2021 by SilverWood Books

SilverWood Books Ltd
14 Small Street, Bristol, BS1 1DE, United Kingdom
www.silverwoodbooks.co.uk

ISBN 978-1-80042-108-0 (paperback)
ISBN 978-1-80042-109-7 (ebook)

British Library Cataloguing in Publication Data
A CIP catalogue record for this book is
available from the British Library

Page design and typesetting by SilverWood Books

Always and all-ways for Jonner
Tooty Toot
Missing you gets harder with each passing day, knowing how
much wonder you are missing, but being thankful for
all the wonder you taught me to see.
I love you, Porgy
Nofe

Acknowledgements

Firstly, thank you to you! Thank you for being brave enough to venture into the world of *The Colour of Marriage*. I hope you enjoy reading it as much as I enjoyed writing it.

Secondly, thank you to my wonderful family – my husband Daz, who I pestered constantly, asking "Is this a word?" "No dear, you've just made that one up!!" and my beautiful daughter Charlotte, who was insistent that a character be named after her. One day maybe, darling!!!

Finally, thank you to my folks – Mum for being the first person to read this, and messaging me at silly o'clock in the morning – "GET IT PUBLISHED!" – after sitting up all night reading it, and for my dad, who hasn't read it yet. Dad, you have no excuse now!!!

Love you all so very much.

Don't forget to visit my website and tell me what you think. www.fionapartridge.co.uk

Enjoy,
Fi

One

How It All Began…

So here we go, an honest, frank, graphic, brutal and captivating story all about the colour of marriage.

Why am I writing this?

Because I need to be accountable, responsible and proud, always and all-ways.

My name is Rob Lawson, husband to Annie, father to Lexie, Louis… Oh and hoomon Dad to Beau, the four-legged final member of our family.

This story begins at the end, middle and beginning of my life as I knew it.

I went to the University of Worcester, where I studied marketing. Those years were the best times of my life, and it is a fantastic city for a young person to be in. Captivating history, architecture, great cafés and bistros and a roaring nightlife, all while being on the banks of the beautiful River Severn.

Being a student, I frequented the local coffee shops within the city walls. The Busy Bean Company was my favourite; it was warm, bustling and welcoming. Sofas and squishy armchairs dotted around the old arched building that rested under the railway line. The whole building would shake when the trains passed overhead. I loved it; if I close my eyes, I can still smell the mix of old oil, brewing coffee and cooking bacon. Now I look back at this period of my life and I know that this is where it began – my two life obsessions, coffee shops and… The reason I loved The Busy Bean Company was the owner's choice of staff. Namely, one Annie Stephens.

To me, Annie was a vision of perfection. I've since found out (via my best friend) that in the early days, I was incapable of having a conversation with anyone else while in the café if Annie was working. Apparently, I would sit there "open-mouthed, catching flies!"

I'm not sure that's entirely true, but I do know I found her captivating. She wasn't like the girls I'd previously been attracted to. She was quiet, shy and entertaining all rolled into a perfect little package.

While working, she always wore her blonde hair up out of the way; she hated when it fell in front of her face. She never wore any make-up, her natural beauty never needing any help. Her gorgeous deep brown eyes always looking from this to that. I could have spent hours just staring into those deep, rich, chocolate-coloured eyes. Her clothes were always functional, never the latest trends. Her sense of humour was one of the things I liked most about her; she was so witty, so dry and so bloody quick. She ran rings around me and I didn't care.

I, however, wasn't a catch, or at least that's what I thought! In those days I was six foot three inches and weighed about eleven stone. It's fair to say I was a bit scrawny. My mop of uncontrollable brown hair took on a different look with each passing day. I'd stopped trying to style it with every hair product under the sun back in Year 10. My clothes, although clean, never matched. I liked to think I was leading the pack rather than following it. Truth is, no one was following me – no one!!!! I've always thought my best feature is my eyes. The brightest blue. People are always telling me they look like the bluest oceans. More often than not, it's also the first thing people notice about me and comment on.

After a few weeks of bravely visiting the café every day, I plucked up the courage and started talking to Annie. I found out that she was working part-time in the café while attending the local technical college. She spent most of her free time focusing on her love of painting. She carried a sketch book in her satchel and when she was on her break, sat outside the café to capture the beauty of the moving river. I started timing my visits so that I could sit outside with her while she painted.

From those early days just relaxing by the river, I can honestly say I have never felt more comfortable with another human, not even my folks or best friend. Annie listened to me, took an interest in me, and I couldn't get enough of her. I wanted to know everything about her, everything that interested her. Being around her made my heart soar. I know it's smooshy for a bloke to say that, but it's true.

We'd been having our little rendezvous by the river for about six weeks before I found the courage to ask her if she'd like to go out on a date with me. God, I was so nervous, I couldn't even eat my breakfast! Who knew that uttering those seven words would be so bloody scary?

"Annie, will you go out with me?"

She stopped sketching mid-stroke, slowly lifted her head and locked eyes with me as a slow smile spread across her beautiful face.

"I thought you were never going to ask, Lawson! 'Bout time. A girl can get bored waiting, you know." She smirked.

Returning back to her sketch pad, she continued: "Although I have one condition: nothing ordinary for the date. I'm not a pub lunch or bowling girl. You need to be creative." Without missing a stroke, she carried on capturing the kids feeding the ducks further down the bank from us.

"Not a problem Miss Stephens, not a problem."

With that, I spent the next three days (seventy-two hours, 4,320 minutes) in utter fear! I had no idea what I'd agreed to. The fact that I was going on a date with Annie Stephens was all-consuming, let alone the fact the date had to be memorable, unique and creative! What the hell…? For those three days I didn't even go to my lectures. I became a hermit in halls. I was frozen with the pressure. I knew within my very soul that Annie was the woman I would marry. Therefore, I had to get this right. For the first time in my life, I had to get it right.

Calling on everything I'd learned from our chats sitting next to the river over the previous weeks, I created what I hoped would be the best afternoon of Annie's life.

Drum roll, folks…

I borrowed my dad's car for the day (a red Nissan Nova called Nikki) and I took Annie to Sanders Park, a quiet park about twenty minutes' drive from Worcester. In the boot of the car, I had my mum's wicker picnic hamper (and was on strictest orders not to lose it, make a mess in it or in any way, shape or form defile it – "it's from Fortnum and Mason, Robert!!!") and filled it with Annie's favourite food – cheese and pickle sandwiches, pickled onion flavoured Monster Munch and of course a tub of cheese and pineapple, apples, green grapes (not red), little cans of lemonade, cherryade and Tizer. Pudding was, of course, sherbet dips.

Taking the picnic blanket, we sat next to the duck pond in the middle of the park and watched the locals enjoying family time together, kids learning to ride their bicycles, older kids learning to pull tricks on their skateboards. No music was needed. The sounds of life and happiness were our soundtrack.

I asked Annie to sit facing the duck pond as I laid all the food out on the blanket, straightening this, fussing with that. Finally, I felt it was as ready as it was ever going to be.

"All ready," I said.

She turned round and gasped, hands to her mouth. Was it a good gasp? A "Holy crap" gasp? Or an "Oh good grief" gasp? I couldn't tell!! My heart was going ten to the dozen as I stared at her, trying, searching for any sort of hint that would tell me if I'd done good.

She jumped up and ran to me, wrapping her arms round my neck.

"You did good, Lawson. You did good." She pulled away from me with the biggest grin on her face.

We must have sat in the park for three hours. Slowly the food I'd prepared with Mum's help disappeared, and the park filled and emptied of people. We loved people-watching. Making up stories about those who walked past. We laughed. We swapped stories. We learned so much about each other. The whole time it was…natural. I never felt like I had to pretend to be someone I wasn't. Never had to put on an act, or try hard to impress her. I was just me. I would find out years later that Annie felt exactly the same. In fact,, her words were that she felt, "It was a connection of the souls", and she was so right.

After we'd eaten, we fed the ducks our scraps and watched the sunset. It was perfect.

We ended the night as I dropped her back to her parent's house. Annie turned in the front seat and looked at me. I knew we were going to kiss. I knew it in my bones, and as I leaned in for it to happen, Annie uttered the words that resonate within my heart to this day:

"You'll do, Lawson. You'll do!"

Then she kissed me. As our lips touched, fireworks went off inside my body. I had never, ever felt anything like it in my life. I had had girlfriends prior to Annie – I'd even kissed girls who hadn't been my girlfriend, but none of them caused such a response within my very core. I have no idea how long our first kiss lasted – could have been seconds, could have been hours. It was amazing.

As Annie pulled away from me, her face no more than an inch from mine, she stared deep into my eyes and repeated, "You'll do." With her lopsided smile, she opened the car door and, with that, she was gone. All that was left was the lingering smell of her perfume, while I remained half leaning across my seat, with the stupidest grin on my face. That grin lasted for weeks.

Eighteen months later we moved into our first home together and it was the happiest day, filled with joy, laughter, lost kettles and boxes breaking open in the middle of the street – like most people's moving days, I assume. Bridge Walk was to me the most impressive combination of bricks and mortar I'd ever seen. In truth, it was a tiny flat in among many other identical flats. But that didn't matter.

I'd got my own place, with my beautiful girlfriend. I was living the life of a grown-up!

The day consisted of much organisation as I was moving from close to the university and Annie from her folks' house near Bewdley. Travelling up the M5 towards Bromsgrove for what felt like the umpteenth time, with my little red Micra rammed to the roof on what would be the final trip, I knew this was the beginning of the rest of my life, and I was so happy. Mum and Dad were loaded up and following me. Life was good.

Annie and her parents were already at the flat when we arrived. They'd clearly had an early start – Annie's doing, I'm sure! She had been itching for weeks to nest-build for us. Constantly talking about where this would go, and how she couldn't wait to own a pantry: "Can you believe it Lawson, an actual pantry. I could make jam and everything!!" That was my Ann, so excited about the little things in life – the things that I wouldn't even think twice about.

Dad and Malc, Ann's dad, wandered up into the village around 2pm-ish and came back with fish and chips for everyone. I can honestly say it was the best meal I've ever had. The six of us squished into the living room of our one-bedroomed-flat, me and Annie on the floor in among the many boxes. It was brilliant – one of my most treasured memories.

After our folks had left and it was just us two and our new four walls, Annie came up behind me and wrapped her arms round me and whispered:

"Lawson, I'll live with you, but on one condition – we never go to bed mad with each other, ever."

In that moment, I couldn't see a time when either of us would ever be mad. I was genuinely happy, content and ready for the rest of my life that I'd share with my beautiful Ann.

Twelve months to the day of our moving in, over an anniversary meal of cheese and pickle sandwiches, I got down on one knee and asked my beautiful Annie if she'd be my wife. I wasn't nervous, I wasn't scared, I was ready. Annie's answer was: "Of course I'll bloody marry you, Lawson, but there's one condition. Every day of our lives should be filled with love, laughter and magic."

I couldn't have agreed with her more. I loved this woman with all my heart and never wanted anything but happiness for her.

Two

How It All Began…To Go Wrong

Fast forward eight years and two children – and Beau, our Cockapoo who loves to steal socks – later.

Annie and I moved on from the flat, to the home we bought together for our family. 16 Chestnut Grove was ideal; all it was missing was a white picket fence. It had room for more stuff than we actually needed! Annie is an amazing home-maker, taking pride in everything – the glasses in the display cabinet always sparkle and we've got more reed diffusers than the air freshener aisle of the local supermarket. She provides for all of us – clean clothes and warm nutritious meals each night. She never moaned once. In fact, I think she loved doing it.

I graduated with honours from University five years ago. After floating from one job to another for a while, I saw an advert for a position at Morris and Co, a global marketing consultancy company that mainly works overseas. However, about three years ago the company had to change its business model and move outside its historical business partnerships. This meant moving further afield and venturing, successfully, into Europe. Thankfully, while being interviewed by the owner of the company, David Morris, I knew nothing of the trials and stresses of the coming years.

Lexie Rose was born six years ago, two weeks after we moved into Chestnut Grove. She was the image of Annie – long lashes. The most beautiful baby I'd ever seen. If I thought it was a shock when Ann told me I was going to be a dad, I was NOT prepared for actually BEING a dad. Our whole world was turned upside down. Life as we knew it was gone. Annie was exhausted, our marriage and relationship was pushed to the back row. Lexie took all our energy, attention and money!

I remember the day we brought Lexie home. Back to our family home. I drove like an old man the whole way from the hospital. I was so scared that someone would hurt my baby. I'd never been so fearful. That fifteen-minute journey was the longest of my life. I vividly remember Annie telling me I was being an idiot: "Lawson, will you stop acting like a plonker! This is a 70mph road. Driving at 40mph is going to get us killed!"

"I'm being careful, Ann. She's the most precious thing in the world."

"Fair enough, old man. I can't argue with you about that." I could see her staring at our bundle of joy in the rear-view mirror. My heart skipped a beat. My girls, my beautiful girls. My two weeks' paternity leave went by in a haze of nappy changes, sleepless nights and endless loads of washing babygrows. But God, I loved it. That bubble of the three of us was fantastic. No, honestly, it really was.

Unfortunately, five days after Annie came home, her midwife was on her daily visit when she said she felt it best if Annie went back to the delivery suite. She was concerned that her section wound had become infected. I called her parents and they came straight away. I'd planned to take Annie to the hospital myself as she wasn't allowed to drive, but when it was time to go, Ann became quite emotional about leaving Lexie, so I said I'd stay with the baby.

Five hours later, they came home, Annie armed with a bag of pills from the hospital pharmacy, Malc with bags from the local chip shop and May with bags of nappies.

"How's our baba?" asked Annie, making a beeline for Lexie, who was fast asleep in her Moses basket.

"Absolutely golden. We played on the floor for a while. She was fascinated by kicking her legs – it was adorable. How did you get on?"

"Yes, it's infected. They couldn't believe that the consultant had stapled me, exactly what Julie, our midwife, said. Anyway, upshot is I've got a course of antibiotics, which need to go in the fridge, and some sort of cream or powder that I've got to put directly on the scar three times a day."

There was more though, I knew it. I could tell by her face, something she wasn't saying.

"What's wrong, Ann?"

She stood up from looking in the basket and stared me in the face. "The antibiotics will come through the milk, Lawson. I won't be able to breastfeed her anymore." Tears began falling. My poor Ann was heartbroken.

"Oh, my love." I engulfed her in the biggest hug and held her as she sobbed. "It's ok. It's ok. Lexie will be fine. I'll go to the supermarket now and I'll buy all the formula food. She's going to be fine. She is, you know, because she's got the best mommy in the world."

A louder sob escaped.

May came in and took her daughter in her arms and consoled her. I went into the kitchen, where Malc had been left to dish up the food.

"It'll be alright, son. She just needs a bit of time to get her head around it. It's just the fact that her choice of feeding the baby has been taken away from her. She's not had a say in it." He grabbed hold of me and pulled me into a hug. "Right, you go and get your shoes on. We'll go in my car to the shop and get everything that's needed. We can eat this when we get back. Let May look after Ann for a bit. Sometimes a girl just needs her mum."

I can't say for sure when it was – but I'd guess at around the time Lexie was ten months old – I started to realise that I was going to work for a rest, a break, and I was staying a little bit longer than I needed to, not much, but the odd half-hour here and there. Don't get me wrong, it wasn't that I didn't want to be with both the girls, it's just that the endless cycle of nappies, bottles and naps was relentless, exhausting and, if I'm honest, a bit grim. Any free time we had when Lexie was sleeping or being looked after by our folks was completely consumed by cleaning, bathing or sleeping!

The magic leaves a marriage once you've seen your wife at 6pm in two-day old clothes, baby-sick-matted hair and dinner stains down her top. That's what I thought.

I couldn't tell her that though, could I? She'd given birth to my baby. She was allowed to look however the damn way she wanted to; trouble is, I realise this now, but I didn't know it at the time. I'm man enough to admit I was an arsehole, and exceptionally selfish and self-centred.

Three years later we were fast approaching Lexie's third birthday and our son Louis arrived. If we thought it was tough with one child, we were entering a whole new madness.

I'm ashamed to say that I didn't do *Driving Miss Daisy* home from the hospital with Louis. That all-consuming fear I had felt with Lexie didn't seem to be at the forefront of my being. Or perhaps I'd grown so used to the feeling that it was just my "norm".

Selfishness approached with such velocity that I had no way of stopping it. It consumed me, evolved, twisted, turned and manifested within my every cell. Hindsight is a bloody amazing thing, isn't it? Sitting here now in judgement, I see how unbelievably selfish and self-centred I became in the months after Louis's birth.

Our marriage was losing its sparkle. Actually, that's an outright lie – it had completely lost its sparkle because I pulled away. I felt trapped and was looking for a peg to hang my "this is shit" coat on. I did the worst thing possible – I moved away from Annie when she needed my support the most. I virtually left her to raise our two young children alone. For this I will forever carry the weight of shame. The shame of letting my wife down in the biggest possible way. Forgiveness was given to me freely, willingly, but I don't want forgiveness. I must carry the weight as a reminder of what I did to Annie.

At the time I told myself that we'd simply drifted apart, that Annie had played her part, but in fact it was my doing. We had no sex life, we never talked about anything other than the children, paying bills and mending things that had broken in the house. I'd moved on from staying late at work to going out to the pub after work. Returning home when I knew the kids would be in bed and Annie asleep from the exhaustion of the day. Knowing I wouldn't have to talk to her.

I'd sit in the pub once all the lads from work had gone home to have their tea with their loving families, and I'd order another beer, a packet of peanuts, and I'd sit in the corner. I knew I was actually making the wrong choices. I knew I was destructing. Could I stop myself though? No! Knowing I was missing out on the kids was a killer, knowing I'd missed Louis's first words and Lexie's little "shows" left me with a weight inside my stomach. But the thought of having to be involved in all that just showed the type of character I actually am.

To see her sleeping on top of the bed, still clothed, hair matted to her head, what I thought was a bib hanging from her trouser pocket, do you know what I felt? Relief! What a fucking moron I am. I was relieved I didn't have to deal with my wife!

Idiot.

I wanted my family, I loved my family, I just didn't want any of the responsibility and nappy changing that went with it.

Grief was trying to sweep up over me as I thought with sadness that my dad never got to meet the kids. He would have idolised them. Their grampy would have been the best.

You know, throughout all of my shitty behaviour, Annie and I never argued, not even once. She never once questioned me, never pulled me up on the fact that I wasn't there, she just carried on providing for our children and keeping our home.

God I was an arsehole.

Three

The Meeting That Meant the End...

She worked in a different section of the company to me, but we came into contact quite often.

Was she pretty?

Compared to Annie? No. Annie always took my breath away.

But she was unattached and that was attractive, very attractive.

It started as banter, nothing more. Chatting a little longer after meetings developed into "Shall I get you a coffee on the way to the kitchen?" into "Just off to grab some lunch, fancy tagging along?"

I have since spoken to Zak about this. As my best mate, he's bound by some sort of universal law that says he's got to tell me if I'm being a knob, and at this stage, he agreed that I wasn't, which was good to know!

However, where I became a monumental knob (apparently) was when the "Shall we grab lunch on the run?" turned into "Off to the pub for a quick drink, fancy coming?" turned into two bottles of wine later and I found myself kissing her with a passion I'd long since forgotten, all in the beer garden of The Rising Sun – fuck!

Jesus, it felt so good, I admit it. She felt so good. She tasted so bloody inviting. Ego kicked in – I was a thirty-four-year-old man who was wanted by a single, unattached twenty-four-year-old. We got interrupted by a rowdy group of students coming out for a smoke, laughing and joking with each other. Pulling me to my senses. I made my excuses, left and drove home.

My house, our family home, was still when I walked in. Even Beau watched me from her cage in the kitchen with sleepy eyes. I looked at the clock on the dining room wall, 11.51pm – God, I'd done it again, missed an evening with my family – just so I could suck the face off a younger colleague.

Climbing the stairs, I looked in on Lexie and Louis, sleeping, dreaming, content. Annie was asleep as well. Climbing into bed, guilt slowly took hold of my heart.

I lay there listening to my honest, reliable, caring, kind, sexy and trustworthy wife. What the fuck was I doing? Why was I jeopardising everything? What the hell was wrong with me? Was I going through a midlife crisis? Round and round my thoughts went. None of them offering me any more clarity as to what was happening in my life. As I lay in the dark of our cocooning house, I knew that I couldn't continue, I wouldn't risk my family.

I'd created a chasm between me and Annie, I'd done it, and I'd fix it. I decided as I turned over and hit the pillows into a comfier position, that in the morning I'd tell Annie exactly how sorry I was and I'd make it right. I'd tell my beautiful wife just how much she meant to me.

Trouble was, the next morning Lexie woke with a high temperature and Louis had decided that today was the day to become a bomber aeroplane. Having any sort of conversation with Annie was just not going to happen.

I left for work with my sandwich box kindly made by Annie the previous night, and a heavy feeling in my heart. When I pulled up at work, I sat in my car, staring out of the windscreen, watching people scurrying this way and that as they went about their early-morning duties. Everyone so busy, so consumed with their lives. Resting my head against the headrests, I felt the pressure behind my eyes, the weight of my actions showing. I was such a pillock!

Dragging my tired body into work, I got my head down and just hoped the time would pass quickly so I could get home and talk face to face with Ann.

It was just before lunch when Bex came to my desk and asked if we could go out at lunch and talk about last night. This was definitely a conversation I needed to have, but not one I was looking forward to. She even suggested her flat, which was just round the corner, and no one from work would see us then.

As we walked to her block of flats I tried, I really did. I tried to remain focused and on topic. I'd apologise for my behaviour last night, I was out of line, and I hoped it wouldn't impact upon our professional relationship. Trouble is, I'm such a fucking idiot.

We weren't in her flat more than thirty seconds before we were pulling each other's clothes off. Fuck!

Having sex with Bex was so freeing. I didn't have to be quick or quiet. It was a new body to explore and I enjoyed it. It wasn't the body I'd grown so used to. It was – honestly? Exhilarating.

As I lay in Bex's bed listening to her in the shower I didn't feel guilty. I know you're reading this cussing me, confused as to how I can say that. But it's the truth. I was propped up, hands behind my head, feeling – comfortable – and not guilty. You see, in that moment I'd compartmentalised my life. Bex in one box, Annie and the kids in the other, and the two never met. I didn't allow myself to think about Annie when I was with Bex, and I tried not to allow Bex to seep into my home life.

I continued to meet Bex three or four times a week, sometimes during the lunch hour. More often than not though, it was after work. My perfect reason for not going home.

I need to say here that I never took Bex out for meals, or to the cinema. I don't believe I was in a relationship with her – it was just physical and freeing. She'd always be asking if we could go out for a meal, or go for a walk in the park. But I knew if I agreed to that, I'd be crossing a line I'd never be able to return from. So, I never did – not that it in any way condones my behaviour. I crossed the line the first time I even considered being unfaithful to Annie, I just didn't allow myself to see it.

The Berlin trip was the breaker for me, and the catalyst for everything that came after. Four nights, five days of onsite work. I needed admin support with me to ensure everything that was discussed was minuted, as we'd had issues in the past with miscommunication. So, I made the biggest mistake of my life. Vanity and pure desire took over and I suggested Bex to David Morris, my boss, and he had no reason to disagree. I had a choice. I could have chosen anyone in the admin team. I could have put a stop to it, but I didn't. I chose Bex knowing full well when we weren't on site we'd be together and alone.

Four

The Lies Came Easily…

I remember the first time I told a *real* lie to Annie.

Bex and I got to Berlin early, after catching a 4.30am flight, meaning we'd have a full working first day. Hiring a car at the airport, Bex and I drove straight to our client's office. Pulling into their pristine car park, Bex pulled me across the centre console and kissed me deeply. My body instantly responded and Bex knew it!

"Not now Bex," I said, pulling away.

"Spoilsport!" she mocked me and climbed out of the car.

The morning was hectic and I hardly had time to breathe. I did manage to squeeze in a quick message to Annie to let her know I'd arrived safely. The day was long and tiresome, lots of tweaking this and altering that. The Germans are very straightlaced folk, so not much banter happens! Thanks to FaceTime, we were able to get a lot of preparation work done back at the office. Emails flew backwards and forwards.

Arriving at our hotel, the Radisson Blu, I felt that Monday had, all in all, been a successful day. Thankfully, the company always uses the same hotel in Berlin, so I've gotten to know the staff well. I asked for an upgrade to the room, and I'd pay the difference personally, ensuring we had a premium room with a balcony. The views across to Berlin Cathedral were majestic. After unpacking, Bex took a shower and I had every intention of joining her, when my phone rang.

It was Annie on a FaceTime call. The kids were ringing to say goodnight.

Now, here is where I say that I absolutely adore my children. Lexie and Louis have command of my whole heart and always will. I may not have always been the most 'there' father, but I adore my children, and will do anything and everything for them.

Sitting on the king-sized bed, I answered the call with excitement. Lexie told me in great detail about the book that her class had read at school that day – how the whole class had to join in with the actions and voices. Louis was less interested in talking to me and more interested in showing me his toy tractor.

After we'd said goodnight, and I'd told them both how much I loved them, Annie came into frame just as Bex shouted from the bathroom for me to hurry.

Annie asked, "Who's with you, Lawson?"

I replied, "Oh, that's the housekeeping lady bringing me more towels."

Even as I write this, I cannot believe how easy it was to lie to my wife's face, her innocent beautiful face that looked tired and a bit strained – or was it confusion?

So, the cycle continued, all week. Each and every day I lied to my family. I lied to hide my deceit, my shame, my selfishness. At the time, I justified the behaviour as a necessity. I mean, who was I really hurting? Annie didn't know, and therefore wasn't being hurt by my behaviour. I was enjoying myself – it was ok, right? Little did I know what I was actually doing. What I was beginning. What I was forming. Not only within my family unit, but within myself.

That week wasn't what I'd imagined it being. I thought being alone would be super sexy, with loads of free uninterrupted time, it'd be great. In reality, we spent from 8am to 7pm in the client's office each day, rushed to eat and shower back at the hotel, and when we hit the hay we were both genuinely knackered.

Friday dawned and instead of excitement about returning home, I truly felt dread. That feeling only grew with intensity as the day drew on. By the time we were sitting in our seats on the plane it was all consuming. The plane finally took off, two hours late. Bex was asleep in the seat next to me and I stared absentmindedly at the inflight movie. Realising that it wasn't dread I was feeling, it was resentment (later, I realised it was actually selfishness) at returning to my perceived chained existence within my family. As we began our descent into Birmingham International Airport, I knew what I needed to do.

Hindsight is a wonderful tool, isn't it? (I know I've said that before, and I'll probably say it again!). In that moment I was totally blinkered. I don't believe anything could have steered me away from what I perceived to be the right thing to do. Now though? I totally ballsed up!

Arriving home (finally) at 11.45pm, I sat for a moment on the drive, staring up out through the windscreen at the house. The home that Annie and I had spotted in the corner of the estate agent's window on that blustery Sunday morning. The house we'd brought both of our babies home to. The house that was our family home. It was in darkness except for the outside light that Annie had left on for me, knowing I'd be home at some point tonight. She has always been extremely thoughtful like that. Opening the porch door, I dumped my bags in the living room and made a fuss of Beau, trying desperately not to make her bark. After a quick scratch behind the ear, she went back to her bed, circled four times and dropped back into her slumber. She never was a great guard dog!

Upstairs I went into each of the kids' bedrooms in turn. Louis first, with his moon nightlight on the wall. He had one leg dangling out of bed and the other resting vertically up the wall! I've no idea how! Rearranging him back under the covers, I kissed him goodnight and moved along to Lexie's room. My princess was actually totally in bed, so I kissed her gently and she stirred awake and smiled when she saw me. After a quick trip to the toilet, I carried her back into bed and tucked her in.

Walking into our bedroom, I listened to Annie's slow rhythmic breathing. I knew I was about to break this beautiful, perfect human. I knew I was. But yet, I couldn't see any other way. Or perhaps, to be more truthful, I didn't want to see any other way.

I woke Annie, gently shaking her. She was so happy to see me, pulling me into an all-encompassing hug, and I uttered the words I thought would make my life better.

"I want a divorce."

Five

The Condition...

I've often heard my mum use the expression "silence is deafening", but I'd never actually experienced it. I'd always assumed it was just another of her 'Motherisms'. However, as Annie pulled away from me and looked me in the face, I realised my mum was spot on.

The silence that followed those four words was deep, cutting, heavy and almost unbearable. I swear even the minimal light within the room got darker.

Her beautiful deep brown eyes flicking left to right, taking in all of my face, searching for something, anything, hoping, I guess, for me to follow up with "just kidding". She swallowed, pulled away from me and dragged the duvet back up over her body and simply said: "Goodnight Lawson."

Turning over, she went back to sleep, leaving me half crouched on our ruffled bed. I pulled back onto my ankles and waited, hoping, desperate for Annie to turn back over and talk to me, say anything to me, hit me even – anything. But she didn't.

I left her, alone in our bedroom, and peeped in to check

on the kids again, almost needing to be near them, to see them, Lexie cocooned in her unicorn duvet where I'd left her, and Louis kneeling – bum in the air with a death grip on his favourite teddy. I dragged myself downstairs and poured a large dark rum and sat in the conservatory as Beau slept on my feet.

Did I feel better for voicing those words? Honestly, I don't know. I was devastated at the hurt I'd caused Annie; she was innocent, and I'd hurt her. That is not what I ever wanted to do. I texted Bex, hoping she was still up, but didn't get a response. No one in their right mind would be awake at that ungodly hour.

As I let Beau out for a quick trip around the garden, I stared up at the night sky and hoped with all my heart that I'd made the right decision. Settling Beau in her bed, I locked up the house and turned off all the lights. Sliding into our bed, I listened to Annie's breathing. She was asleep. I would miss her, of that I was certain, but we simply weren't working.

Surprisingly, I fell asleep easily.

I woke up at 10.30am to a very quiet house.

Going downstairs, I was greeted by Beau, who I let into the garden. I came back in towards the kitchen, and it was then that I saw the letter propped up against the fruit bowl on the dining table.

Dear Lawson

I have taken the kids to my folks where they'll have a sleepover tonight.

I feel it is important that in the next few hours to come we be free to be ourselves and not distracted, to talk freely, openly and honestly.

I will be home around lunchtime.

I have given your request a lot of thought and ask that we say nothing to our children at the moment.

I will graciously and quietly grant your wish for a divorce. I do not want anything from you, Rob, not the house, or money, the children will spend their time equally between us but I ask for one condition.

My condition is:

You delay proceedings for thirty days and each of those thirty days you eat dinner with your family at the dining table, no excuses.

Annie

Six

Tea Will Help Right…?

I stood stock still, rereading the letter as Beau darted in and out of house like a mad thing.

Shit, she'd called me Rob. She hardly ever called me Rob, always right from the start of our relationship it had been Lawson, that's what struck the most. I could hear Annie's words in my head, I could hear her calm approach to everything, could feel the undertone of hurt. It was so Annie, non-dramatic, yet emotion-filled.

Looking away from the paper, I stared into space as I considered what it meant. She would give me what I wanted?

I walked into the kitchen, its surfaces shining in the morning sunlight. I flicked on the kettle and grabbed my favourite mug from the cupboard.

I looked down at the paper in my hands and saw for the first time that it was shaking – I was shaking.

Shit!

I heard the post box go as the post lady shouted, "Morning" as she always did on the weekend. Leaving the letters where they lay,

I just couldn't move, couldn't speak, couldn't understand what Ann had written.

Finally, realising the kettle had finished boiling, I made my morning tea.

Taking the steaming cup, I sat in my favourite chair in the conservatory, staring into Annie's beloved garden, which had been trimmed to within an inch of its life.

I rested my head back against the soft leather of my chair, hoping the warm sweet tea would help me get a grip on what was going on.

Dinner? What?

Why wasn't she mad?

Why wasn't she hitting me?

Why wasn't she throwing things around the house?

Shouting?

Raging?

Why prolong it? I simply didn't understand it. What would delaying everything for a month achieve? Dinner? What?

My phone beeped in my pocket. I pulled it out and saw "1 unread message from Ben", my code name for Bex.

Lying in bed all alone is not how I like to wake up, especially when there's nothing between my skin and the sheets...

My body responded to her hinted suggestion. I adjusted my seating position and pressed FaceTime, and she answered, hair tousled around her head:

"Morning," she said.

"Hi."

"I miss you..."

"Me too... I've got some stuff I need to deal with here, I might be quiet for a while..."

I could see the look of confusion on her face. "Oh ok...well I'll have to...please myself I suppose...?"

"How will you do that?" I enquired, knowing exactly what was about to come.

Seven

Dinner Number 1 She Knows...

After Face Timing Bex I needed a shower, and a long one. I shaved and put on fresh clothes, all before loading the washing machine with my dirty clothes from the week away in Berlin.

Annie arrived home just as I began unloading the dishwasher. I may be a shit husband but I'm not lazy! There aren't any chores around the house that I won't do. I didn't believe that this is his job or her job. I believe that if something needs doing, I'll do it. My mum and dad raised me to be able to look after myself, mainly because my mum refused to be greeted with a black bag of washing on Sundays when I visited from uni.

Annie went straight upstairs and then came back down a few minutes later, arms laden with the bathroom towels.

"I've just put a load in. My clothes from last week."

She dumped the towels in front of the washing machine, walked to the sink and filled up the kettle and flicked it on.

"Are the kids ok? I'd liked to have seen them this morning."

"They're fine. They're going to the cinema to watch the latest

LEGO movie with my brother. They both came and saw you sleeping before we left. They know you are home." She continued to fuss around the work surfaces, wiping away imaginary crumbs.

"Annie please…can we talk about this?"

She moved to the vegetable rack and started putting potatoes and carrots in the sink drainer. Finding her peeler in the cutlery drawer, she pushed it closed slowly, purposefully.

"Honestly, Rob, there isn't a lot to say. You've made your decision. That pretty much wraps it up, doesn't it? Now would you like cottage or shepherd's pie for your dinner tonight?" she said as she looked in the fridge.

I was shocked, stunned, I didn't know how to respond to her. I didn't understand the way she was taking this. I was baffled.

Annie was simply indifferent to it. Non-judgemental, non-committal, just Annie.

"Cottage pie would be nice. Annie, please, I'd like us to be able to talk about what I said last night. I need to know that you are ok."

Returning to the sink, she looked over her shoulder at me and smiled her lopsided smile. "Me? I'm absolutely fine Lawson, absolutely fine," and returned her attention to peeling the potatoes.

I went to our home office and began going through my work emails, catching up on what I'd not had a chance to respond to last week. Always the downside to being away is the inbox filling up.

Two hours whizzed by and then Ann called to say the food was ready. We sat across the dining room table from one another. She served up the most delicious cottage pie and fresh bread, gluten-free obviously. It was bloody delicious.

There is something comforting about home-cooked food. Annie always was a great cook. "Sumat outa nothing." That's what she used to say!

"How was your trip?" she asked as she spread some butter on her bread.

The question genuinely floored me. There was no malice, hatred or even spite, she was truly interested.

"It was a long week with long days. But it was successful. I think we made real progress. They even commented that they think we're now ahead of schedule and should be able to hand over earlier than planned. I suggested modifying Sub Section 2 for the more environmentally accepted DonMite product and it was a big hit. The Radisson has had a makeover, it's very swanky now. Much more in line with its prices!!!! The flight home was awful though. The plane was delayed by two hours, and we had to just sit on the runway and wait as we'd all boarded by then. And then so much turbulence."

All of this was truthful, and it felt nice to talk about something "normal".

"Did she enjoy it?"

I actually choked on my mouthful of cottage pie. I had to compose myself and have a big drink of water. I stared into my wife's face. Again, not a hint of anger. She hadn't even stopped eating, she was... content?

"I assume she went with you?" she followed up.

Another simple question, but I couldn't answer. I felt like my stomach had dropped out from underneath me and I was going to vomit all at the same time. My face felt hot, my hands began sweating. Shit!

"I'm not blind, Rob! There was a time when I could make your face light up. I suspect though that those days are far behind us now."

Something stabbed me in the pit of my stomach.

Christ! Guilt. It engulfed me. I was hurting Annie. I was stripping her bare and leaving her raw. I never wanted this, not for a single moment.

"I simply ask that you don't discuss her within this house, and especially when the children are around. I don't want her to be 'present' physically or any other 'ly' at our dinner table, or within these four walls – ever."

Annie carefully moved her food around her plate, not looking me in the eye.

Christ, I am a selfish bastard. I'm hurting her and all I wanted to do was sweep her up in my arms and take away her pain – pain I caused.

I couldn't find any words to respond to her. Her calmness to this was disconcerting.

"Eat up, your food is getting cold!" she said as she picked up her bread and pushed her food around her plate again.

When did my wife become so strong? So focused? So sure? I honestly didn't know she was so capable and I was so not.

Saturday evening Annie and I barely spoke. Looking back, I think I realised now that I was anticipating and waiting for the fury that should have erupted from Annie, but didn't. Instead, she went and had a bath.

After Annie had gone up to bed I sat alone in the garden. It was a warm(ish) evening. Beau was mooching around the garden, chasing the last few butterflies that were awake. I sipped on the last of the beer I'd opened earlier that night. I just sat there for a good couple of hours, watching daytime retire and night-time arrive, flowers closing their heads, and nocturnal animals waking up.

I couldn't help but think back to my dad. He'd been gone more than seven years at that point. It was a big shock to everyone when he passed away. He never stood a chance really.

Life was ok, growing up. I am an only child, so at times it was a struggle, as there was no one else to deflect the ever-present stare of expectation from the folks. I tried hard at school, sometimes having to try even harder, and Tim Harris, who was in my class and lived next door to us – he was just one of the obnoxious people who found everything so bloody easy.

As I grew, the level of expectation, particularly from Dad, grew too. He knew I'd go to university, and he hoped I'd follow in his footsteps and study Engineering. I wasn't all that keen if I'm honest with you. In those days, I'd got a secret burning desire to become a café owner. The appeal of brewing fresh coffee, the beans, the froth. I think it came from my childhood visits to barista shops with my nan and grandad, whose treat each week was a cup of freshly made coffee each, while I had a glass of milk and my pick of the freshly made cakes. Those days truly hold a special place within my heart, carefree, happy and loved. Though I never vocalised this desire to

Dad, I have done so in more recent years to Mum.

On the day of my graduation (not Engineering), we went to a local pub to celebrate with a pint and some food. I was walking past the bar and happened to overhear my dad giving the woman behind the bar our home phone number. In my naivety I never really thought much about it. But (again) hindsight now tells me that this was my first exposure to my dad's infidelity.

Mum and Dad's relationship had always been fractured with arguments; however, throughout it all there was overriding love. Dad worked at a local engineering company and Mum worked part-time in the office at the local school. Looking back now, I realise that Mum knew about Dad's other women, she just chose not to actively notice.

That is until Dad died. He was two months off his sixty-ninth birthday when he suffered a major heart attack while in the shower at home. The coroner and GPs I've spoken to since all said the same thing, "He would have been dead before he hit the floor." One even said, "It wouldn't have mattered if he'd had the heart attack in the middle of A&E, he would have gone."

At the time, Annie and I had just started to think about looking for a bigger home. We'd been married just over a year and had talked about trying for a baby. We were actually due to go and look at the first house the day after he died. Annie was fantastic, she even slept over at Mum and Dad's, being a shoulder for Mum to cry on. I've never been good with emotional outbursts, I don't know what to do with myself, especially my hands. My hands always seem to get in the way. But Annie just swept in and looked after Mum. May (Annie's mum) swept in and looked after me.

At his funeral two weeks after his sudden passing, the family car pulled into the crematorium behind the hearse and we were all stunned to see the throngs of people. They were standing five-deep in places. None of us had realised just how many people Dad knew, or how popular he was. He was always a sociable creature, happy to stop and have a chat with the neighbours, nipping down to the pub for a quick pint with the boys from work. He was a great laugh, always cracking a joke, and able to laugh at himself.

We held the wake in the garden room of a local craft centre. It was a beautiful setting overlooking a large pond filled with ducks and sculptures by local artists. Mum, Annie and I stood by the door welcoming everyone as they arrived, listening to stories about Dad and how he impacted all those present. I'd no idea how many people were there – we catered for 250 and there was only a little food left after everyone had gone home! The line just seemed to go on and on.

Towards the end though, a few stragglers came in, including a woman dressed in very dazzling dress (I was later informed by Annie that it was more of a cocktail dress; a dress is a dress to me!)

"What the hell do you think you're doing here, you bitch?"

Until that moment I'd never even heard my mother swear. I didn't even know she knew any swear words! I stared between the two women, the woman in black smirking at my clearly seething mother.

"Janie, nice to see you," she responded. Swinging her handbag.

"You need to leave – NOW." My mum stepped out of our little line and stood in front of the unknown woman.

"You can't ban me from his wake! I'm allowed and entitled to be here. So, wind your neck in, I'm off to get a white wine."

"The fuck you are! Get your skanky ass out of this building before I kick it out, you disrespectful slut!" My mum moved closer to the woman, who was at this point becoming redder in the face.

"How dare you speak to me like that, woman! Who the hell do you think you are?"

"I'm his fucking wife, bitch. You, however, are nothing! Do you hear me? NOTHING!"

"Oh really? I'm nothing, am I? If I'm nothing sweetheart, then why did he spend Christmas Day with me? How come he saw in the New Year with me and not you?" she spat at my mother in response.

"Mum?" I said calmly and quietly, hoping not too many of the guests had heard the disruption. "What's going on? Hello. I'm Rob, Ken's son." I extended my hand to greet her, but she just continued to stare my mother down.

It was Annie who broke the deadlock.

"Right ladies, obviously we need to have a proper chat, perhaps we could all move into the kitchen?" She moved to start ushering both women away from the ears of the mourners.

"No Annie love, it's fine." my mother said. Straightening herself up, she stood, shoulders back, with a smile across her face. "Rob, Annie, this woman is Leanetta Driver. She was your father's latest bit on the side. However, she seems to be under some sort of misconception that she actually meant something to your dad!"

Ann and I both stared open-mouthed as my mother dropped the biggest bombshell ever.

Leanetta began laughing – hysterically.

"I did mean something to Ken, he was going to move in with me. He'd had enough of you. You bored him. I excited him. Enriched his life and soul," she bragged.

All three of us stared wide-eyed at her.

"Oh, you poor cow! You really believe that, don't you? Ken went and spent an hour with you on Christmas Day because I told him to. He was getting under my feet while I was cooking the turkey. He was with you from about 11am to 12pm? Right? As for New Year's Eve, I took poorly during the day with a streaming cold, so I told him to go to you."

Now it was Leanetta's turn to stare open-mouthed.

"That's right sweetheart. Me and Ken had NO secrets, ever! I knew when he was with you. He'd even show me some of your text messages! Ha! They were hilarious. You fell for him hook, line and sinker, didn't you? Unfortunately love, you are just one in a long line of other women that my husband has had over the years. So, I think perhaps it's time for you to turn tail and go home. You are not welcome here."

A small squeak escaped Leanetta's mouth, a huff, and then she actually stomped her foot, turned and left, slamming the door on her way out, leaving me and Annie staring at the door, completely stunned by the interaction.

The rest of the wake passed without incident. People were so kind to tell us their favourite stories of Dad, or how they knew him, so many stories of how Dad had helped people. He was a good man; it would seem he had just one fault – remaining faithful.

After the wake, I drove Mum home while Annie went back to ours in her car. After we finished loading the car with Mum's share of the remaining food, we headed back. After a few minutes I couldn't help myself. I needed to understand.

"I'm so confused. Dad was unfaithful and you knew?"

"Oh yes," Mum responded so nonchalantly.

"You didn't mind? You didn't care?" Trying hard to keep my eyes on the road, and not stare gobsmacked at her.

"Well really, when all is said and done, what's to mind?"

"Well quite a bit really! Your husband was seeing other women, Mum!"

"Yes. But it was only ever fleeting liaisons, Robert, never great romances. That was saved for us. Me and your dad. I was his great love, always had been, always will be. These other women were... distractions? Mere whimsy."

"Whimsy?"

"Yes. They hardly ever lasted more than a few months. He'd always treat them nicely. He wasn't a cad. He was always a gentleman. That was always part of the deal. I never wanted hear that he'd behaved ungentlemanly. A woman always deserves respect."

"WHAT?" I was exasperated by what I was hearing.

"Robert, I know it's hard for you to understand darling. But I really didn't mind. Your father adored the bones of you and me, and he always came home to us at the end of each day. It was always us he'd sit at the kitchen table with of an evening when he'd finished work and eat his tea with us. He loved us, loved his family with a passion."

"But Mum, he was unfaithful to you!" Concern filled my words.

"I know, son. The first time it happened and I found out I was utterly broken. I even took you and left our family home. We went and stayed with Nan and Grancher for a few weeks, while I tried to work out what to do."

I knew none of this. How was it that I knew none of this?! I could barely drive, let alone take in what my mother was telling me on the day of my dad's funeral.

"I realised that I had a choice. A choice to allow your father's behaviour to define me, and the rest of my life. Or I could choose to recognise my own self-worth. I chose the latter and we returned to our family home. I sat your father down after you'd gone to bed that first night back, and I had a very frank and honest discussion with him. I told him that I intended to live my life the way I saw fit, and if he chose to walk that life with me, then great; if not, then he could leave. However, if his choice was to remain with us and continue his behaviour, I wanted to know every single detail about who they were, where he'd been and for how long. Never ever were they allowed to know where we lived, or my or your names. I could not, and would not, try to control your father's behaviour. Trying to change someone's behaviour to suit your own needs is selfish."

She went silent for a moment, perhaps summoning more strength to continue telling me all that had been hidden for so long.

"Years passed before he told me he'd met someone. We were in bed one night, just about to turn the lights off to go to sleep, and he just came out with out. I recognised my choice again, and I chose to say, 'Nowhere near here. Never at the dining room table. Most importantly, don't be a dickhead.' Kissed him goodnight and went to sleep."

"Good God!"

"I felt ok with the arrangement, Rob. Hindsight, of course I'd have preferred it to be different. But he was true to his word – always, and it worked out. We made it work out. There were eight different women in total. So, please don't think he was out sleeping with anything that moved because he wasn't. He would go months, even years without doing anything, then it would start."

"Mum..." I was lost for words.

"Rob, please don't think any less of your dad. He adored the bones of you, and Annie. He was, however, human, and sometimes we mess up. It's what we do when we realise that we've messed up that defines us."

"I love you Mum."

"I love you too sweetie, and I love your dad."

We arrived back at the house and went inside and helped her put fresh water in the many (many) vases of flowers she'd received since Dad's passing. We talked about the ceremony, and the people who had been kind enough to come and pay their respects, never once mentioning Dad's infidelity, and we haven't since.

"I'm going to have to nip back home and grab the bag I've packed. In the rush this morning, I forgot to put it in the car," I said as I refilled the jug with water and headed into the dining room, where the table was covered with hand-tied arrangements.

Looking up, I saw Mum standing still in the doorway to the lounge.

"Oh sweetie, no that's ok I'm fine, don't worry." She insisted that she'd like to be at home on her own.

"It's no bother Mum. I shouldn't be more than an hour." I carried on topping up the vases.

"Rob, I need to do this now. Dad's gone, I need to grieve him, accept that he isn't coming back and start to find a way to live a life that isn't the two of us, that is just me now. I don't know where to even begin any of that. But if you and Annie keep loving me the way you have, I won't need to begin any of it. Do you understand?"

I was pulled up short by what she said. "Mum, are we stopping you from grieving?"

"Of course you're not darling, more..." she fumbled for the word, "delaying it? Sweetie, first and foremost, I'm your mum, and I always will be. But I'm also your dad's wife, and I always will be, but now I have to learn how to be a widow. I've never done that before. I don't know how to be that..."

Her tears began to fall silently.

"I'm so sorry that your dad's gone, Rob. I wish I could scoop you up like when you were little and take away your pain. But I can't, darling. We all need to start to find a way of dealing with the

43

pain. Find a way to begin to see the sunshine in the day. Begin to live again. He will always be a part of us. We will always treasure our memories, but we must individually find a way to make room for new memories that are to come."

I left Mum that night as requested, but only after we agreed I'd call her later on that evening to make sure she was ok, and then again in the morning, which I did. We also agreed that nothing would happen inside the house until Mum was ready.

It was around six weeks after the funeral that I had a text message while I was at work:

Hello sweetheart
How are you and my lovely Annie?
I've sat for some time in my and your dad's bedroom
staring at his open wardrobes.
I think it's time to dive head first into his clothes.
There are lots of people who are worse off than we are,
who may really value the use of his clothes.
Would you like to help me? I understand if it's too much
for you. If it is, but there's anything of his you'd like me to
keep, just let me know.
Love to both of you
Mum
Oh, also how did the house viewing go? Do let me know.

And so it began, the slow process of passing Dad's things on to other people who would get use of them. The house viewing was of Chestnut Grove. I told her all about it that evening as we stood in their bedroom. After I'd called Annie at lunchtime to tell her about Mum's message, she'd insisted that I go.

As I went into detail (at Mum's request) about the house, I said that we liked it, but that we'd only really gone to see it to gauge a better understanding of bedroom sizes. The cost was out of our price range, realistically, so it was never going to be a serious contender. But at least we knew what we could afford with our budget.

"How much more is it than your budget?" I remember Mum asking casually.

"Twenty K. It is beautiful though. There was a lovely little park just off the next street. Great walks as well. But we've both accepted that we need now to just wait and the right house will come along." I couldn't bring myself to tell Mum that Annie had said as we walked around the house that she could see herself bringing our baby home here.

"Put in an offer, Rob," she said. "I'll give you the extra money. Call it a final gift from Dad. As long as it won't stretch you, mortgage-wise, to have a bigger house, so bigger bills. It's a gift, I don't want it back. Your dad would want you and Annie to be happy, in a house that makes you happy. In a place that makes you happy. So just go and do it. Let me know when you need the money and I'll get Clive at the bank to transfer it to your account."

What a truly remarkable woman my mother was and is. Now I am seeing the striking similarities in the woman I chose to be my wife. They are so alike and I hadn't even noticed until that night in the garden, not one hour after I'd told that remarkable woman that I didn't want to be with her anymore!

Eight

Dinners Number 2 and 3 Pizza Off…

Sunday morning dawned and Annie wasn't there when I woke up. The house was empty. I was grateful that Annie hadn't banished me to the spare room. Actually, she'd probably have sent to the sofa, the spare room was only for guests! Although deep down I knew I deserved it. I think I wanted to be punished for my behaviour; it would have made me feel better for what I was doing. I couldn't seem to stop the behaviour though. I was a total contradiction.

There was no note this time. Her car was gone. It was only 8am. Where on earth could she have gone?

I rang her mobile but there was no answer. A sense of foreboding began to rise within me. I still cared deeply about her, perhaps more than I was acknowledging.

I tried her mobile again. Still no answer.

Slapping my hand to my forehead, of course. Her mobile had stopped syncing with the car's Bluetooth system. She'd asked me two or three weeks ago to have a look and see if I could fix it before she took it to the garage.

Going to the Find my Friends app, the little pointer showed that Annie was moving up the B4549. She was heading towards her folks' house. She must be on her way to collect the children – and breathe, Rob!!

While she was out of the house, I made myself useful. I stripped all the beds and put on the first load of washing. I ran the hoover round upstairs.

Then I went into the office-cum-study and switched on my laptop. Opening up the internet browser, I sat staring at the blinking icon. I intended to search for local divorce lawyers, but couldn't seem to get my fingers to work.

Instead, a million and one thoughts were whizzing through my head, all logistical problems. How would it work? Where would I live? How would we divide our belongings? Annie said she didn't want the house or anything. I'm not an utter arsehole, Annie, and the kids must stay in the house, it's their family home and I will not take that away from them. So instead of divorce lawyers, I Googled local letting agents.

Just as I was about to submit my email address to receive notifications of new properties I heard Annie's car pull up on the driveway. Turning off the computer, I rushed to the porch, sweeping Lexie into my arms as she ran from the car to me. Louis was too busy explaining the complexities of the inner workings of a tractor to his mum. As she tried to unload their bags from the boot, I rescued the towering piles of belongings from Annie's arms and carried everything inside the house.

Anyone with children will understand the battle that is a family trying to get into a house, accoutrements and baggage and all. It's like *Mission Impossible*. But once we were inside the house filled with chatter, laughter, shouts and noise.

There really wasn't time to be alone with Annie and talk about the divorce or her condition. If it wasn't Lexie taking up our time, it was Louis wanting to know why you can only harvest at certain times of the year, then it was both of them wanting to know why they have to have a shower every day, when cows don't shower at all!

Dinner was a traditional Sunday roast, and it was bloody delicious – lamb. Annie had done all the trimmings, roasties, carrots, cauliflower and to top off this combination of wonderfulness, Yorkshire puds – I know, controversial.

As we all sat around the dining table, the kids talked non-stop, even with their mouths full. We heard in great detail about the LEGO movie they'd seen yesterday with their Uncle Andy, about eating chocolate in bed and going in the bath fully clothed. Oh, and the water fight they definitely didn't have with Gag! They always have so much fun at May and Malc's house. They are fantastic grandparents and have always been good to me.

Lexie and Annie had their heads together as they discussed which nail-polish they would use on each other after dinner, and Louis floated off into his own tractor-filled world. I sat and watched Annie and Lexie giggling together. I hadn't really noticed how similar they'd become. Not just their features but their demeanour. Both were beautiful, that was undeniable.

After dinner was tidied away, I sat with Louis on the couch, looking at the picture book he'd been allowed to bring home from nursery, *Farming Through the Year*. He had always been obsessed with farms, animals and vehicles. His favourite place to visit was the local petting farm. Annie and Lexie sat on the floor in front of the log burner, painting each other's nails and talking about what Lexie had got up to with her nanny.

Putting the children to bed that night was – enjoyable, not a single argument or protest. It felt comfortable, like we were safely cocooned in our warm home.

As we said goodnight to the kids Annie turned and said she was going for a shower. I headed back downstairs, closed the office door, and kept myself amused with the computer, my phone and Bex.

11pm arrived and I went to bed, after spending an hour answering emails and preparing for the next day at the office. Annie was already asleep. Again, no anger from her at all.

Was I feeling put out? I was so confused. Why hadn't she got angry with me? Didn't she care? Didn't she want to fight for the marriage? But actually, who the hell was I to say anything about fighting for our marriage. I wanted to leave! I was so confused by her response.

Monday dawned and I returned to work. The kids were still asleep as I left the house. Annie was awake but was in the bathroom as I left.

I was straight into the thick of it when I arrived, as I had a recap meeting with David Morris regarding the week in Berlin. He was so happy with the progress we'd made, and how much had been accomplished. I have a lot of time and respect for David. He built the firm up from just him in a shed in his back garden to a multimillion-pound organisation that employs many local people. David's values are woven into Morris and Co and I'm proud to say that I have grown professionally and personally since being taken under his wing all those years ago.

The meeting broke off after about four hours, at midday. My phone beeped. A message from "Ben":

Now or (and) tonight?

Just as I was about to reply another message arrived, this time from Annie:

Lexie has decided we're all going to make our own pizzas tonight and then judge each other's creations. I'm off to the Co-op for provisions, would you like any specific toppings?

I held my phone in my hand, torn between who to respond to, which way to turn.

I surprised myself by replying to Annie's message first:

Onion, chilli and sausage. Looking forward to beating you all – LOSERS.

I turned my phone around and around in my hand, then responded to Bex:

Now, but I only have 20 minutes.

I got to Bex's flat ten minutes later and she was waiting for me, patiently. I couldn't help but make the comparison of a faithful pet – God, I am an arsehole! I made sure not to go anywhere near her bedroom. I felt like I just needed to 'do the deed' and leave, so I had her over the back of her sofa. I didn't even want to look at her that day. Something was shifting in me, and it felt like that shift had absolutely nothing to do with me.

Looking back now I know I didn't enjoy it. I didn't stay afterwards, I just left, returned to work and shut the door to my office and lived with the sadness that was growing deep in my stomach.

I arrived home at 4.50pm that Monday night. I couldn't remember the last time I'd been home before 5pm on a work night, I simply didn't do it. But Annie's condition weighed heavy on me, therefore, I was home in time for dinner.

The "Pizza Off" was a ridiculous mess of laughter, crying and mozzarella-smooshed hair. All the ingredients were laid out on the dining room table and each contestant had fifteen minutes to create their masterpiece.

I was so proud of my creation, carefully carrying it to the oven. Annie went for a traditional approach of cheese, onion, sweetcorn and chicken. Lexie went wild and crazy with cheese, pepper, onion, peas, bacon and ham. Louis triumphed though, with his bizarre concoction of tuna, pepper, ham and sweet chilli. Reluctantly, I conceded it was bloody lovely. We all agreed we'd be having it again!

As we sat among the carnage of creation at the dining table we talked, we laughed, we felt sick, we found a love of different combinations of food, we smiled, we were a family.

After showering the kids and putting them to bed, the hour spent cleaning up the dining room and kitchen was totally worth it. Annie and I worked in comfortable silence; she was humming and I was…content?

Nine

Dinners 4–7 Chippers...

Tuesday is always a busy day in the office. It is Project Meeting day, with solid meetings from 9am–3.30pm, so never time for lunch.

Therefore, Bex's suggestion of a Chinese takeaway back at her place was tempting, but I declined and said truthfully that I wasn't sure if I'd be able to meet up with her this week as I needed to finalise the Berlin project, ready for handover next week. She stormed out of my office and slammed the door behind her.

Finally! An emotional response! That's what I'd expected from Annie. But she had still been so calm and collected, it was a bit unnerving.

I was home a little after 5pm as traffic was heavy. When I walked through the door, I could hear the three of them in the kitchen having a very in-depth discussion about why a sunflower can bloom in the garden but not the cupboard under the sink. As I leaned my weight against the lounge doorway and listened to them, I couldn't help but smile. Annie always allows the children to have and form their own opinions, to rationalise and explore topics with such depth that they don't even realise that they are learning! She's always calm with them, very patient with them. Something I'd always noticed about her as well is she scoots down on her knees and talks to the kids at their level; very rarely will she stand and talk down to them. I remember once her telling me that, "It's not their fault they are short!"

The aroma emanating from the kitchen was amazing and I couldn't wait to sit down with all of them and eat it!

Turns out it was one of my all-time favourites, spag bol à la Annie, and tear and share garlic bread – YUMMMMMM – get in my belly. Unfortunately, it did result in Louis having to be placed fully clothed in the shower after we'd finished eating as there just wasn't any point in stripping him beforehand!

I wanted to talk to Annie that evening, but she seemed distant and took herself off to our en suite for a bath and early to bed. I don't believe she was avoiding me, just needing some time to herself, and I fully respected that.

After answering a few quick work emails, I completed my registration for a few local letting agents and felt positive ticking something off the to-do list. I even sent off a couple of enquiry emails to ask about potential properties.

Wednesday passed slowly in a blur of report-writing. Getting everything ready for the handover the following week takes time. Making sure every scrap of information is accurate, printed and presented. These days are few and far between and, unfortunately, the downside of my position. I love my job and all it entails – the front-facing aspect, connecting with clients and suppliers and the in-depth analysis that pulls on my marketing knowledge.

I caught myself staring blankly at my computer screen. I was thinking about that evening's dinner. I was looking forward to going home. It took me by surprise. I was enjoying their company, all of them – even Annie's.

At 3.59pm I was ready to log off at exactly 4pm and be out the door and on the M5 as quickly as possible. David Morris poked his head into my office to ask on the progress of the handover report and if I'd be ready, and I was pleased to be able to say that I would be. As I packed away my stuff, I asked him if he was ok. I thought he looked a bit peaky.

"Thanks for asking, Rob, just a bit tired. It's been a busy few weeks, hasn't it? Me and Sheila are thinking of having a break down in North Devon for a few days. It's just finding a good time to slot it in."

"Oh, I love North Devon. Whereabouts are you thinking of going?" I asked, as I closed my office door and walked down the corridor with him.

"We have a house on the coast, between Combe Martin and Ilfracombe. It's bloody gorgeous. Really recharges the old batteries."

"I know that part of the world. Me and Annie had our honeymoon in Watermouth, do you know it? It's just a perfect part of the world, isn't it?"

"Know it? That's where the house is! You're not wrong though son, you're not wrong!" He put his arm around my back. "When all this Berlin stuff is put to bed and we've had the evaluation meetings, I'd like for us to put a date in the diary. I want to meet with you and discuss what's next. Email Glenda, she knows you'll be in touch and she'll set it in stone."

"Oh, ok Dave. It will certainly be good once we've handed over. It feels like we've been doing Berlin for so long now!"

"Yeah, but such a boost to our confidence and reputation. Good eggs, the Germans. Anyway, I'll let you head off back to that lovely family of yours. How's Annie? Shelia always asks after her."

"She's well thanks. Always busy, you know Ann! The kids keep her on her feet!"

"Well give her our love, won't you, and I know Sheila would love to meet her for coffee one day."

"Will do Dave. Have a great evening." I waved goodbye as I got into the lift and headed downstairs to the car park.

When I walked through the front door, I was greeted by a whole farm laid out in the hallway. Clearly Louis had been busy!

I tiptoed my way across the collection of cows and soldiers (?) as Louis came running in clutching a toy fire engine.

"Fire in the barn, Dad."

"Hi champ! Have you had a good day?"

"Yep, better than the farmer!"

Lexie shouted down from upstairs that she couldn't come down right now as her Barbies were having a shower.

I found Annie in the kitchen finalising dinner – ooooooooooh, bangers and mash with onion gravy, it reminded me of my Nanny Teague.

I walked over to her and, putting both hands on her shoulders, kissed the top of her head and asked if I could do anything to help? She said it was all under control here, but could I round up the kiddliwinks and get them washed and seated?

Annie was quiet throughout dinner. She said she was just tired, but she hardly ate any of her food.

After putting all the dishes into the dishwasher, we sat in the living room and watched CBeebies. Both of the kids denied being tired; only their yawns gave them away. I carried both of them upstairs, Lexie on my back and Louis clinging to my front, both giggling the whole way. Showering and teeth-cleaning was tense, but we got there in the end. After tucking the kids into bed, I offered to run Annie a bath; she seemed like she needed to relax and rest. I lit candles and made sure to add her essential oil smelly stuff.

As she came into the en suite, I told her to simply relax and enjoy the quiet and that I'd be on hand for the kids, as I kissed her forehead.

I lay on our bed, reading the news on my phone. As I was browsing the sports pages a message arrived from Bex asking if I could come round tonight.

Without missing a beat, I typed my reply:

Not tonight. Busy.

and deleted her message thread.

I must have fallen asleep where I lay because I woke up in the night to find Annie asleep next to me under the duvet and a blanket over my still-clothed body. I climbed under the covers and reached over and put my arm across Annie's warm body and fell back asleep quickly.

Thursday was, thankfully, busier at work, with more actual work, less paperwork, lots of toing and froing with new projects coming in and finalising the handover. I agreed to go to lunch with Bex. She wanted to go to her house but I was hungry, so we went to the Sandwich Box instead.

On the way back to the office she tried to hold my hand. Thankfully, I was shuffling my chicken tikka baguette between my hands. It was becoming clear that Bex wanted more from our situation than I did. Could I blame her? She didn't have any other commitments or responsibilities. She was twenty-four years old, with A LOT of disposable income, the freedom that I felt I was missing out on.

Was I though?

Was I missing out? I was so confused.

The past few nights had made me realise that actually I had been missing out – I had chosen to exclude myself from the most precious times. Fucking idiot.

3.50pm arrived before I knew what was happening. It was then that I remembered David's request from the previous afternoon to book in to see him in a few weeks. I emailed Glenda:

To: glenda.willis@morrisandco.co.uk
From: robert.lawson@morrisandco.co.uk
Date: 21 April 15.53pm
Subject: Proposed meeting

Hi Glenda

David mentioned last night that he'd like to meet with me

once we've handed over the Berlin project. He said you'd know all the details.

Kind regards

Rob Lawson
Global Marketing Manager
Morris and Co
Tel: 01905 769769
Email: robert.lawson@morrisandco.co.uk
"No project too big, we'll always deliver your vision."

My laptop bonged just as I was about to close it down and put it in my bag. One new message received.

To: robert.lawson@morrisandco.co.uk
From: glenda.willis@morrisandco.co.uk
Date: 21 April 15.57pm
Subject: Re: Proposed meeting

Hi Rob

Thank you for your email.

Indeed, I do know about the proposed meeting. David has requested that you clear your diary for a whole day. He would like to take you off site, but you're to meet here in the office in the morning.

I have two dates available for him at the moment:
Monday 16 May
Wednesday 18 May

Please let me know which of these dates is convenient?

You will not need to prepare anything prior to your meeting, or indeed bring anything with you. All information will be provided, including refreshments.

Regards
Glenda

Glenda Willis
PA to David Morris
Tel: 01905 769769
Email: glenda.willis@morrisandco.co.uk
"No project too big, we'll always deliver your vision"

Clicking open my calendar, I had a look at both proposed dates and then hit reply:

To: glenda.willis@morrisandco.co.uk
From: robert.lawson@morrisandco.co.uk
Date: 21 April 15.59pm
Subject: Re Re Proposed meeting

Monday 16 May please Glenda

Thanks for your help.

Rob
Rob Lawson
Global Marketing Manager
Morris and Co
Tel: 01905 769769
Email: robert.lawson@morrisandco.co.uk
"No project too big, we'll always deliver your vision."

That night's meal wasn't quite ready when I got home, so after snuggling the kids and breathing in their unique hair smell, I offered to help Annie finish off. It might not seem like much. A husband offering to help make the family dinner? Right? Except never had I ever offered to help make any dinner. Never.

As she had it all under control, I laid the table as she assembled the enchiladas and dips.

As always, the food was delicious, and I really enjoyed watching the kids pick from each other's plates and construct their meals. My heart seemed to expand with joy.

Annie seemed brighter throughout the meal and even chit-chatted with me about my day, and we talked about Lexie's day at school. All in all, it was just a wonderful evening. Astoundingly, I even remembered to pass on David's wishes.

That evening after the children were asleep, Annie sat in the conservatory working her way through the many letters and flyers that had come home with Lex from school. I watched her as I stood waiting for the kettle to boil, perhaps looking at her for the first time in a long time. I saw the beautiful woman I'd married, but she was tired.

Was I responsible for that tiredness, the heavy look about her shoulders? Come on, Rob, of course I was. I'm a fucking idiot! Selfish, self-centred, idiotic excuse for a husband. I had fucked up, I knew it. But I had no idea how to unfuck it!

Friday is frigging awesome. Early finish day! YES!!!!!

But rather than my usual habit of texting "I'm running behind" to Annie I texted to say that I'd collect Louis from nursery and Lexie from school. You know what? I actually wanted to do it. I wasn't trying to get in Annie's good books; I wanted to collect my children and spend a bit of time with them.

Annie didn't respond, but I knew she'd read the message, so I finished work at 1pm and as I was leaving my office, I caught sight of Bex standing down the corridor, staring at me. She looked… 'simmering' is the only word I can accurately use. Yep, she was a pot ready to boil over! I didn't hang about for her to explode over me. I left and headed to the nursery and Louis.

I collected my boy with ease. The nursery functions like a military operation, with passwords required even before they'll unlock the door to you! He was so excited to see me that he ran straight through his sandcastle he'd been constructing.

Collecting Lexie was an altogether different story. Good God, the playground is a strange place. It's almost reminiscent of the animal kingdom. You have your dominant pack, the lesser herd and then, finally, the timid creatures that hang back for fear of being spotted. Having little or no experience of this place, I stood on my own with Louis constantly trying to drag me towards the mums and dads who Annie obviously stood and talked to and who, therefore, he knew. But I stood my ground and bravely stayed away from all of them!

After we'd successfully retrieved Lex, we went down the road to the local play park. The kids love it here because it's got a wibbly-wobbly slide. As they ran up the steps and screamed all the way down, I texted Annie:

Shall I pick up chippers for tea?

She responded almost straight away:

Sounds nice. Just a mini fish and chips for me please.

The kids and I had such fun at the park, real unconditional fun. No computers or phones to interfere, just us and their imaginations. I loved it.

Fish and chips were eaten out of the paper as we sat on the living room floor with *Willy Wonka* playing in the background. Louis even asked for seconds – well, Annie's food became his seconds anyway!

I can honestly say, hand on heart, that night was the best family night we'd experienced for a very long time. Some days I yearn to go back to that night, to the simplicity of it and the magic that love created.

After everyone had gone to bed and I'd got back from taking Beau for her last walk, I couldn't help but compare how much had changed within a week. One week ago, I woke Annie and effectively told her our marriage was over. I meant it as well. At that moment I'd believed that I couldn't and wouldn't remain in the constraints of my marriage, I was suffocating, drowning in a sea of mundanity, regime and predictability.

Now as I cleaned Beau's paws in the utility room, I had no fucking clue what I wanted or what the hell was going on.

Ten

Dinners 8–9 The Realisation…

Saturday dawned bright and breezy. I felt refreshed for being in bed last night before 10pm. Totally unheard of for me. I reached across the bed to find the space empty and cold. The *en suite* door was closed, but I could hear Annie. She was being sick.

"You ok?" I asked as I gently knocked on the door.

"Must have been last night's fish. Can you sort the kids out please?" she asked, as she opened the door clutching a hand towel to her mouth. She looked utterly awful, ghostly white and gaunt. Dark circles hung under her eyes, and her whole demeanour spoke of someone being drained physically and emotionally by sickness.

She almost crawled back into bed and, with effort, pulled the duvet back up over herself.

I refilled her glass and went to the cupboard in the bathroom where we kept a spare washing-up bowl, collectively known as the sick bowl, and put it beside her.

"Just try and sleep, I'll have them all day. Maybe we can go and see my mum? I'll take Beau as well. The house can be quiet and you can recover."

She murmured a response, but I've no idea what language she was speaking!

Organising two children under seven isn't easy, let me tell you – especially when you're a rookie like me! Christ those two can't half run rings around me! Chocolate somehow made it into breakfast, and as a snack afterwards – I've no idea how! Louis dressed himself as Superman, although I'm sure when I left his room, he was putting trousers and a top on. Lexie emerged dressed as a Disney princess, but I know for sure she had had on a playsuit. Good Lord, how did Annie do this every day and maintain order?

Visiting Mum was great. She was so surprised to see us, and I was so thankful to find her at home! After kisses and cuddles, the kids made a beeline for the massive dollhouse that dominates the dining room. Dad made the house for me and my cousin Alison when we were about eight years old, and now my kids absolutely love it.

With apple juices all round and a plate of chocolate fingers to keep them going, Mum and I went and sat in her conservatory with a cup of tea. I pulled on my big boy pants and uttered the words I knew I'd end up saying.

"I've ballsed up, Mum," looking her in the face, "I mean, really messed up."

For the next ten minutes my mum listened without interruption, never once giving away what she was thinking about me.

"So that's about it, Mum! I've messed up and I don't know how to make it better, or what the hell to do." That's when it happened, the tears fell. I couldn't control them. I didn't even know why I was crying. Was it the grief for the end of my marriage? The guilt for the hurt I'd caused? The shame? The pain? The relief of talking about it? Oh, it was everything!

Moving from her chair, Mum came and sat next to me on the sofa and put her arm around me, just like she's always done.

"Oh, my darling boy. It's ok. It's ok," she just kept saying over and over again.

When I'd finally regained myself, she offered me a box of tissues.

"Well, Robert, you certainly don't do things by half, do you?" She chuckled. "Do you want my honest advice or just someone to massage your ego?"

I stared at her, knowing full well I was in for it! I was going to have a serious telling-off.

"You've made a mistake, Rob. Right now, I'm not sure if the outcome of that mistake is in your hands. It's really sitting at Ann's feet. You've been unfaithful to her, and she is well within her rights to tell you to shove off. I know you said you wanted a divorce, but I'm not sure that's exactly what you want, Rob, is it?"

"I don't know, Mum, I'm so confused. My head hurts, my heart hurts, my stomach hurts."

"Well sweetheart, the question is simple really. Do you want a life that doesn't include Annie?"

Instantly I responded, and the response took me by surprise, "God, no!"

"Well, there you are then, son. Seems to me that you've got some serious work to do in order to make it up to Ann and repair the damage to your marriage."

At that moment both the kids and Beau came running in to show us that one of the doll-house people had lost their leg!

BOOM! Back to it.

After a few hours visiting my mum, the kids, Beau and I returned home to find Annie still asleep upstairs. So, shutting the living room doors, and telling them that on pain of death neither of them were allowed to venture upstairs, I set about preparing that night's meal, while simultaneously allowing them to paint and craft at the dining room table. After a conference-like discussion, us three Lawsons decided on a picnic-style meal in the conservatory, blanket on the floor and all! I'd got the hang of this multitasking malarky.

Around 4.30pm, just as we were carrying all the nibbly bits through to the blanket in the conservatory, that Lou had proudly laid out with added assorted farm animals, Annie appeared wrapped in her dressing gown. She had a little more colour to her face, but just watching her every move you could see she was in pain.

However, she sat with us in the conservatory and although she didn't really eat anything, you could see how much she enjoyed being there. She listened intently as the kids told her how they'd made the jam sandwiches and rice crispy cakes all by themselves!

After the meal, the kids put on the little show that they'd been practising all afternoon, in the hopes that it would make Mommy feel better. As instructed, Annie and I sat next to each other on the sofa as the attentive audience, and the show began. Somewhere around the second act (or about five minutes in) Annie placed her hand on my leg and left it there. This simple act by a wife to her husband reverberated deep within me. She was literally and figuratively leaning on me.

I put everyone, Annie included, to bed, made sure they all had fresh drinks and returned downstairs to tidy up the carnage that had been the day's activities. As I reassembled the lounge cushions, I decided that tomorrow I wanted to do something with the kids. I wanted to spend more time with them. It was clear that whatever had knocked Annie sideways had really taken its toll, so the peace and quiet would only help her. Thank goodness it hadn't spread around the house. Grabbing myself a bottle of beer out of the fridge, I went hunting under the sink and pulled out a packet of antibacterial wipes and went to do battle with the bathrooms.

On Sunday, I got the kids up, fed and dressed with relative ease. I think because I'd warned them that Mommy still wasn't feeling well, they knew they needed to be on their best behaviour. Lexie was a little sad, as she said her tummy had been hurting in the night, just like Mommy's, but it was feeling better now.

Lexie is such a sweet-natured child. She has always been the same. She will, I'm sure, grow up to work within the care industry. She loves taking care of you when you're poorly, making sure your pillows are plumped enough, bringing many drinks, and simply asking after your wellbeing every ten minutes.

We left the house by 9.05am and headed to our local leisure centre and their amazing leisure pool, with slides and chutes. What's not to love? Oh, my goodness we had a blast! Not a cross word from any of us, just fun. Lexie's swimming lessons were really starting to pay off; she was confident in the water, although she still preferred being able to touch the bottom, but was more than happy to venture down the slides by herself now. Louis, who was still in the beginners' classes, was content to spend the whole time clinging to my arms and splashing me as much as possible!

We had lunch in the onsite café that overlooks the pool. Both kids opted for a sausage roll and mini hot chocolates and I settled on a coffee and a slice of cake. Life was just gently passing by. I can't say I felt that we were in any rush to be anywhere or do anything, and it was great. We finished lunch with a very intense game of I Spy. I've no idea who won!

Annie was up by the time we got back home. She was in the kitchen preparing the veggies for dinner tonight. Apparently, we were going to be having a roast chicken dinner – yumm.

"I'll do that, you go and sit down," I said, as we bundled in.

Annie was still in her dressing gown, but her hair was damp after she'd managed to have a shower, which she said had made her feel better. She looked fragile, but better than yesterday.

"No, it's fine, everything is under control. The chook is in the oven. Veggies are just about done. Besides, it's nice to be a little occupied by something else. Takes my mind away from how rough I've been feeling!"

I occupied the kids with football and tag in the garden for the rest of the afternoon. We even lay on the grass, Lou one side of me, Lex the other, staring at the clouds, shape-spotting.

"Hey you bunch of hooligans, your dinner is ready, time to come and wash up!" Annie called as she hung her head out of the conservatory door.

The kids rushed into the downstairs toilet to wash their hands and faces. I followed and grabbed hold of Annie's elbow before she entered the kitchen.

"Are you ok Ann? Shall I dish the food and you sit down?"

"I'm much better, just still a bit washed out. Another early night for me and I should be right as rain tomorrow!"

Dinner was bloody gorgeous. I'll say something for my wife, she makes a banging roast.

The kids told Annie all about our adventure at the swimming pool, including how Lexie had definitely mastered being a mermaid!

"I'm sorry I missed it. It sounds like you had the most fun."

"We're sorry you missed it as well Mommy. You would have loved seeing Lou being a shark!" I laughed in reply.

I meant it as well. I wished that Annie had been with us, our family all together. I couldn't remember the last time I'd missed Annie. She was always there, never far away. It was me that had moved far away.

As I watched her help Louis tackling his "trees" (broccoli) she definitely looked tired. The food poisoning had taken it out of her but she was naturally beautiful, my beautiful wife. The way she interacted with the kids; she was a natural mother, she never got angry with them, always patient and calm, always listened to everything they had to say, playing endless combinations of made-up games. She didn't have an ounce of negativity within her, fuelled by love and kindness.

It was at this moment, precisely this moment, that I acknowledged the little voice inside my head that kept repeating over and over again: "You've fucked up, you idiot. You've fucked up, you idiot."

Gasping to regain my breathing, I passed it off as a cough, as Annie looked towards me and smiled. I realised that with all my being I loved my wife, and I wanted my family.

Eleven

Dinners 10–12 The Meadow...

Monday dawned again and as I lay warm and comfortable under the duvet, Annie sleeping next to me, for the first time in a long time I decided that I didn't want to go to work. I simply couldn't muster the energy to go in and do the daily political battle of the workplace. I wasn't sick, I wasn't incapable of going, I just couldn't face it.

I must have nodded off again, because the next thing I knew, Annie was shaking me.

"Lawson, you're going to be late! You've slept through your alarm, you gommo! Get up old man!"

Rolling over, I stared bleary-eyed at her. "I'm not going in today."

"You're not going in? Since when? Are you sick?" She moved further across the bed at the prospect of my being sick.

"Nah not sick, just not going in today," I said, running my hands through my hair and shifting to a more comfortable position.

"Phew! Well, that's ok then. Do you want some tea and breakfast?" she asked as she got out of bed and put her slippers and dressing gown on.

"Yes please, I'll get up now. It'll be nice to eat breakfast with the kids before school."

Breakfast turned out to be A LOT more enjoyable in my head. Rice Krispies flew through the air like missiles, toast crusts ended up in my hair. But there wasn't a single cross word, just screeching and laughing!

As I saw Annie and the kids off to school, I called the office and left a message that I was sick and wouldn't be in.

I grabbed Beau's lead and as we walked down Chestnut Grove, I pulled out my phone and texted Zak to meet us in the Meadow in ten minutes.

It's at this time that I must acknowledge my best friend, Zak Matthews, and how he has held me accountable for my behaviour and everything that has happened as a consequence.

Zak and I have been friends since Year 2 of first school. We would run around the playground every break, pretending we were superheroes. He was always Batman and I was Superman. Neither of us was the better hero; we were, and always have been, equals. I love him and respect his opinion about everything. I even asked his opinion before I asked Annie to marry me.

"You are kidding right?" he nearly choked on his beer.

"No! Of course, I'm not joking. I'm going to ask her. She's definitely the one." I felt very offended by his remark.

"Lawson, I've been telling you since the two of you started going out, you are punching mate! Annie Stephens is well out of your league! Christ, let's be honest, she's well out of my league as well! Why the hell does she even hang out with us? Mystery!"

Pondering what he'd said, I asked, "Do you feel like that, Liv?" and turned to look at Zak's fiancée, Liv Adlington. The four of us often double-dated, and got on so well.

"Lawson, it doesn't matter what I think, or Zak for that matter. Do you love Annie?"

"With all my heart."

"Will you hurt Annie?"

"Never intentionally."

"Will you remain faithful to her for as long as you both shall live?"

"Of course, Vicar," Zak and I sniggered.

"Then that is what matters. No one else's opinion or belief should have any bearing on the direction of your life." She took a long swig of her beer.

"Thanks Liv, you're so wise."

"Yeah, I know! But for what it's worth, Lawson, Zak is spot on, you are punching!" With that we all fell about laughing.

As we left the pub that night and said our goodbyes and then walked in different directions, Zak and Liv shouted back at me, "Oi, Lawson."

"Yeah?" I turned to face them.

"We both think she's quite possibly THE most perfect person we've ever met and she'd be crazy not to say yes."

Thankfully, they were too far away to see the tears that they brought to my eyes. I loved my best friends dearly.

After finishing high school, Zak and I went in different directions, but never lost our friendship. Zak followed in his dad's footsteps as he joined the Matthews family business and became a first-class plasterer. Me with marketing.

I was best man at his and Liv's wedding, and gave a banging best man speech that still gets spoken about today – and for the right reasons!

As Beau and I climbed the stile and walked through the Meadow, Zak and his dog, Poppy, were already pushing through the long grass.

"Alright bud? What's up?" he asked as he hugged me.

"Mate I need your advice. I've fucked up big time."

"What the hell now! I'm not covering for you with Annie because you've been buying secret KFCs again! Liv gave me such a rollicking last time!" he chuckled.

We carried walking deeper in to the Meadow, a beautiful community pasture that is loved by local dog walkers and nature enthusiasts. "I asked Annie for a divorce, and I've been seeing someone else."

Zak stopped in his tracks, turned and stared at me open-mouthed, his eyes flicking from side to side. I didn't see his punch coming, it got me square on the side of my face and I hit the ground like a ton of bricks. I deserved it.

Crumpled on the grassy floor, I sobbed like a child, like my heart was breaking. Zak had continued to walk on, leaving me in my crumpled mess. Beau came over and licked my head, loving me unconditionally. Tears blurring my vision, I rubbed our dog's head until she was distracted by Poppy's barking and ran off to join her.

"OFF your arse NOW, Lawson!" shouted Zak. He'd doubled back and was now standing behind me. His loud voice made me jump up in the air.

"You do not get to sit there feeling sorry for yourself. Get up, dust yourself off and shut the fuck up!"

Taken aback by his bluntness, I did as I was instructed. I knew he'd be disappointed in me, but even by Zak's standards this was bad. He walked back and joined the girls, who were investigating the hedgerow.

Catching up to them, I apologised as I blew my nose.

"It ain't me you should be apologising to, is it? So, spill it, bell-end!"

"Mate, come on! I get I've messed up, but God, you're being a bit harsh on me!"

"I'll let you know when it's time to not be harsh on you. Now spill it."

"I've been a selfish dick. I thought I was trapped by domesticity, but I wasn't, I was just blind to seeing how amazing my little family is."

Silently simultaneously nodding his head and rolling his eyes, Zak listened without interruption.

"I had my head turned by one of the younger staff. Honestly though mate, it was just sex. I don't even know if it can be classed as an affair? She was just a…release?"

"Idiot!"

"I know! When I was away in Berlin, Bex was with me. I enjoyed the freedom that came with her, the lack of responsibility.

God, she practically offered it to me on a plate – every single day. Whenever and wherever I wanted it. So, when I got back, I woke Ann up and told her I wanted a divorce. She looked shattered, Zak, like I'd just ripped her heart out and stomped on it."

I dragged my feet, hardly able to look my oldest friend in the face, shame filling my every cell. I couldn't find any more words to explain my behaviour.

"Well, Rob, I'm not surprised."

I stopped short and stared open-mouthed at my best mate. Firstly, he'd called me Rob, secondly, "What do you mean?"

"Well, anyone with any sense could see that you'd pulled away from your relationship with Annie about six months ago. But I've no idea why! You just seemed bored, with everything. This Bex woman sounds like an easy out, sex with no strings. Annie? She is Annie and she comes as a package deal – your package!!"

This felt like a knife through me. He was absolutely right, and I knew it. I hated (and loved) how bloody right he always was! He had my number and there was nothing I could do about it.

"What did Annie say? Does she know about 'her'?"

"She guessed! And she guessed that I was with her in Berlin! Not much gets past her. Her reaction has been the thing I haven't been able to get my head around. She hasn't shouted at me once Zak, not once! She hasn't hit me, thrown anything at me, or even cried! Nothing! She said that she accepts my request and will grant me the divorce, quietly. She doesn't want anything from me, not even the house."

"Bloody hell!"

"I know! I was miffed to begin with, like, why isn't she fighting for us? Then I felt selfish because I'm not exactly fighting for us. I'm so confused. Then she follows it up with one of her conditions…"

"Aghhhh, this sounds like the Annie I know!"

"She said that she will grant my request in thirty days' time. However, during that time, she wants us to sit down each evening as a family and have dinner together. In other words, I'm to come home in time for dinner and we're all to be together each evening!"

"Ummmmm, ok? Wait! That's brilliant!" smiled Zak.

"This past week I've been so confused, mate!"

"Of course, you have, because let me guess, for the first time in a long time you're seeing how amazing your family is? Because, Rob, you really don't look like someone at the end of their tether trying to leave a relationship. You sound like someone realising they've ballsed up big time!"

"For fuck's sake, do you have to be so right all the time!"

Chuckling to himself, Zak added, "I'm not wrong, am I?"

"No, I don't think you're wrong, and I don't know how to undo what I've done. Help me. Please."

"No, pretty boy, you made your bed – lie in it." With that he called Poppy and walked back to the exit of the Meadow and off towards his home. Leaving me and Beau alone in among the long grass.

Alone with my thoughts, my swirling confusion of thoughts.

When we got home, I sat for a while just staring into space, trying to find some sense in the midst of the mess. Dinner this evening was going to be simple, simple is my middle name when it comes to cookery, so it was jacket potatoes and salad all round!

As I methodically cut all the ingredients for the salad, I found the process very cathartic, very focusing.

At around 3.30pm, the peace of the house was broken by everyone coming in, and they were all super pleased to see me, and even more happy to see the food weighing down the dining table. As the kids tucked in, I leaned across the table and took Annie's hand.

"Are you ok? You haven't been home all day."

"Oh yeah," she said, pushing her food around her plate, "I'm really busy with the PTA at school at the moment, lots of planning ready for September term, Christmas Fair and stuff. Did you have a good day working at home?"

"I didn't work from home. I just didn't go in today. I'm going to email David after the kids are asleep and tell him I'm going to take the week off. I need a rest, Ann. I feel like my brain is turning to mush!"

Annie's face creased with shock. I couldn't blame her. Never in my whole working career have I ever just 'not turned up'. She sat silently for a few moments.

"Of course, you deserve a break. Look, I know there's a list of jobs that probably need doing around the house, but don't even bother with those either. Just relax – properly. Take Beau for long walks, lie on the floor playing puzzles with Lou. Sleep in. Just rest. You need your strength." She patted my hand and intertwined her fingers in mine.

I sat on the sofa in the lounge with my laptop on my lap rather than sitting alone in the office. Annie was curled up on the other end of the sofa under a blanket, snoozing and half watching the latest episode of her murder mystery programme.

To: david.morris@morrisandco.co.uk
From: robert.lawson@morrisandco.co.uk
Date: 25 April 20.39
Subject: Annual leave request

Evening David

Firstly, my apologises for not being in today. I hope everything went smoothly with the handover to Berlin?

I would like to request some time off work. I have a few personal issues that have come up that I need to deal with. I am happy to use my annual leave for this period. I'm looking to come back to work next Monday.

Rob

Rob Lawson
Global Marketing Manager
Morris and Co
Tel: 01905 769769
Email: robert.lawson@morrisandco.co.uk
"No project too big, we'll always deliver your vision."

Staring blankly at the telly after I'd hit 'send', I felt a small weight lifted off my shoulders. I'd given myself some breathing space. Some time to think. Now I just had to work out what the heck was going on! The bong of an email arriving pulled me back from the telly. It was an email from David.

To: robert.lawson@morrisandco.co.uk
CC: bryony.micham@morrisandco.co.uk
From: david.morris@morrisandco.co.uk
Date: 25 April 20.42
Subject: Re Annual leave request

Rob

Of course! We'll see you next Monday. Don't even think about turning your laptop on this week. We will all still be here when you get back.

On a side note, if there is anything I can do to help or support, please just ask. You have my personal mobile number, just call day or night.

Much love to Annie and the kids. Rest up son.

David

Bryony – please can you accept this email as authorisation for Rob's absence over the coming week. We'll fill in all the necessary paperwork when he returns. Today will be given as paid leave, the next four days as annual leave.

David Morris
Managing Director
Morris and Co
Tel: 01905 769769

I have a lot of respect for David and his work ethic had passed on to me, although I wasn't sure I could permanently keep up the pace with which he worked. I once heard a rumour that he only slept for four hours a night! God, that is something I couldn't emulate! I love my sleep!

Annie had gone on up to bed and I locked the house up after letting Beau out for one last time. I took my mobile out and used the torch to light my way up the stairs so as not to wake the kids. When I was two steps up the stairs, I noticed I had messages and missed calls from Bex. I must have flicked my phone to 'do not disturb' at some point today. Standing on the stairs, listening to the rhythmic breathing of my family, I felt with a sense of certainty that I knew what I needed to do. Without even reading the messages I deleted the thread, closed my phone and carried on up to bed, to my Annie. To what I truly wanted. But I needed a sounding board, I needed to make sure I didn't hurt her anymore. I'd text Zak in the morning.

Tuesday began in a wash of heavy rain and, because I wasn't rushing out the door to get ahead of the traffic, I offered to take the kids to school and nursery.

Annie said she was meeting her friends today so wouldn't be home for much of the day, so I had the house to myself.

I made the kids breakfast and noticed a few empty spaces in the food cupboard, so, after making sure they were safely delivered to school, I headed for the supermarket to top up on provisions.

I couldn't remember the last time I'd been to a supermarket to actually shop, rather than to quickly buy lunch. The notion that I wasn't on a time limit was strange as I wandered around the aisle. As I rounded the bakery aisle, standing in front of me was Liv, Zak's wife. She stared open-mouthed at me, and I knew instantly that Zak had told her what I'd done. She was obviously deciding what she was going to do or say.

Pushing her trolley past me, she spat through gritted teeth, "I cannot believe your selfishness. Annie doesn't deserve this in her life. Your children deserve a better role model. Have you no shame? Don't you care?" Holding up her hand to shush me, she carried on as I hung my head, knowing full well that anything she had to say to me, I deserved. "Your level of disrespect is truly astounding. What the hell are you thinking, Rob? Forget that – I know exactly what you were thinking! Idiot!" and she walked off, leaving me alone in the aisle, surrounded by bread.

God, everything she said was right. I was an idiot.

Suddenly, from behind, I was enveloped in a hug and Liv wrapped me in cocooning warmth.

"We love you with all our hearts and always will. You're a fucking idiot, but you're our fucking idiot."

And, just as quickly as the hug came, it went again.

I was left bereft, bare and broken.

Arriving home, I took Beau for her walk, sticking to the paths, as I didn't fancy traipsing through the wet grass, although when we returned, I still had to clean her muddy paws. I spent most of the walk in a daze. I know I didn't fall in a hedge, or in anyone's wheelie bin, so I must have been paying attention, but I can't tell you what I saw, or where we walked. I just put one foot in front of the other and moved. Trying to make sense of the jumble of thoughts, what my mum had said, what Zak had said and now what Liv had said. Trouble is, none of it made any sense.

Sitting in the lounge after making a cup of coffee, I opened my laptop, got up a document with two boxes in front of me, and started to fill them in:

Divorce

PROS	CONS
Sex with Bex is more active	Break my family unit up
	Have to move house

76

Beginning 'dating' again
– do I want that?

Comfort of partner who
I know

Love my children

Love my wife?

Sadness

Loss

Upset

Pain

Here's where I stopped...

Was the reason I wanted a divorce because being with Bex made me feel twenty-one again?

I did, at one time, believe I'd fallen out of love with my marriage, with Annie.

Maybe I hadn't fallen out of love, maybe that love had changed? Had the love changed? Matured?

Annie and I hadn't had sex in a while, but was that the foundation for a long-term relationship?

Did I want a divorce?

Zak was saying no I didn't! Liv was saying no I didn't! My list was saying no I didn't! My heart was saying no I didn't! My head was...confused.

Why was I so confused?

I exited the document, not saving it, closed the laptop and pulled out my phone. Time to bite the bullet and grovel to Zak.

"Alright dude? You talking to me yet?" I texted.

"No," came the reply. Smiling, I knew I was in. My mate could never stay mad at me for too long.

Ok great. Cause I need your advice.

I ain't helping you clamber out of the shit! You dug your hole, now sit in it.

You're right. I have dug my hole. I've made a massive hole. So big that I can actually entertain while being in said hole. So, would you like a metaphorical cuppa while in my hole?

Coffee please... Now what the fuck do you want knob, I mean, Rob!

I think I have messed up. I think I made a mistake telling Ann I want a divorce. I don't think that's actually what I want at all!

No shit Sherlock!
Good God, Lawson,
I could have told
you that right from
the start. You are
a first-class knob!
You have one of
THE most perfect
wives and you want
to give that up? Go
and find Annie and
tell her you made a
monumental fuck-up
and please will she
forgive you.

I felt like I almost whispered the reply "What if she won't mate?"

"Then buddy, you will and forever more be known as Mr Knob. TTFN."

It was time to collect my babies.

When we got back, Annie was elbow deep in dinner preparations – tonight's feast...homemade fish pie and veggies.

Oh, come on, I think we can all agree by now that there is no way on earth I'd be able to make a fish pie from scratch! A fish pie from the microwave yes, no problemo! Annie is most certainly the chef in our house.

While the kids were devouring their food and, can I point out, barely breathing between mouthfuls, I leaned over the table to quietly talk to Ann.

"I was wondering, as I'm not going to work tomorrow, if you fancied going out, just you and me? I mean after we've dropped the kids off?"

She seemed genuinely taken aback by my request but, without hesitating, she said she'd like that.

Fantastic, I was so chuffed! As I kissed Lexie goodnight, it dawned on me, I had absolutely no idea where I'd take her!

Idiot!

It was Wednesday, halfway through my self-imposed week off and I was starting to feel less tired. I managed to have a good night's sleep. The weather was a complete contrast to yesterday, with not a cloud in the sky and blazing sunshine.

We both took the kids to school. Divide and conquer being the motto of the morning, I took Louis to nursery while Annie walked Lexie around to her classroom. We met back at the car, and locked our seatbelts while simultaneously releasing a sigh of relief that they were both where they should be, by the right time. After all, that was what parenting is all about!

"Where are we going?" Annie asked as she shifted to get comfy in her seat.

Focusing on pulling out into the road at drop-off was like navigating the streets of a war zone! They come at you from all angles, and you've got to drive for everyone else on the road.

"Well, after giving it some thought last night and after a few scrapped ideas, I decided it should actually be your choice! And, no, it's not an easy cop-out. I thought it would be good to go somewhere you want to go."

Stunned palpable silence followed. I couldn't really look at her face as I was travelling in downtown Bromsgrove with its rogue SUVs!

"I'd like to go to the lake with the little boat café and blankets outside," she responded after a couple of minutes.

"Right you are, then that's where we're going," I replied, turning right and heading in the direction of the lake.

"Thank you, I do understand and appreciate you letting me choose."

We arrived just as the owner was opening up.

"Morning folks," she greeted us as we got out of the car, with a big smile.

"Morning," Annie and I smiled back.

"Go on round and grab yourselves some blankets, guys. I'm just opening up and then I'll come and get your order once I'm up and running." She manoeuvred the "ice cream for sale" sign onto the edge of the car park.

Grabbing a blanket each from the massive woven willow box, I followed Ann as she chose where we'd sit. Close to the edge, but not near the steps. It really was a glorious spring morning, bright sunshine, still a hint of winter in the breeze, but a promise of something warmer on its way.

We sat in silence staring out over the lake. A couple of brave open-water swimmers were doing their thing in among the reeds and fish. Two of the lake's employees were in the water tending to the inflatable obstacle course that would open in a few weeks' time. We had taken the kids last year and they loved it. I, however, had spent the whole hour in the water swinging from joy to terror as I made sure that neither of them drowned!

The silence between Annie and I wasn't really awkward, but I think we both knew what was coming.

"Are you still seeing her?" she asked.

I didn't turn to look at her, I couldn't look at her, I focused on a duck out on the lake.

"Yes," I answered honestly and heard her gasp, and quickly followed it up with, "but not since last week though." I turned to look at her as she stared out across the water. "I've so enjoyed the last few days, Annie. I think that's why I didn't want to go to work."

"She's at your work?"

"Yes."

"Sorry to keep you waiting, folks, what can I get you?" said the owner, who had appeared beside our table, notepad and pencil in hand.

"Two hot chocolates please," Annie answered for both of us.

"Coming right up." The owner walked back inside her cafe to bustle about making our orders.

"I am truly sorry Ann, I never, ever meant to hurt you. I've been incredibly selfish, and I see that now. I'm so sorry."

"I know."

That's it. That's all she said. But there was an all-consuming sadness that spread across her whole body. Almost like she'd accepted her fate and that in her mind our marriage was done. She'd taken me at my word and was done, and so she should. It is, after all, what I said I wanted.

I'd caused this misery. I couldn't do it anymore. I was breaking her.

Our drinks arrived and brought welcome warmth with them.

"Mum and Dad have asked if the kids would like to have a sleepover next weekend. What do you think?" I don't think she was changing the subject, simply asking my opinion.

"Sounds great, they always love it there."

We continued to drink our scrummy hot chocolate in relative silence.

"I'd like to go home now. I'm still feeling the effects of that sickness."

So, I took Annie home and she went upstairs to have a nap before the kids needed to be collected. I prepared that night's tea, simple, chicken kebabs.

At 2.30pm Annie was still sound asleep, so I walked the five minutes to collect the kids. They were thrilled that I'd picked them up again. It was noticeable to me how much I missed out on simply by always being at work. When we got back, Annie was still sleeping, so the three of us attempted to combine ingredients to produce something edible.

Once everything was cooked (I checked the chicken three times to make sure it was cooked all the way through), we put the food on a tray and I carried it upstairs and surprised a sleepy Mummy with dinner in bed. We all piled under the duvet and scoffed away, it was great. Even Annie was crying with laughter.

I left the kids and Mummy snuggling under the duvet as I took the plates downstairs and loaded the dishwasher. I stood staring at my reflection in the kitchen window, I looked... happy.

I'd not felt happy for such a long time and it physically took my breath away. I gasped as I realised how my self-imposed isolation had stolen my happiness, insight and self-worth.

When I went back upstairs to get the kids ready for showers and bed, I found all three of them fast asleep. They looked... angelic. I took my phone out and took a picture and made it my screensaver.

Tiptoeing back downstairs, I got Beau's collar and took her out for her walk.

Twelve

Dinners 13–16 Such a Shock…

I set my alarm for earlier than normal. We'd have to bath the kids before school, and that definitely needed more time! I left the kids to sleep with Annie in our bed and I spent the night in Lexie's single bed.

The next morning, Annie was feeling much better and bathed Louis while I helped Lexie in the shower with the spraying shower head! I'm not sure who was more wet, me or her!

After the quickest breakfast in history, Annie ushered the kids out the door. I kissed each of them on the head and stopped Annie in her tracks and kissed her goodbye on the cheek. She wouldn't be back after drop-off as she was meeting her PTA chums, leaving me alone and with no excuse or reason not to answer Bex's multiple messages.

Sorry for being quiet lately, got a lot going on here.

Almost instantly a reply came back.

No biggie… I'm free later if you want to meet up?

Did I…?

My body responded with a yes. However, my heart said no. My head again was conflicted.

My finger hovered as I pondered my reply. The phone buzzed in my palm. One message received from Annie.

Your mum has just messaged asking if she can collect the kids from school tonight? I said yes, of course she can, and asked if she'd like to stay for dinner with us, will be nice to see her.

It is one of the things I have always been lucky with. My wife and my mother actually like each other; they love spending time together. Before we were married, Annie and Mum would spend Sundays together, watching movies, baking or shopping. Annie is friends with everyone! She never has a bad word to say. I closed Bex's message and opened Annie's.

Sounds like a plan, Batman. Let's order a pizza delivery.

I stopped typing, held my thumb over the screen and then added,

I miss you

and hit send.

I then went back into Bex's message, again hovering, and wrote,

See you in the office on Monday.

Send. I sighed – actually sighed, because in that moment, I knew.

I needed to end it with Bex. I loved Annie with all my heart, I'd just forgotten that for a while. I wanted my family. I wanted my wife. The question is, did she want me?

Not long after I returned from a long walk with Beau, everyone bundled through the door, with noise, bags and coats galore.

Mum, a sun worshipper, looked well, and a bit tanned. Lexie sat at the dining table and showed her nanny her reading book, while Louis sat on her other side trying to show her the latest tractor he'd got for his collection.

Annie arrived home and greeted Mum with love and excitement.

The pizzas arrived and we had enough food to feed half the street. The kids were so excited. It was lovely to have Mum there, it was lovely to see Annie smiling and laughing.

Mum helped us bathe the kids. She adores being a nanny, she's a natural. She often speaks about how much Dad would have enjoyed being a 'pop'. After we'd tucked both of them safely into bed, we waved goodbye to Mum and Annie went upstairs to have a soak in the bath and read her book.

I put away all the leftovers (there were a lot!) and instead of isolating myself as I always had done before, I went upstairs, had my shower and then got into bed next to my wife and drifted off to sleep holding her tight.

Friday morning was quiet and relatively stress-free. I took the children to school and nursery and then went home via the local florist, where I bought their biggest bouquet. I'd chosen today to be the day I'd begin to make amends.

The lady in the florist was so helpful, offering suggestions in terms of arrangements and flower combinations. Also, I think she might have seen me coming, because twenty minutes later I was the owner of a fancy bouquet and £65.00 lighter.

But getting home didn't go as I planned.

As I turned the corner into our road the blood in my veins turned to ice. Bex was standing on our doorstep and Annie was holding the door open to her. I dropped the flowers where I stood and felt actual pain in my chest. I was struggling to catch my breath.

What was she doing? Was this because I rejected her? Her way of paying me back?

Should I go and get rid of her? Should I hide? Annie didn't know Bex, so she might not know that this was the other woman.

Should I pretend I never saw her? Fuck!!

I stood staring down at the flowers I'd spent a small fortune on, picked them up and had a word with myself. Grow up!

I marched up the Grove and in through the front door. Into my own home. My sanctuary. I could hear them in the kitchen. Kicking off my shoes, I pushed open the connecting door from the living room. I stood and stared at them both.

"Hello love, these are for you." I handed the flowers to Annie and kissed her cheek.

"Oh, Lawson they're beautiful, thank you. Rebekah is here to talk to you," Annie said as she moved to the sink, grabbing one of our wedding vases on the way, and began unwrapping the flowers and rearranging them.

"Thanks love," I responded.

As she lifted the vase filled with the blooms and walked past me, heading towards the living room, she whispered, "You promised me."

F-U-C-K! She knows! Of course, she knows! Why on earth did I think my Annie wouldn't know! Nothing escapes her – ever. Had she guessed? Or been told? I had promised her I'd never bring 'her' here.

"What are you doing here?" I spat at Bex through gritted teeth, pushing the doors closed slightly.

"What's the matter?" she asked, not moving off the bar stool she was sitting on.

"What's the matter? What the hell are you doing here?" I rounded the kitchen island and grasped the edge of the sink, trying to steady myself.

"This needed to be done face-to-face rather than on the phone." She stood up and moved towards me.

"For fuck's sake! How dare you come to my home." I spun round – and pulled back. She was right behind me.

"Don't take that tone with me, Rob. I'm free to see and speak to whomever I choose and I bloody well will!" She slammed her hands on her hips, her anger clearly rising.

"What the fuck do you want, Bex?" I asked. I couldn't keep the exasperation from my voice as I moved away from her.

"To tell your wife, maybe?" She mocked me! She actually mocked me in my own kitchen! I couldn't fucking believe it. She really was showing her true colours. I couldn't believe I'd been sucked in by her. She was an immature, self-centred and self-absorbed, ugly, argumentative human. She even had a smirk on her face! All the qualities I recognised in myself lately.

I opened my mouth to respond but was stopped in my tracks by the living room doors slamming open and Annie marching in.

"She already knows, sweetheart, so what's your next move?" She positioned herself in between Bex and me and wrapped her arm round my waist. Annie hadn't even raised her voice, but she'd won the argument.

You could have knocked Bex over with a feather. Her face was a picture. Utter shock! Horror! She was out of moves – my clever ever-amazing wife was right.

My next move was so uncalled-for and totally immature, but I couldn't help it. I just started laughing at Bex.

Her eyes moved between me and Annie. Bex was staring daggers at both of us, her face growing redder by the second. She was shuffling from one foot to the other. Huffing and opening her mouth as if to say something, but nothing came out.

Annie touched my stomach and I stopped laughing, realising my behaviour was massively inappropriate.

Staring at Annie's hand on my stomach, Bex didn't take her eyes away. She just stood there staring at my wife's hand on me. Suddenly, as if realising what she was doing, she coughed, stood up straighter and stared me in the face.

"David Morris died last night! You need to go to the office now. His family and solicitor are waiting for you. I stupidly volunteered to come and tell you." She turned around and started to storm off towards the front door, but reaching the living room, she turned round and shouted, "He's left the whole business to you." She slammed the front door behind her, and it metaphorically slammed the door on our relationship, and I was so relieved.

I stood stock still. Annie's arms released me and she cupped her mouth, moving to stand in front of me, tears filling her eyes.

David was dead? He'd left the business to me? What? David was dead? I couldn't help it; tears began falling.

Annie put her hands on mine. My Annie stood waiting to comfort me, advise me, love me, my Annie, my wonderful Annie caught me as I broke on the kitchen floor. Broke for my friend, broke for my boss, broke for my mentor, broke for my mistakes, broke for my marriage, broke for my stupidity, broke for my selfishness. As I fell to the floor out came the past few months of my life.

Annie just held me. She didn't let go of me. As I lay crying on the kitchen floor, she just held me. She stroked my back and told me she loved me, over and over again. Just telling me how much she loved me and how she was so sorry, so very sorry.

I don't know how long we lay on the kitchen floor, but Annie's strength and love nurtured me back together. I dried my eyes, pulled myself together and went and washed my face and changed my clothes. Annie came into the bedroom as I straightened my tie in the mirror. Sliding in behind me, she put her hands round my neck and helped me finish off straightening it. Then, coming round in front of me, she slowly and lovingly kissed my lips. Just the briefest of touches but it was a kiss filled with so much promise, so much unsaid. It was exactly what I needed. I needed my Annie, and she was there, ready to catch me if I fell again.

The drive to the office is a journey I've taken for the past five years; I could probably do it with my eyes closed! However, the journey that Friday was like no other I'd ever experienced. It was like I was super alert, focusing in on the strangest little things – a discarded coffee cup on the embankment of the motorway, a stripped tyre from a wagon.

The car park at the office was busy, but I managed to squeeze in beside the fence and took a deep breath before pushing open the reception doors. I took the lift up to the main office level and the door dinged open at Level 3. I emerged into the glass-fronted open vestibule emblazoned with the Morris and Co logo. I could see my colleagues huddling together talking in groups, people sitting at their desks, crying.

Using the fingerprint scanner, I pushed open the double doors and entered the office. Glenda emerged from the conference room and beckoned me to join everyone. She greeted me with a warm hug. She'd clearly been crying. I entered the room to find Sheila Morris sitting in one of the chairs, and next to her was a man I thought I'd seen in the office before. He stood up as I entered.

"Rob, this is Irvin McGuire, David's solicitor, and of course, you know Sheila," Glenda said. I shook Mr McGuire's hand, and moved round the table to Sheila and, as she rose, enveloped her in a hug while telling her how deeply sorry I was for her loss.

"Rob, thank you so much for coming. Glenda has told us you're on annual leave this week," Sheila said, clutching a tissue. She gestured for everyone to sit around the table.

"I can't believe it's true. Is it true?" I knew it was a stupid question, but I needed to hear it from a more reliable source. I'm not saying that I believed Bex to be a liar, but I couldn't be sure.

"Yes, Rob, David passed away last night at home. I was with him," Sheila confirmed.

Ivan McGuire coughed and spoke. "Are you Robert Lawson, Global Marketing Manager of Morris and Co?" he said directly to me.

Pulling my gaze away from Sheila, who was utterly bereft, I properly acknowledged the solicitor for the first time. Struggling with my emotions: "Umm...yes, I am." Shaking my head in the hope of regaining control: "Sorry, yes, that is me."

"Can you please confirm your home address?"

"Uggh, 16 Chestnut Grove, Bromsgrove. Can I ask why you need to know that?" Confusion setting in.

"I just need to establish your identity, Mr Lawson."

"Rob, it's just standard procedure to ensure that you are who we say you are," Sheila confirmed.

"Mr Lawson, David Morris left a detailed and very specific last will and testament that has been implemented as a result of his death. I have been instructed to carry out the instructions of that aforementioned will and testament, and support executer Sheila Morris to the best of my abilities. As such, we have asked you here today to inform you of subsection 4 of Mr Morris's will that directly impacts you."

Glenda placed a glass of water on the walnut table in front of me, pulled a chair closer to mine, sat down and reached over and grabbed hold of my hand. In that moment, it was exactly what I needed, to know that someone was there to support me, to offer me unspoken words of encouragement.

"Robert Charles Lawson, David Wilbur Morris has willed to you his one hundred per cent shares of his company Morris and Co, without reserve. Therefore, in layman's terms, you are now the outright owner of Morris and Co; you are its new Managing Director. There is also a financial buffer of £500,000, should it be required, to see you through this transition period of unease and uncertainty. David has also stated in his will that he would like to gift to you and your wife Annie Lawson the sum of £10,000 with the specific instruction of 'To either have the best holiday ever, or finally convert your bloody loft!'"

I knew I was crying. I knew I was. I just couldn't help myself. Not even if someone had told me to stop. I just needed to cry.

"Mr Lawson, I would like to congratulate you on becoming the owner of a multimillion-pound organisation. I wish you every success. In terms of the legalities of the bequest, all appropriate paperwork will be submitted to the company solicitors and accountants, who in turn will notify HMRC and other appropriate organisations. The second bequest will take a little longer to honour, but I see no reason why you won't have the funds before the end of the month. If I can just have your signature on these two forms, agreeing that we have discussed Mr Morris's wishes."

He slid over an open folder that contained a summarised version of what he'd just told me and at the bottom was space for my signature with my name printed under the line.

Picking up the Morris and Co pen that was waiting next to the glass of water, I read the form from top to bottom, knowing that this could be THE most important piece of paper I ever signed.

Looking up at Sheila, who had been silent this whole time, I asked, "Sheila, are you sure?"

Stifling a sob that seemed to escape, she grasped the tissue to her mouth and composed herself.

"Rob, this is what he wanted, what he'd planned. He knew he couldn't keep going the way he had done in the past. 'Running a company is a young man's game,' he'd say to me. The day he interviewed you all those years ago, he knew it was going to be you who would take over. He even rang me up to tell me, 'She, I've found him! I've found the one I'm going to get to take over the business. He's a bit rough around the edges, but I'll soon mould him into shape!' He was so excited. Never for a single second did he doubt you and what you're capable of, Rob. He knew what an amazing leader you'd be. He knew that you'd push Morris and Co on to bigger and better things."

I couldn't believe what I was hearing. "I had no idea."

"That meeting he asked you to arrange with me? The one offsite? That was to tell you of his plans, Rob."

I turned and stared at Glenda, totally gobsmacked.

"You knew?"

"Of course, Rob. This has taken a lot of planning! Many meetings, discussions and far too many conversations with accountants and solicitors. But finally, we had the go-ahead about three months ago. All the paperwork and folders are ready for the handover process. David had ultimately planned to semi-retire, and still be around while you gradually took over," Glenda said.

"We've just completed on the purchase of a house in North Devon, it was going to be our retirement home, so we'd split our time between here and there," Sheila offered as a way of confirming what Glenda was telling me.

"Mr Lawson, I do understand what a shock this must be for you, and especially at such a heart-wrenching time. However, by law, I need your signature for the bequest to be implemented." Ivan McGuire gestured towards the sheets still in front of me.

Knowing I was so unsure, Sheila added, "Come on, Rob, what on earth am I going to do with his business? I'm not even sure I know exactly what it is you guys do!" She laughed, a genuine laugh, and I laughed too.

I clicked the end of the pen and signed my name twice with purpose, closed the folder and slid it back across the table to the stern-looking solicitor.

"Thank you, Mr McGuire. I appreciate your time today, and your honesty." I stood up and shook hands with him as he packed the folder into his briefcase.

"If that's all, Mrs Morris? I'll see you at the house tomorrow as agreed?"

"Yes, thank you, Ivan. See you in the morning." Sheila touched his arm as he left the conference room, and Glenda showed him out, leaving me and David's wife alone.

"Sheila. I'm not sure that any words I have are going to be enough, but I am truly sorry for your loss. David is, was, a great man. Such an inspiration to me, and so many in this company. That's why we have such a low staff turnover. Once someone starts working here, they very rarely want to leave! I've no idea what the next few days, weeks, months even are going to look like for me and the company, but I swear to you I will do everything within my power to ensure that Morris and Co thrives and flourishes, just as it did when David was steering her."

"I know, Rob. I know."

I arrived home five hours later, having organised a full staff emergency meeting for the next morning. With Glenda's capable hands steering me, we'd pulled together a brief script of what I would say, hopefully to offer reassurance to everyone.

"This is what I do, Rob, you've got to trust me when I say I'm better at this than you'll ever be! Now bog off home and let me do what I'm good at," she said, and she ushered me out of the building.

*

Everyone was in the dining room, eating dinner. I apologised to Annie for not making it back in time. The last thing I'd wanted to do was break my promise to be there for dinner each evening.

"I didn't expect you back. This is much more important. Shall I make you some food?" She stood up and wrapped her arms round my waist, holding on tight to me. Louis jumped up from the table and grabbed hold of my left leg and hung like a monkey, laughing loudly. Lexie joined in and grabbed my right leg.

This...this was what I needed, and I never wanted it to end. I held on tight to my family, telling each of them I loved them.

After the kids were settled into bed, Annie and I sat together on the sofa in the conservatory, as Beau rushed in and out.

"David died of a massive heart attack last night. He has willed me the entire business. I'm the hundred per cent owner of Morris and Co. I'm the sole owner of a company with a turnover of seven million pounds!" I couldn't believe it. I just sat there, my hands in Annie's, and she stroked them, letting me know that she was right there.

"Sheila was wonderful and grateful to know the business will go to someone of worth." I added, I'm not someone of worth though, am I? Good God, I can't even remain faithful to my darling wife.

"What the hell am I going to do, Ann? What the hell are we going to do? David's gone." I broke down again, tears falling freely. I was barely able to control my breathing.

"You listen to me, Robert. You're going to go into the office tomorrow, and you're going to talk to the staff and reassure them, because they are going to be devastated, and fearful for their jobs. Then you will come home and play football in the back garden with your son. Have a colouring competition with your daughter. Climb into bed and hold me tight as you drift off to sleep knowing how truly loved you are, Lawson, because we do love you. I love you."

She held me as even more grief released from my body, but not just grief, it was relief. My Annie loved me. She loved me, even though I'd put her through hell these past weeks. She loved me, and I loved her.

I'd been awake most of the night. Annie refused to let me go downstairs and instead simply held me tight as she slept and I lay there trying to make sense of the last twenty-four hours.

Saturday morning was a struggle. Glenda had done a fantastic job of getting everyone in early; the car park was full as I pulled in. They were all expecting a leader, direction, clarity, stability. None of which I felt I could deliver.

I stood in the conference room with fifty-eight pale, worried and fear-etched faces watching me as I explained what had happened and what would happen. It had become clear that there were a number of false rumours spreading like wildfire around the offices, and they needed to be stopped. I could only hope that I sounded confident because, deep inside, I was shaking with fear and uncertainty.

After everyone had gone and I was alone, I told Glenda she must go home and be with her family, and I promised to lock up. I walked down the corridor past the now-empty conference room to the big double doors that held David's office – my office.

I pushed open the door and was hit by the smell of David's aftershave. I walked around the desk touching this and that. Returning the other side of the desk, I sat in the visitor's chair, facing his chair.

"David? What the bloody hell am I going to do?" I just sat there, and stared and hoped and prayed for inspiration.

I won't bore you with the intricacies of the this's and that's of learning you own a business, and you must learn (quickly) how exactly to run that business, but it was…overwhelming, and that's an understatement.

The drive home was actually helpful. I had the window down and allowed the sound of the engine to be my soundtrack. As I pulled up on the drive, I could hear the kids screeching from the back garden, and it brought a smile to my face. No matter what else was happening, my kids could and would always bring a smile to my face.

Walking through the house, I found everyone in the garden, the kids jumping and running through the octopus sprinkler as

Annie sorted out the BBQ on the patio – great idea, BBQ for tea. I encased her in my arms from behind and held her tight. She patted my arm and asked how it went.

"Worse than I expected, and better than I hoped. Everyone is just numb and shocked. No one can believe he's gone. Glenda had done a great job prepping me and all the info I needed was ready for me. I think she'd going to be a godsend!"

"It's going to be ok, Rob, we'll work it all out." She turned round and embraced me, and I could feel her strength passing to me. "They've been very patient waiting for you all day," she nodded towards the kids.

Kissing the top of her head, I jogged over to the kids. "Right then, kiddliwinks, what's this octopus doing?" I said, as I dashed through the spray and the kids howled with laughter. Annie laughed watching us, and carried on preparing the BBQ.

Two hours later and we'd destroyed many burgers, sausages and chicken strips, not to mention a massive bowl of salad and countless chunks of fresh bread. We all slouched on the garden sofas, too stuffed to move.

"You know, guys, I just want to tell you all how much I love you. I'm sorry I wasn't here much today. But I promise I'll try to be around more, and we'll definitely do more things like running through the octopus, spraying water!"

"Aaaaah, Daddy – I love you too. But we can do other stuff, you know?" Lexie said.

"I know, sweetie, and we will!" I kissed the top of Lexie's head and vowed silently to myself to never let any of them down ever again.

I spent most of the evening exchanging text messages with Zak as I told him what was going on.

Sitting across the living room from Annie, I could see her give me sideways glances every now and then.

"Ann, come and sit next to me." I tapped the cushion next to me on the sofa, purposefully not touching my mobile.

As she sat down, I said, "I need you to see what I'm doing."

"No, Lawson, I don't need to or want to," she said, trying to stand back up.

"No, Ann. It's important that you know exactly what I'm doing, and who I'm doing it with. I'm messaging Zak. I've been telling him what's happened. He has offered advice and help if I need it."

She looked me in the face, smiled her cute half smile and simply said, "Thank you."

On Sunday, I was up before dawn. The house was quiet. Beau didn't even stir as I made my way from the kitchen armed with a big cup of coffee and sat in the home office and opened my work laptop. I needed to get serious about the next few weeks, and get a head start on what I needed to do and who I needed to be talking to.

I opened the first of the files, marked *Rob #1*, that Glenda had given me. It contained all the contact information I needed, and I began working my way down the list emailing each person in turn. Introducing myself, explaining what had happened and that a representative from the organisation would be in touch shortly. Accountants asking for the last-period accounts and summaries, main suppliers for a meeting to discuss going forward. Senior managers to have a meeting Monday morning. I sent many, many emails to Glenda; the poor woman's inbox was going to be rammed when she got in tomorrow. I was lucky that I always got on really well with Glenda; she and I had a similar dry sense of humour. My final email to her was sent as I heard movement upstairs. I expressed my eternal gratitude and informed her that I was at her mercy for the foreseeable future and to show my appreciation I would come armed with many biscuit-based products tomorrow.

Annie offered to bake a big batch of shortbread biscuits that I could take in to the office the next day as, without my even telling her, she knew how busy and fraught the coming days would be. I was lucky to have this remarkable soul standing next to me.

Sunday lunch was roast pork. Unfortunately, I couldn't seem to manage it. But I didn't break my promise to Annie, and I sat at the table as the kids scoffed like they hadn't eaten for two weeks! Annie didn't seem hungry either. The loss of David had hit us all hard. It made us appreciate what we had and who we had.

We both watched our gorgeous children with such pride. Somehow us two crazy kids who met nearly twenty years ago had brought these two amazing souls into the world and, look at them, so perfect, so original, so full of life, so utterly wonderful.

Thirteen

Dinners 17–21 The Longest Week…

After another restless night, day dawned with the realisation that I was now the boss. The buck stopped with me, I couldn't hide behind anyone, I was front row and centre. That came with a big weight of responsibility.

Annie and I had sat in bed, lights off, for a long time the previous night, going backwards and forwards, talking about what had happened, what was going to happen. The logistics of owning a multimillion-pound organisation. How it would impact on our family, on us. After many times round the Wrekin, we came back to the same answer – mostly thanks to Annie's clear thinking and rational brain – we knew absolutely nothing. The only thing we knew for certain was what we could control. Which was our family unit. Our home. Everything else was out of our control and, therefore, we could not pre-empt it, control it or even guess what it would consist off. Stick with what we can control, and allow it to anchor us.

I left before the kids woke up, wanting to be in the office before anyone else arrived. I felt it was important that I had those few moments to compose myself, to centre myself, to get ready!

Annie stood by the front door wrapped in her dressing gown, holding my travel mug filled to the brim with a strong coffee, and the Tupperware box of biscuits.

"Good luck, Boss! It's going to be a tough day, so just accept that right here and now, and look for the positives instead."

"Thank you. I just still can't believe it's happening! This time last week I was racked with guilt because, for the first time in forever, I pulled a sickie. Now I'm the bloody boss!!"

Pulling my coat around my front and holding each side together, Annie looked me in the face and offered me the best advice I have ever had. "Yes, you are the boss. But you're not a tree. If you don't like it – move! You don't have to stay being the boss if you don't like it! However, that said, David wouldn't have left the business to you if he didn't think you could handle it. He believed in you, and so do I."

Nodding my head, as I realised she was right, I added, "You're right, thank you for your calm perspective on life, as always." I was about to add "goodbye" to the end of the sentence when, after a couple of seconds of uncertainty, I leaned in and kissed her on the lips. The first time I'd actually kissed her properly in a few months, and it felt…wonderful, and she didn't pull away. I pulled her closer and hugged her. She felt so thin and small, even through the dressing gown. Another wave of sadness and guilt passed across my heart. I knew that my actions had played a part in that. But not anymore. Never again.

"I promise I'll be home for dinner," I said, as I unlocked the front door.

"My condition is flexible. This isn't what we'd planned. None of this is what we'd ever planned. Poor David. I understand that other things must come first, and they must, Lawson," she responded.

I got in the car and cranked up the heater a bit and waved to her as I reversed off the drive. She was so understanding. How could she be so understanding? There hadn't been an ounce of anger from her. Not even when Bex was in our house. Annie was calm, composed and straight to the point, but she wasn't angry, malicious or vindictive.

As I sat at the traffic lights before the M5 junction it dawned on me that Bex wasn't in the room on Saturday. She wasn't there and I hadn't even noticed!

The day passed in a mish-mash of meetings that seemed to merge into one! God, by about 2pm I thought my head was going to explode. Thank goodness for Glenda, who periodically brought me cups of coffee, biscuits and paracetamol, along with little handwritten messages from Annie. The first one said that she had rung in but didn't want to disturb me, that she just wanted me to know how proud she was of me. My heart leaped. The second said that she was still proud of me!!

On one of my trips back to my old office to collect a file, I passed Bex's desk and it was empty. Retracing my steps, I asked the other admin support, "Andrea, where's Bex?"

"She called in this morning. She was odd. She just said she won't be coming back in again. I emailed Bryony to tell her. It was weird, Rob, she sounded…weird."

"What do you mean, weird?"

"Just toneless," she clarified.

"Toneless?"

"Yeah, you know when someone has no emotion? They're kind of flat." She gestured with her hand.

"So, she's left the company? What about all her stuff?"

"Yep. Gone! She never mentioned her stuff actually!" Andrea shrugged.

"Oh! Are you ok to pick up a little of the slack for today, Andrea?" I enquired. "Are you happy to box up her belongings and put it in the bottom of a cupboard in case she should want it back in a few weeks?"

"Oh yeah, no worries. She hardly did anything around here anyway!" Andrea casually waved her hand in the air.

"Thanks, you're a star!" I walked back, closing the double doors of David's office – I mean my office – and slumped in the visitor's chair. I still hadn't been and sat in his chair yet. I simply had my laptop open and was working at the desk the wrong way round. I couldn't believe it. Bex was gone. She was out of my life! I felt so much relief I actually laughed out loud. Thank God!

I quickly composed an email to Bryony and IT to make certain all the appropriate measures had been taken.

To: bryony.mincham@morrisandco.co.uk;_darren.donal@morrisandco.co.uk
CC:_glenda.willis@morrisoandco.co.uk;_louise.low@morrisandco.co.uk
From: robert.lawson@morrisandco.co.uk
Date: 02 May 14.55
Subject: Rebekah Green

Hi all

I've just seen Andrea and she has told me that Bex has verbally handed in her notice with immediate effect over the phone.

Bryony – HR specific
As there hasn't been a notice period, I just wanted to ensure that everything can be done in her absence, paperwork-wise?

Darren – IT specific
Can you please remove all her log-in details to our systems, and ensure that Louise is passed all information from her files?
Can you also ensure that her fingerprint registry is removed?

Lou – Admin specific
Let me know if there's anything you need in terms of

picking up the workload in her absence? Do you feel you need to replace the position? I'm happy for you to liaise with Bryony about placing an advert.

Glenda
FYI

Rob Lawson
Managing Director
Morris and Co
Tel: 01905 769769
Email: robert.lawson@morrisandco.co.uk
"No project too big, we'll always deliver your vision."

It was the first time that day that I actually noticed my new job title under my name on the email signature. WOW!

The final meeting of the day finished just after 4pm and with it the knowledge that I'd seen the accountant, bank and all the important people I needed to. Today had been a successful day, just like Annie had said it would be. I'd survived.

By 4.15pm I'd packed up my stuff and told Glenda she needed to go home to her family, life is too precious to be in front of a computer, but not before thanking her for all her help and saying that I couldn't have done it without her.

I got home just after 5pm and the house smelled amazing and I realised just how hungry I was. There seemed to be noise, light and what appeared to be singing and dancing coming from every room! Walking into the kitchen, I found all three of my loves dancing to *Last Christmas* by Wham!

"What on earth? It's not Christmas, you crazy bunch!"

They all answered at the same time, "It's always time for Christmas!" and carried on dancing. Lexie grabbed my hand and pulled me into the madness. Annie said she'd plated me up a dinner but, even though I was hungry, I couldn't quite face food just yet. I needed to unwind a bit first. As it happened, I didn't eat the dinner

Annie had made me. I ended up with a plate of toasted tiger bread (and bloody gorgeous it was too!).

The kids were bathed and in bed after one extra bedtime story. I sat with each of them on their beds and told them how much I loved them.

"Daddy," Lexie said, just as I was about to get up and turn her light off, "Has something happened? You and Mummy seem sad."

My ever-observant Lex, how could we ever hope to get anything past this switched-on girl! I sat back down on the bed next to her. "Oh sweetie, it's nothing for you to worry about." I stroked her forehead. "Mummy and Daddy have had some sad news, that's all. Sometimes in life we receive news that makes us happy, news that makes us laugh, news that makes us cry, and news that makes us sad. There's nothing we can do about that. But what we can do is choose how we respond to that news. Does that make sense?"

She seemed to give it some serious thought and responded, "Yes Daddy. But I know that I'll never have to do any news without my momma and daddy."

"You're absolutely right my darling. We will always be beside you. We'll never do anything without one another. I love you Piggy. Have wonderful dreams."

"Night night Dadda."

I was showered and in bed by 8pm, absolutely exhausted. Annie lay next to me as I told her about my day and what had happened. She listened and offered tentative advice when I seemed lost. She didn't interrupt me, or tell me I was doing it wrong. She just held my hand and listened to the madness that had become my life in the last few days.

"There is something else I want to tell you. Now I know you made me promise not to bring her into the house. But I felt it important that you know. She quit. She wasn't there today. She phoned in this morning, spoke to one of the administration support team and quit. She won't be back at Morris and Co again."

Silence fell in our room. Annie squeezed my fingers a little and said, "Thank you for telling me. I'm sorry she felt she needed to resign from her job. No one wanted her not to have a job. I hope she finds something more suitable quickly."

Knock me over with a feather, what the actual...?

I turned over in bed and stared her straight in the face, "ANN! What the hell? How can you? Why aren't you? How? What??"

She looked at me, utter confusion spreading across her face, "Are you ok, Lawson?"

"No, I'm not ok! How can you be so calm about everything? So nice? So understanding? Why haven't you shouted at me? Why haven't you hit me with a saucepan?"

"Saucepan? My saucepans cost a lot of money, I'll have you know! I'm not going to ruin them hitting you! What is the point in getting angry? It isn't going to change anything, is it? Anger doesn't serve any purpose, other than by hurting the person who is angry. Do you think I've been understanding? I don't wish ill on anybody, Rob. I do hope she manages to find another job. I do. As for Morris and Co and you, Lawson, you just need to take one thing at a time, not take on the whole lot in one go – that would drown a person. One thing at a time."

"Oh, Annie, I love you." I scooped her up into my arms, reached across her and turned her bedside lamp off and fell asleep holding on tight to her, almost immediately, safe in the knowledge that my Annie would stand beside me and give me the strength I needed to get through this awful and strange time.

I didn't make it home in time for dinner on either Tuesday or Wednesday. I didn't walk through the front door on either day until after 9pm. However, I made sure to keep in contact with Annie the whole time. I felt terrible. I'd broken my promise to her, even though she told me it didn't matter, that work came first, but I still wanted to make it right with her. I wanted our family to be together.

Those few days were just awful. At times I simply couldn't take in the amount of information that was being thrown at me. Corporation Tax this, PAYE that, Annual Returns, the sheer volume of leads that needed migrating into sales and projects –

BOOM, by Wednesday afternoon my head felt like it was going to explode.

I left the office after the umpteenth meeting. I sat on one of the picnic benches that edge the car park nearest the river and stared out across the moving water, watching the ducks diving head first into the water looking for something scrummy to eat.

Was I really cut out to be a boss? Self-doubt was oozing from my every pore. I really didn't know if I could do this?

I hadn't seen the kids since Monday night, I still hadn't returned a call from my mum from two days ago. My marriage was still hanging by a thread and needed me to mend it. At that moment it felt like everything was getting on top of me.

I heard the gravel crunching underfoot and turned to see Glenda approaching with two steaming cups of something warm. She sat down on the bench next to me and handed me a cup of coffee. She didn't say anything at first, just sat and stared across the water, just as I had been.

After taking a sip of her tea she said, "You know, Rob, I've been working for Morris and Co for fifteen years. Twelve of those directly with David. I love my job. I love this company. It's more than a company, it's a family. We all look out for one another, we support everyone, we push those who we see will sparkle, we reassure those who are doubting and, above all, we are comfortable to say when one of us is dicking around!"

I stared at her. Never in my time at Morris and Co had I ever heard Glenda speak with such…freedom? I hadn't even been sure she knew any swear words!

"You're dicking around, Rob. We've lost the head of our family. We need you now, Rob. The company needs you. The family need you. We've lost David, we can't lose you. So put on your big boy pants, shove your shoulders back and get a bigger notepad." She stood up and walked back across the car park to our building, leaving me alone, her words bouncing around my brain. Was she right? Was I the new leader? The only way I'd know for sure was to give it the best possible go I could. Stop bloody moping around and get on with it.

As I stood up and tipped the dregs of my coffee onto the grass in front of me, I set myself a goal. One month. I'd give myself one month. In that time, I'd devote everything I had and more to Morris and Co. If, after that time, I still felt I wasn't good enough, I'd look to pass the company on. I needed to be realistic and know that any longer than that could jeopardise the business and, above all, I was not prepared to do that – ever.

I awoke at 5am on Thursday. Everyone was still sound asleep, and the only noise in the house was Beau's deep snoring! Light crept around the edges of the pulled curtains. It was so peaceful.

As I pulled on my coat, I saw a note taped to the back of the front door:

"Fridge."

Walking back into the kitchen, I opened the fridge and light flooded the dark room. Beau snorted in disgust, then proceeded to go back to sleep. Inside on the top shelf was a lunch box filled to the brim with food, and another note resting on the top:

"One thing at a time. A x"

That's exactly what I did that day, I took one thing at a time. I didn't mither about my ever-filling inbox as I sat in the conference room listening to the Management Team giving their updates. I listened, I took notes (in the bigger notebook that Glenda had left on my desk for me), I asked questions – not fearful of looking thick. This was, after all, my first week in a brand-new job! I offered suggestions, alternatives and even recommendations.

I am thankful that each one of the managers had emailed me individually over the previous few days to offer me their support and reiterate that they understood this was all new to me. Glenda was right when she said this business was a family. As a result, for the first time that week, I actually felt like I was making progress. I was starting to understand the intricacies behind running the business.

As I was finishing off the last bits of work before closing down my computer for the day, I realised just how sheltered I'd been within the organisation. I had no idea about finance spreadsheets or corporation tax. Being the boss isn't a job, it's a combination of every single job that you employ someone else to do on your behalf, because you have to know a little about all of those roles, in order to effectively run a successful business.

I actually left the office early, as I was visiting David's wife Sheila. Glenda had kindly been to the florist at lunchtime and bought two bunches of flowers, one from the entire staff and one from me and Annie.

Given their wealth, the Morris family home was understated – a semi-detached on the outskirts of Worcester, a pristine garden and a lawn that dare not sprout a single blade of grass higher than its neighbour. After I'd pulled up outside, I sat for a while in my car, totally unsure of myself and exactly what I was going to say to her, even though we'd sat together a few days earlier in the conference room. Her husband had effectively changed my life forever. Thank you didn't seem good enough. This was the time where I wanted to express my gratitude.

I needn't have worried. Sheila was as gracious and welcoming as always. Rather than being consumed with her grief, she wanted to hear about how I was, how I was getting on and, most importantly, how Annie and the children had been with the news.

My drive home from Sheila's was sombre. A wonderful woman, in the midst of her grief, who just wanted to make sure I was ok. God, if only she knew what an utter arsehole I was, how selfish I'd been of late. I'm not sure she'd have greeted me with such compassion. I felt ashamed of myself.

I phoned Zak from the car.

"Yo dude – what's up?"

"Mate, am I a bad person?"

Clearly spluttering whatever drink was in his mouth: "Lawson! What? No! Of course not, you idiot! What on earth would make you think that?"

"I've made a serious fuck-up, serious. I have been so selfish, self-centred and a total dick!"

"Well, I can't argue with you there, mate. You have been a total knob! But you're not a bad person. You've made a mistake – everyone makes mistakes. For most people, it's buying the wrong brand of baked beans. So, I'll admit your mistake is monumental. But still, it's just a mistake."

"What if Annie can't forgive me? What if she doesn't want me? What if the damage is irreparable?"

"Have you asked her?"

"Have I asked her what?"

"Have you asked Annie if she'll forgive you, knob? Have you asked her if she still wants you? Your marriage?"

"Uggghhhhhhh." A light bulb was coming on inside my head. "No!"

"Idiot!"

"As always, it's been a pleasure conversing with you."

"Pleasure's all mine, knob! Sorry, I mean Rob – God I've no idea why I keep doing that! TTFN."

The house smelt amazing as I walked through the door at 4.45pm. I was so chuffed to be able to be home in time for dinner. It was full of laughter and Beau was barking.

I walked into the kitchen to find them all jumping around – even Beau. Laughing and jumping. So much happiness.

"Hi you lot!"

"Daddy!" squealed Lexie, running over and grabbing me by my middle.

"Yo Daddyo!" shouted Louis as he retrieved his Thomas the Tank Engine model.

"Daddy! We didn't expect you back so early." Annie had the biggest smile on her face. "Are you home now?"

"Yes. Home now and I'm not planning on opening my computer until tomorrow. I think some family time is well overdue!"

"YAY!" Both kids cheered and clapped.

"That's great, I'll put some more spaghetti in the pan," Annie said with a smile.

Lexie and Louis dragged me into the living room and pushed

me onto the sofa as they both told me about their day (at the same time!). Annie called us into the dining room about ten minutes later. Four plates awaited us, covered in pasta tomatoey goodness. Gosh, I was so hungry, even with Annie's lunch box having helped me through the day. The kids both ended up looking like circus clowns with big red smiles on their faces. We had to carry Louis straight up to the shower as his spaghetti had apparently, "Jumped off my plate into my lap, Daddy."

Annie was lying reading and writing in one of her books when I climbed into bed next to her.

"How was your day?" she asked as she closed the purple cover and turned to me.

"Much better than yesterday, thanks to your words of wisdom. I took one thing at a time. Oh, plus Glenda got me a bigger notepad." I chuckled.

"Glenda seems like an angel for you?"

"She really is. She pretty much has all David's knowledge stored in her brain. She knows exactly how that company is supposed to be run. I just need to pull out all the right stuff that will help me. She's also not afraid to tell me when I'm being an idiot. I think I need that!"

"How was Sheila?"

"Clearly broken. But putting on a good front. She loved the flowers, and was very grateful. She spoke about David again and how he'd always planned to hand the business over to me, but wanted more of a transition, he'd wanted to semi-retire, so that he could hand over the day-to-day running to me, while still being by my side until I was comfortable. I still can't believe it, Ann. I simply had no idea he'd planned to do this. He never mentioned it. Not once."

"He always had a soft spot for you though, Lawson. He was such a forward-thinking man. He must have been moulding you in his image for a while. Getting you ready, so to speak?"

"Glenda passed me all the AGM info today, and it's in there, in black and white, that within the next twelve months he would promote me to Assistant Managing Director. So, he'd planned to begin this transition soon. I'm so sad that he didn't get to tell me himself." A silent tear fell down my cheek.

"He cared for you, Lawson, and he's now placed before you the opportunity of a lifetime. It's your choice what you do with that opportunity." Annie turned and placed her arm across my stomach. "What do you want to do?"

"What do we want to do, you mean. This impacts all of us," I corrected her.

"No Rob. This is your choice. We will support you no matter what you choose. If you want to continue running the business, then I will be your biggest cheerleader. If you choose to walk away, I'll still shout for you. But for what it's worth, I don't think you'll ever be presented with this opportunity again."

Kissing the top of her head, smelling her coconut shampoo, I just wished with all my heart that I'd never messed up. "Thank you. You're amazing, really you are. I sort of made the decision last night to stop moping and give myself one month. One month to have a full bash at it. If I can't get it within a month, I'll never get it!"

"That sounds like a great idea. David obviously had complete faith in you, you just need to have faith in yourself. Clearly all the staff are on your side and that's going to be so important."

"Yeah, you're right. I'm very lucky to have some amazing team members. There's an air of sadness though, throughout the office. It's all just so sad."

"It's your job to ensure that everyone knows that Morris and Co is stable, strong and will continue even though David's gone. It's you they will look to."

"That's what I fear the most, letting them all down."

"You won't do that, you could never let anyone down," she said sleepily.

My heart sank, sadness washed over me with such ferocity. "I let you down, Annie," I whispered barely audibly, for I knew she'd nodded off.

*

Friday began calmly. Everyone was up with the lark, and we all sat around the breakfast table as the clock ticked to 5.45am. Lexie and I had a teeth-cleaning competition, I'm still not sure how it was judged but, needless to say, I lost! Louis was deeply engrossed in a spider climbing along the skirting board as I went in to say goodbye.

"How do you think a spider moves house, Daddy?" he asked.

"Good question mate. I'm not sure. I don't think spiders have many things, so it probably doesn't take them much work to move. What do you think?"

"Oh, they just get the moving people with their vans."

From the mouths of babes and all that! Can't argue with the logic! Kissing the top of his head, I told him how much I loved him and that I'd see him later.

Annie had another lunch box waiting for me at the front door.

"Thank you. I guess I can kiss goodbye to the early Friday finishes now!" I said solemnly as I pulled on my jacket.

"Things will settle down, Lawson. You can't expect everything to slot into place instantly. Who knows what the future holds? Now off you go. I've got two horrors to get ready." Annie was always so wise. Sometimes it was like listening to a self-help book!

"Thanks for the food," I said, as I took my travel mug and lunch box from her and kissed her cheek. But she had other ideas and pulled me into a deep and lingering kiss. As I pulled slowly away, I heard her barely audible "I love you." She didn't stop to wave goodbye that morning; the kids had taken it upon themselves to have a pillow fight.

As I look back, I know that I shall always remember that moment. The moment I reversed out of the drive to go to work, and seeing Annie closing the front door while smiling and fondly telling the kids she was going to eat them for tea if they'd made a mess. I shall always remember it because I felt so happy in that moment, real genuine happiness.

The whole day turned into one crazy hour after the next. The Management Team had agreed yesterday on the wording we would use to inform our suppliers and customers of David's passing and my becoming Owner/MD. We wanted to strike the right tone between devastation and positivity for the future – a very tricky thing to do!

Although crazy, it was again another productive day. I felt my confidence growing. I was starting to see the light; bit by bit, I was gaining a better understanding of what the business was and how we would move forward. That became our priority and as I sat in front of all the staff on that Friday afternoon, I reiterated to them all that every single one of them mattered, they were all valued and that we would all push Morris and Co into the new era.

I also told them, after agreement from all the Management Team, that no more overtime would be approved, unless in exceptional circumstances.

"As you all know, at the very heart of Morris and Co we are a family, and we will always support each of you to achieve our full potential. However, losing David so suddenly has made us all stop and realise what truly is important in life." I stood up at this point, wanting to make sure I could see each set of eyes that was watching me, wondering where I was going with this speech. "Therefore, we have made an executive decision that, across the board, no more overtime will be paid."

I heard a sharp intake of breath from some employees. Having spoken with Belinda in Finance, I had already got a fair idea that some employees used their overtime money to top up their wages – they had almost come to rely on the additional income. That was not a situation that I felt comfortable with. Although we'd always had a small pay rise each year, we'd never really had a pay review. Now was the time.

"Please don't panic. I know those of you who kindly undertake overtime will have many questions, but all of those questions will be answered individually by your managers. Right now, I want to explain our decision to you. As I'm sure you're all aware, we have always been given a small pay rise by Morris and Co, but we have never had a pay review. I asked the simple question, are our staff being paid the right wage? The answer came back – we don't know! So that must change now. A full pay review of every employee's role will be conducted and

I make this personal guarantee that, within that framework, Morris and Co assures each of you that your annual salary will not decrease. My hope, my goal, is that each of you sees a substantial and sustained increase in the money you take home. You work hard for this organisation and we want to reward that dedication."

Smiles and murmurs of approval swept across the room. "That dedication comes at a cost though. That is why overtime will be scrapped for all but exceptional circumstances, because I don't want you guys to sacrifice one minute longer than is necessary from your families. No one knows what's round the corner – for any of us – that's why I want to make sure that the balance of your lives tips in the favour of your loved ones. We value and appreciate everything you do for us, and we want you to be happy. Let's take David's vision and make it happen."

Cheers and clapping erupted throughout the conference room as the entire staff agreed and shouted with joy. I knew in that moment that my first executive decision was the right one. We needed to make sure that our people knew how much we valued them.

Back in David's old office I was still sitting on the wrong side of his desk, laptop open. I was scanning though the emails I'd received while in the staff meeting when Glenda came in clutching a few folders.

"You did well, Rob. I could see it was a struggle at times talking about David, but you did well. I see now what he saw in you. You will be a great leader, we're very lucky to have you."

"Thank you, Glenda. That means a lot to me. You're right, It was difficult at times. I think because this company is – was – David's baby and I feel a little bit like an imposter taking over. But the last couple of days I feel like I've got my head around a few more things. Everything is becoming clearer, and I sort of know what people are talking about!"

Glenda smiled as she sat in the visitor's chair across from mine. "You know I hear rumblings from the office floor, don't you?"

Of course I knew! There wasn't anything that didn't get back to Glenda! "What's the word then? Go on, hit me with it!" I slouched back in my chair, the anticipation almost too much to bear.

"They love you. They're devastated by David's death. But you've done exactly what was needed of you. You reassured them. You listen to them and you're making your mark, while still being totally respectful to David's memory. They really like you, Rob." She slapped my arm as I took in what she'd said.

They liked me! The staff actually liked me as their boss. Well stone me! Who knew!!

"Have a look at these over the weekend. You'll need to be familiarised by Monday when we have Ian Packham from NRH coming in to discuss the possible relocation project in Iceland," she said and handed me the two manila folders in her hand.

"Thanks Glenda. You know I couldn't have done ANY of this without you?" I said as she got up to leave the office.

"Oh, away with you! I haven't done anything really. Just shown you the door. You're the one who had to walk through it! Oh, and another thing. Please can you sit on the right side of the desk next week? Have a great weekend. See you Monday."

My final act of the day was to email Finance.

To: belinda.barr@morrisandco.co.uk
CC: managementteam@morrisandco.co.uk
From: robert.lawson@morrisandco.co.uk
Date 06 May 15.59
Subject: Glenda Willis Bonus

Afternoon Belle

Please can you accept this email as official confirmation of our discussion earlier today. The Management Team and I would like to add a 5% bonus to Glenda Willis's May pay packet, in recognition of the invaluable assistance she has shown to myself and the whole management team over the past week. We appreciate all the work that she has done.

As I discussed, I would like the money from this to come directly from the MD's personal budget.

MT – As discussed, Belle will issue the bonus in Glenda's next pay packet. I think it might be nice to issue a formal letter and attach it to her wage slip – perhaps we can all sign. What do you think?

Rob

Rob Lawson
Managing Director
Morris and Co
Tel: 01905 769769
Email: robert.lawson@morrisandco.co.uk
"No project too big, we'll always deliver your vision."

Closing down my laptop, I packed my bag, making sure to include the folders ready for next week. I also turned my pen pot around before leaving the office. Next week would be a new week, full of new prospects and possibilities and a new chair for me!

Hitting call on the car's Bluetooth, I turned the volume down as the ringing sound blasted throughout the car.

"Yo dude – what's up?" Zak always answered my calls in exactly the same way he had done since we were ten!

"Just calling to say hey!"

"Liar! What do you really want?" I could hear the smirk in his voice.

"Advice... I'm thinking about maybe cooking, or taking Annie out for a meal, to talk honestly with her and tell her I've made a massive fuck-up. What do you think?"

"I totally agree, mate."

"What? No! Not that I've made a fuck-up – I know that! I mean about the meal. Do you think it's a good idea?"

"Oh right! Umm then, yes, I think it's a good idea. Stay at home though, wouldn't want to have any unpleasant scenes in the middle of the Mint Lounge. Not that I'm saying there'll be any unpleasant scenes – oh, you know what I mean!"

I did know what he meant. As always, he was very sensible, it's why I valued him so much. "Is she going to forgive me, Zak?"

"Honestly? I've no idea. Me and Liv have been talking about it – sorry to be discussing you. She doesn't know either. Neither of us can call it. Annie's played this one very close to her chest. We both feel it could go either way. You've really hurt her, knob. Not just with that chick, but with the lies. If she doesn't forgive you, I don't think anyone will blame her. But if she stays, you will be one lucky fucking knob! She's got to work out if she can trust you again."

"Always a pleasure conversing with you!"

"Pleasure's all mine, knob! Sorry, I mean Rob – God, did it again! TTFN."

I got home at 4.45pm. The house was deathly quiet. I stood in the conservatory watching my family in the garden. They were clearly setting up a picnic on the lawn. Those guys own my heart.

"Hi you lot, what's going on?"

"DADDY!!!!!!!!!!!!!!!" Both kids dashed across the garden and jumped at me, knocking (well, I did a staged knocking) me over. "Daddy, we're having a picnic in the garden, all my teddies are coming!" shouted Lex.

"And my cows," added Lou.

"That sounds like a very busy picnic blanket! Will there be room for us?"

"DADDDDDDY don't be silly, of course there will be room, I'm going to have to sit in the middle of them to help them eat their food!" Lexie clarified.

"Oh right, well that's cleared that up!!! How was your day, guys?"

"Great," beamed Lexie.

"Ok," grunted Louis.

"Oh, good to know! Thanks for the update!"

"Come on monsters, go and wash your hands. Food is ready." Annie shooed them towards the downstairs toilet.

Offering me a hand to get back up, she smiled at me. "Welcome home. How did today go?"

"Today was a good day. I really think I might be able to do this, Ann." Taking my coat off, I threw it over the conservatory sofa. "What do you need me to do?" I turned up my shirt sleeves.

"Oh nothing, it's all done. But you could help carry it all into the garden?" She walked into the kitchen where lots of bowls and plates had been set out.

"Mommy. Louis has shoved a cow down his trousers and it's stuck!"

"Ok sweetie, you help Daddy carry everything into the garden, I'll go and retrieve the cow." She kissed the top of Lexie's head.

"Daddy, can I carry the plate of biscuits?"

"Sure you can, Piggy." I handed her the plate. "How was school today?"

"It was ok. Millie is back after being poorly, and we had fish and chips for lunch with ice cream."

I never had fish and chips for lunch at school. We were lucky if we got soggy spuds and some sort of unidentifiable meat-based thing!

Putting the food down on the picnic blanket, I said, "Come and sit with me, Pig." Pig is the name I will always call Lexie, ever since she was a little toddler and obsessed with Peppa Pig. As we sat down together, I said, "I just wanted to let you know that I love you. I'm sorry I haven't been around much this week. Thank you for being such a grown-up girl and helping with your brother." She swelled with pride.

"It's ok Daddy. Sometimes Mommy lets me help look after Louis and I like it. It's like pretending I'm the mommy!"

"I'm so proud of you. Never forget that, sweetie," I said, as I kissed the top of her head.

We had such an enjoyable picnic. We sat in the garden with blankets wrapped around our shoulders as we watched the sun set. When the kids began falling asleep, we knew it was time to pack them off to the land of Nod. I carried Louis upstairs first, leaving

Annie alone with Lex. Tucking him into bed fully clothed, I pushed back his hair and wished him sweet dreams.

I returned to the garden to find Annie softly singing to a sleeping Lex.

"Twinkle twinkle little star,
how I wonder what you are.
Up above the world so high,
Like a diamond in the sky."

"You used to sing that to her when she was first born."

"I love singing it to her now. I still struggle to believe that this perfect soul belongs to us. She's perfect, isn't she?"

"They're both perfect," I agreed.

"Take her up."

I lifted Lexie's heavy sleepy body, and carried her to bed. I tucked her in and made sure she had her teddies close by.

Annie had begun taking all the boxes and plates back into the kitchen by the time I came back down.

"I'm going to leave these till the morning. I think all the fresh air has made me sleepy!"

"Go on up to bed," I said. "I'll lock up." I kissed her forehead as she made her way upstairs.

Fourteen

Dinner 22 My Rescue Plan…
(Saturday 7 May)

I didn't even know 5am existed on a Saturday, but I can confirm it does! Lexie was pulling my feet, Louis my arm. I had to use my free arm to grab the headboard, otherwise I'd have been arse-deep in shagpile carpet!

"Come on Daddy, it's breakfast time."

"Daddy, it's chocolate toast day!"

"Ok! OK! I'm getting up!" They jumped around, running in and out of their respective bedrooms. "You stay in bed love," I said to Annie. "Go back to sleep. I'll take them to your parents'." Thankfully the kids' excitement hadn't disturbed Ann; she was still fast asleep.

Three rounds of chocolate toast, one bowl of shared cornflakes and a cup of apple juice each and we were ready to head off to Nanny and Gag's, but not before an in-depth discussion in Lexie's bedroom about why superheroes can definitely wear tutus and cat ears, as well as fluffy socks and gloves, followed by Louis running into her bedroom in just his underpants, proclaiming to be Pant Boy, saviour of the world! I can only liken the experience to some form of UN peacekeeping envoy job because, man alive, it was tough! Keeping those two happy, quiet and calm. Annie had packed their overnight bags the previous day, so that was one less job I needed to battle with. She'd even put them both by the front door.

Once we were all washed, teeth cleaned and dressed, we blew kisses to Annie, who was still sleeping (amazingly), although I think the offer (bribe) of some chocolate *en route* helped keep the volume levels down. I promised the kids we'd stop at the farm shop on the way and pick up some punnets of fruit to take with us (and their chocolate!). After bundling them and Beau into the car, we headed to the shop. Much debate was had about which fruit would be best, but they settled on grapes, strawberries and a single mushroom! Don't ask – it's best not to.

Decisions over the chocolate took even longer. That poor bar of milk chocolate had been handled so much I could only assume it had turned to mush! Finally, we arrived at the checkout with our punnets of strawberries, grapes and the single mushroom. When the lady on the till opened the brown paper bag to see what was inside, she simply raised her eyebrow at me, as if wanting an explanation. I didn't have an explanation for that single mushroom that I felt was good enough. One bar of milk chocolateand a packet of gummy bears. That little shopping excursion took 45 minutes. Was that good? I'd no idea, but I felt exhausted!

When we arrived in the beautiful town of Bewdley, where May and Malc have lived for over twenty years, it was relatively quiet. The town is a hotspot for tourists even in the low season. The draw of a historic riverside town always pulls folks in from far and wide. Even at the ungodly hour of 9.30am both Nan and Gag were up and, thankfully, ready to receive the terrible twosome! The kids had their own bedroom at their house. Well, it was Annie's old bedroom, but the kids had unquestionably put their own stamp on the room. Farm animals adorned the windowsill, and mermaid cushions were scattered across the top bunk of the bunk beds.

Somehow, we all managed to have a second breakfast. We sat

around the large farmhouse-style wooden table, which was weighed down with bowls of sausages and bacon, plates of toast and croissants and every jam flavour under the sun. The biggest teapot I'd ever seen sat proudly in the centre, and it never seemed to get empty – witchcraft, I'm sure!

Both May and Malc seemed distracted and a little bit distant. After the kids had consumed their own body weight in toast, they ran off to get art supplies from their toy boxes.

"Are you guys ok?" I asked.

"Yes son," said Malc. "Just not used to so much noise this early in the morning! I think once your own kids have grown up and flown the nest, so to speak, you get used to the quiet again! It's a bit of a shock when suddenly there's noise coming from every room!" He smiled.

"I'm with you on that! When I had that week off work and I'd taken the kids to school, coming home to the quiet of the house was just – bizarre. There were a few times when I caught myself wondering if I'd actually gone deaf, because I'm so used to being at home and there being some sort of commotion going on! Hopefully, they'll both sleep well tonight with being up so early."

"They are both angels when they're with us, never a bother, are they Malc?" May said, a smile spreading across her face.

"Well, not until it's teeth-cleaning time!" Malc laughed.

"Ohhhh," I chuckled, "You have that battle too, do you?"

"What battle, Daddy?" asked Lexie as they both reappeared laden down with armfuls of glitter, pompoms and pipe cleaners.

"The battle of Toothbrush Mountain. I didn't realise that the fighting had spread all the way from Bromsgrove to Bewdley! This is terrible. I think we should call the newspapers and tell them," I teased her as I grabbed her round her middle and lifted her onto my knee.

"Oh, Daddy you are a fusspot, aren't you! Now what do you think, pink or green glitter for a fairy's wings?"

A long-drawn-out goodbye from Lexie followed – Louis was too busy investigating the new packs of stickers that Nanny had bought. They were terribly exciting stickersapparently. May helped me escape the clutches of my daughter by promising to make cakes once I'd gone. Lexie only agreed on the condition that they had chocolate chips in!

As she stood on the doorstep seeing me off, May called to me, "Rob?"

"Yeah?" I turned round.

"Give our Ann a big hug, won't you?"

"Of course! I'll get her to video call this afternoon. I'm glad I let her have a lie-in this morning," I smiled.

"Yes, she needs her rest, that food poisoning seemed to take it out of her, didn't it?"

"Yeah, knocked her right off her feet. Hopefully she can rest up while the kids are here. Just lie on the sofa and watch rubbish on the telly!"

"Fingers crossed, Rob, fingers crossed. We love you!"

"Love you too," I replied as I loaded Beau into the boot of the car. I climbed into the driver's seat, switched off the Disney CD we'd been listening to on the way over and reversed off their drive, waving as I went. I could see May still standing in the doorway as I drove off. There was definitely an air of sadness about her.

The drive back from Bewdley can be a tricky one. You can take the more direct route through the town of Kidderminster or the more countryside road via Stourport-on-Severn. I opted for Kidderminster as I needed to get provisions for the meal that was pivotal to my master plan.

Pulling into the big supermarket car park, I grabbed my pre-written list, telling Beau I would be quick, and ventured inside. They had all the ingredients I needed – not that I needed much. I'd planned on keeping it really simple – steak, chips and salad. I made up for my simplicity with flowers – tulips, Annie's favourite – a box of what I deemed to be posh chocolates (they'd better be the best bloody chocolates ever, given the price!) and a bottle of her favourite drink, dark rum.

Right, Operation Make it Right was underway.

With the car loaded, I headed back out of Kidderminster on the fairly easy drive back home, and enjoyed listening to classical music on the radio, which is something I hardly ever do! I even plodded along at a steady pace, not dashing, not rushing, just enjoying the sunshine and the music.

I remember looking at the car clock as I pulled onto our drive. It was 11.41am. I can still remember that moment. The peace I felt. I was calm, relaxed and looking forward to making the food I'd bought for Annie. I was quietly optimistic. For the first time in weeks, I felt as if I could do it. I could make it right again. I could save my marriage.

As I grabbed the bags from the back seat and walked up the drive, I noticed that all the blinds were still drawn – strange! Dumping all the bags in the hallway, I went back to the car and opened the boot, releasing the hound!

She ran straight into the house and began howling at the bottom of the stairs. We'd always been very strict with her that upstairs was out of bounds. Then she started scratching the floor and howling even louder.

After shutting the boot and locking the car, I went back into the house to try to calm Beau down. Unfortunately, it didn't work. She was extremely agitated, darting backwards and forwards across the bottom of the stairs. Dragging her by her collar, I took her through the house and opened up the conservatory so she could go out in the garden, but she refused and rushed back to the bottom of the staircase.

"I give up! You are officially the craziest dog I've ever met!" Pulling the blinds in the kitchen and then moving into the living room, I called out, "Ann, I'm home."

No reply! Maybe she was in the shower.

I grabbed all the shopping and took it to the kitchen and put it away. I pulled the price tag off the flowers and carried them with me as I bounded up the stairs, giving Beau's ears a quick rub as I passed her.

"Ann, love, I'm back, these are for you…" I walked into our

bedroom, which was pitch black. She was still in bed. The curtains were still pulled, the blackout blind down.

"Annie, are you ok?" I asked. I could hear Beau's whimpering getting louder. I flicked on the landing light so I could see better. Annie was facing away from the bedroom door.

I walked around the edge of the bed to the side she was facing, hoping she was ok, to see if there was anything I could do to help.

The light in the room was still pretty dim, even with the landing light on.

"Annie love, are you ok?" I asked again, and gently shook her duvet-covered legs. She didn't respond.

"Annie? Annie, love?"

Putting the flowers on the bottom of the bed, I touched the base of her bedside lamp and it illuminated the whole room, bathing it in a warm yellow glow.

Annie's face was white. Her lips were blue. Her eyes were closed.

Reaching down to my beautiful wife, I began to try to gently shake her awake. Touching her shoulder, I recoiled.

She was ice cold.

"ANNIE!" I screamed and I shook her harder.

Fifteen

Ann… (Saturday 7 May)

I remember every detail about the next few hours. I will always remember every detail.

I pulled my mobile phone from my trouser pocket and tried desperately to see the screen through oceans of tears that were raining down on our bed.

"Which service do you require?"

"Am… Am… Ambulance, I need an ambulance," I managed to spit out.

I waited for what felt like forever…

Constantly repeating Annie's name, over and over…

Hoping she'd hear me calling her…

"Ambulance service. Is the patient breathing?"

I couldn't get the words out; I couldn't even get my breath…

"Hello caller? Ambulance service. Is the patient breathing?"

"My wife… It's my wife… Please, I need help… My wife… I think my wife is dead… I don't… HELP…" I know I screamed the last word. I know I did.

"Ok sir, what is your address?"

"Sixteen, we're number Sixteen Chestnut Grove, Bromsgrove. OH MY GOD, please help me, PLEASE!"

"Ok sir, help is on the way. We need to ensure that the crews can gain access to the property. Can you open the front door, sir?"

I didn't have a clue what the woman on the end of the phone was saying, I was staring down at Annie. She looked so peaceful, but not.

"What?"

"Sir, I need you to listen to me. Go and open the front door so that the crews can get into the house. Whereabouts is the patient?"

I began running downstairs, rushing past Beau who was still whimpering at the bottom of the stairs. As I hit the last step, she dashed past me and bolted up the stairs, two steps at a time. She needed to be with Annie. I opened the front door and both of the porch doors wide.

Running out of the house and down the drive into the middle of the road, I desperately searched the close entrance, looking for the ambulance.

"Where is the patient, sir?"

"In our bedroom, she's in bed. Upstairs."

"Ok, we need you to begin CPR, sir. Can you ensure that there is nothing obstructing her airway by tilting her head back and lifting the chin."

"I'm outside... So, they know where to go... I left her alone... Oh God, I left her alone... NO!" I ran as fast as I could back up the drive, up the stairs and into our bedroom, dashing around the end of the bed to my Annie's side. Beau had her head and front paws on Annie's arm.

Sinking to my knees, I grabbed Annie's exposed hand.

"Sir, are you still there? We need to begin CPR. The crew will be with you in a matter of seconds."

"CPR? What?" That's how frazzled my brain was, I couldn't even understand that the operator was telling me to begin CPR on my wife, in an attempt to bring her back.

"Yes CPR, sir, put the phone on speaker and place it where you can still hear what I'm saying."

"Ummm, ok." Beau's whining was becoming unbearable, as was the pain emanating from my heart.

"AMBULANCE... Hello?"

"Sir, the crew should be with you now, can you hear them?"

"Please hurry, we're up here," I shouted at the phone and the voice coming from downstairs.

In rushed two paramedics, armed with massive backpacks and machines.

"My wife, please help my wife." I grabbed Beau's collar and tried to move out of the way, which was tricky, given the size of our bedroom.

The first paramedic climbed up on the bed next to Ann. "Hello, can you hear me? My name's Mike, can you hear me?"

The second medic was rummaging through the bags, and pressing buttons on one of the machines.

"Sir, are you related to the patient?" The second medic addressed me.

"Yes, I'm her husband, Rob, she's Ann, Annie Lawson, my wife."

"Ok Rob, I'm Alex and that's Mike. We're going to do everything we possibly can to help Annie, can you tell us what's happened?"

I watched as Mike, the paramedic closest to Annie, began pulling things out of his backpack.

"I umm... I just came back. I'd taken our children to their nan and grampy's for a sleepover. All the curtains were pulled, so I thought she was having a lie-in. But when I put the light on, she was cold, and her lips were blue. Why is she so cold?"

"Ok Rob, you're doing really well. Does Annie have any medical conditions? Does she take any medication?"

"Ummm no. She was poorly last week, we thought it might have been food poisoning from some fish from the chip shop. She hardly ever goes to the GP." Right then was a light-bulb moment.

"Oh my God! A few months ago, we were chatting about getting our wills written and Annie made me promise that if anything were to ever happen to her, if she was poorly, or taken into hospital, I was to ring Dr Pacey, our GP." I looked with searching eyes at Alex, "Should I ring him?"

"Yes, I think that would be a good idea. Why don't you go downstairs while we look after Annie?"

I manoeuvred out of the bedroom, I was reluctant to leave Annie, but I knew she was in safe hands. Dragging Beau by her collar, I headed downstairs. As I went, I heard: "De-fib Mike?"

"Negative."

I put Beau in her crate, and she whined. Grabbing the house phone from its cradle on the kitchen work surface, I scrolled through the built-in phone book and hit call on our GP surgery.

"Welcome to Hillwood Medical Centre. For medical emergencies press 1, for appointments press 2, for repeat prescriptions press 3, for all other enquires please hold…" I waited.

I was pacing the living room, backwards and forwards. Alex, the second paramedic rushed downstairs and out to the waiting ambulance. I stood in the living room doorway, watching as he rushed back in and upstairs.

"Hillwood Medical Centre, Sarah speaking. How may I help you?"

"My name is Rob Lawson. My wife, Annie Lawson, told me to ring for Dr Pacey if anything happened to her. Something has…is happening to her. The paramedics are with her now."

"Ok Mr Lawson, what is Annie's date of birth?"

"Seventeenth of the fifth, 1982."

"Thank you… I'm just transferring you."

"To where?" I replied but it fell on deaf ears; the receptionist had already hit the hold button. Pacing backwards and forwards. Tears falling. I believed in those minutes downstairs that my whole life was hanging by a thread.

"Mr Lawson?" An older-sounding gentleman interrupted the hold music.

A sob escaped. "It's Annie," was all I could manage.

"I'm on my way." The call ended.

Alex the paramedic ran downstairs again, only this time I wasn't on hold, so I rushed to the door: "Is she ok?"

"We're doing everything we can for your wife, Rob. As hard as it is, remaining down here is the best thing you can do for her, and us." With that, he was out to the ambulance again, and then running back up the stairs.

Moving back into the living room, I stood staring out of the windows. I knew all the neighbours would be wondering what was going on. An ambulance with its lights flashing on the road was just not what happened around here!

Then I noticed a BMW pulling into the road and heading straight for the drive. Out jumped an older man who ran up to the house. I went to the front door.

"Mr Lawson, I'm Dr Pacey, where is she?"

Gesturing up the stairs, "She's upstairs in bed, the paramedics are with her." Dr Pacey pushed past me and started to ascend our stairs. "Doctor, what's going on?"

"I will be back in a few moments, Mr Lawson." And with that, he rounded the corner to our bedroom and I couldn't see him anymore.

I moved back into the living room and returned to my pacing. Up and down, up and down. Stupid the things you remember at times of extreme stress. But I remember pacing while we waited for Lexie to be born. I must have walked miles that night. I was an old hand by the time Louis came along.

Back and forth I went again, only this time my Annie wasn't there laughing at me, she was surrounded by strangers, doing goodness knew what to her.

Minutes passed. I had no idea how long the doctor was upstairs; it could have been one minute, it could have been fifty. I let Beau out of her crate and she walked beside me back and forth, back and forth, her tail between her legs and an occasional whimper escaping.

"Mr Lawson?" The noise startled me. I'd almost cocooned myself in that living room, tuning out the medical noises from upstairs and the drone of the diesel engine of the ambulance running just outside the porch. All I could hear were my own footsteps and Beau padding on the laminate flooring.

Rushing to the GP, who was standing in the living room doorway: "Is she ok?"

"Shall we sit down?"

That's when I knew. That's the moment I felt my stomach physically move inside my body. That's when the instant sensation of nausea rose from deep within me. Nothing good ever came from someone being told to "sit down".

"She's dead, isn't she?" I don't actually remember deciding to say that. It was almost as if something took over me. It wasn't autopilot, it was something else.

The doctor's glanced shifted from my face to the floor, almost as if embarrassed by what he was about to say. "I'm so deeply sorry, Mr Lawson. Annie has passed away."

Time stood still. The world stopped turning. The sun stopped shining. I stopped ageing. I stopped breathing.

Sixteen

The Truth…

A loud noise filled the living room. It was a noise that sounded almost primeval, gut-wrenching. In the months since, I've spoken to Dr Pacey a lot about that day, and he told me that the noise was actually me. This is the only element of that day that I simply cannot remember. I don't remember screaming. I don't remember sinking to my knees. I don't remember it. I just don't remember and I should. I should remember every single second of the day my wife left me.

The next thing I actually remember after Dr Pacey uttering those words to me was rising from the floor and rushing over to the doctor and grabbing his coat.

"What has happened?" I demanded, "What has she done?" I almost shouted. "Why has she done this?" Anger rose in me like a wave, taking over my every atom.

"Mr Lawson, please." Dr Pacey tried to remove my hands from the front of his coat. "You need to calm down and have a seat. There are some things I need to explain to you."

"What's to explain?" I was definitely shouting now, "My wife has killed herself, for fuck's sake. Did I make her so unhappy? Oh my God, what have I done?" My hands on my head. I couldn't believe it. "What the hell is going on? What the hell am I going to tell the kids?" Tears. "What the hell has she done? I didn't mean it... I didn't mean to hurt her... I love her so much".

Raising his voice with the authority of years of public service, he said, "MR LAWSON! Will you please sit down?"

Standing still, Beau at my feet. She knows. I know she knows that her hoomon mum has gone.

I moved and sat as instructed in the big cuddle chair in the big bay window.

"Mr Lawson, I need you to try to control yourself and I need you to listen to what I'm about to tell you." As if suddenly processing what I'd said, "You hurt your wife?"

"What? NO! I mean yes! But not like that!" I was sweating under his intense gaze. He thought I'd been harming Annie! "I made a massive mistake. I told Annie I wanted a divorce, I hurt her terribly. I saw her heart break when I uttered those words. But Doctor, it's not what I want, I didn't mean it. I never wanted to hurt her. I love her so much! Oh God! I hurt her so much she didn't want to live anymore!"

Dr Pacey sat patiently on the sofa opposite my chair, as tears continued to stream down my face. Beau lay across my feet and whimpered. Wiping away the fresh tears, I tried to compose myself. How can Annie be gone? It's not real. It's not true.

I didn't even hear the footfall on the stairs. "We're going to head off now, Doc."

"Yes, thank you, you guys, really appreciate your help." The doctor addressed the two paramedics.

"We're so sorry for your loss, Mr Lawson. Our thoughts are with you at this time," Alex said to me, as he moved out of my house, and my life. How quickly he came, how quickly he left. What devastation in his wake.

I whispered, staring down at Beau, "Annie...it's not true."

"Mr Lawson... Robert... Annie didn't take her life. She didn't kill herself."

My head shot up, and I stared wide-eyed at this older man sitting in my living room, who up until an hour ago I'd never even met.

"What?" I rubbed my snot-producing nose across my sleeve.

"Annie didn't kill herself, Mr Lawson. She has – had – terminal cancer. She knew she was dying. I've been seeing Annie a lot recently, and she grew to trust me. She asked that if anything should happen to her, I was to give you this."

He rose from the sofa, walked across the room and handed me an A4 envelope. "Mr Lawson, I'm truly sorry for your loss. If there is anything I can do, please just call. If there are any questions you need answering, I'm here. Please know that you are not on your own."

I stared at the envelope lying across my legs. "What?" That's ridiculous isn't it! But that was all I could spit out.

"Annie has been battling, Mr Lawson, but she knew she didn't have long left."

Giant massive drops of tears splashed on the envelope. I couldn't take it in.

"What?"

Dr Pacey knelt down beside me, making sure to stare into my eyes. "Rob, I need to know that you are understanding what I'm saying to you. Annie didn't kill herself. She didn't want to leave you. Annie was sick."

"Ww…wwwwhat?" My voice failing me.

"Annie had terminal cancer, Rob. She was, I'm afraid to say, very poorly. She did NOT want to leave you or the children. Do you understand that?"

"No… Yes… I mean, no, I don't understand."

"Then why don't you let Annie explain," the doctor said gently, tapping the envelope on my lap. The silence was broken by a knocking on the front door. Beau's head didn't even move; she couldn't even summon the strength to protect her house.

"Doctor?" called a voice from the hallway.

"I'll be back, Rob, ok?" said Dr Pacey, as he stood up and walked into the hallway, leaving me and Beau engulfed in the silence of the living room. Beau was shaking and I could feel every shake trembling through my feet. Instinctively, I reached down and patted her. Comforted her. Reassured her. The trembling slowed.

"Rob?" Dr Pacey came back into the room. "Rob, I've spoken with the Coroner's Office already, and the guys from the Home Office Pathology department are here. They are going to take Annie to the local hospital. We need to establish exactly how she died. Rob?" He raised his voice slightly.

"Yes. Sorry. Ummm, ok?" I'd no real idea what he'd just told me. "What? What? No, you can't take her. Annie belongs here. I don't want you to take her. You can't take her. NO!" Grief was consuming me. I couldn't stop it, I couldn't.

"Rob, we need to look after Annie now. She can't stay here with you. We need to take her."

"But she's my Annie. I… We… I…" Tears falling again.

"I know, Rob, but we have to take her." His tone was final. I knew I couldn't and wouldn't argue with him anymore. At that moment, I heard footsteps descending the stairs. Beau wrapped herself around my legs. Dr Pacey put an arm round my shoulder as a trolley holding a black bag appeared in the hallway. I know a loud sob escaped. Beau whined.

"Rob, is there someone I can call for you?"

Staring at two strange men wheeling the body of my cold wife out of our house for the last time, I grabbed the house phone from the cradle and simply whispered, "Zak."

"Thanks Doctor, we are all done, and will be on our way. I'll be in touch," said one of the men manoeuvring my wife's body. Her cold body. Her non-moving body. "We're sorry for your loss," he added.

"Thanks Phil, we appreciate you coming so quickly," the doctor said in a friendly tone, not removing his arm from my shoulder as he took the phone in his other hand.

"STOP! Please. Just a second. Please." I stared between the two men who, in turn, took their cue from Dr Pacey. I didn't look at him, but he must have nodded, as they didn't move.

I went into the hallway. My voice was barely audible: "I love you Annie, please know I love you so much. I'll make sure our beautiful babies know how much they are loved every day. I love you, I'm so sorry... I'm so so sorry." Pain enveloped me, real piercing pain, debilitating pain.

"Thanks gents." Dr Pacey gently guided me back into the living room, so I never actually saw Annie leave for the final time. "Sit down Rob, I'm going to go and put the kettle on and call Zak."

I couldn't sit down, I just stood. In the middle of my living room. My pain in the arse Beau whimpering at my feet. I could hear the engine of the van outside. The van carrying my wife's body. I heard the engine fade away. Taking my Annie with it.

"Rob, here, drink this. I've spoken to Zak and he's on his way." The Doctor had become something stable in my stormy sea and handed me a cup of steaming tea. "Rob, I need to return to the surgery. Are you going to be ok for a little while until your friend gets here?"

He was leaving as well. Everyone is leaving. Why is everyone leaving? Is this my punishment? I needed to pull myself together. This perfect stranger had shown me so much kindness over the past hour, in the most horrific moments of my life. "Yes, of course. Thank you so much, Doctor. Thank you for looking after Annie." A single tear fell.

"Rob, I can truthfully say that it was my pleasure. Annie was a remarkable woman. She brightened any room."

I wanted to smile in recognition of that statement, but my body wouldn't respond. It was like I'd become detached from the external me.

"Who were those people? Where are they taking Annie? I need to go with them." I started to move around looking for my car keys.

"Rob, they work for the Coroner's Office. Annie will be transferred via private ambulance to the local hospital, where an autopsy will be performed. We need to establish the cause of death. They won't let you see her just yet, Rob, so there's no point going anywhere. You need to be here. Ok?"

"Yeah, ok. Thank you, Dr Pacey, again. Thank you." Some sort of inbuilt manners surfaced as I realised I needed to shake this man's hand.

I walked to the front door, which was still wide open, and saw him out. Then I closed the door on the outside world. For the first time, it was just me and Beau. The house was eerily quiet. No, I was wrong, I could just about hear the boiler firing up. That was it. No other noise. Such a contrast to the last hour when radio traffic, beeping, talking, running and wheeling bounced off the walls. It was as if Annie leaving had taken all the sounds with her. Beau was still attached to the side of my leg, and I mean attached, every movement mimicked.

I stood at the bottom of the staircase, staring around the curve of the stairs up to the landing, still lit by the light I'd turned on what felt like hours ago.

Taking one step at a time, the wood creaking underfoot. Beau followed me. I didn't even stop her. I needed her close to me. I turned left and stood in the doorway to our bedroom. The bedclothes were a crumpled mess where she had lain. Where she had... died.

I just crumpled right there in the doorway. Straight down to the floor. I screamed, I sobbed, I screamed again until my throat felt raw. The whole time, Beau was edging her head into my lap and bending the envelope that Dr Pacey had given me. The envelope that he said would allow Annie to explain what had happened. At that moment, though, I didn't believe any explanation would make any difference. She was gone.

Hindsight. I'll keep referring to that as we move on, because it's something I've come to recognise isn't actually 'a thing', it's just your brain's way of punishing you for your failures!

But still, with hindsight and reliving that moment more times than I'm prepared to admit, I now recognise that Beau was helping me. She was nudging me to the envelope. I believe that she could smell Annie's scent on the paper of the envelope. She knew that Annie was still there with us.

Moving from my crumpled mess, I pushed my back against the bedroom door, stuck my legs out in front of me, and Beau positioned herself across the threshold of the room, head in my lap. Never once taking her eyes off me.

I picked up the envelope and saw, for the first time, Annie's beautiful script in blue ink.

"Lawson"

drawn in large letters across the front. I pulled open the sealing tab and turned the envelope upside down. Out slid lots of loose-leaf papers and an A5 hardbacked purple book. I began sifting through the loose papers and saw one labelled in big letters,

Read me first

It was dated two days ago.

Thursday 5 May

Lawson

If you are reading this, then my time has come to an end. Please don't be sad I'm gone, be happy that I lived.

I know you're going to be angry that I never told you I was ill, but please try to understand my reasons:

1. *I wanted to live a life without pity*
2. *I wanted to live a 'normal' life with you and the children, not consumed with hospital visits and medical appointments*
3. *I wanted to continue to be your wife*
4. *I wanted to continue to be our babies' momma*
5. *I wanted to be more than this illness*
6. *Selfishly, I don't think I have the strength to tell you. Every ounce of my energy has been going into fighting, fighting to stay with you all.*

I have pancreatic cancer (which I fondly refer to as Hector!!). Hector's gotten too big, he's too far gone to be treated. He's S4, Stage

4, which means he's travelled beyond my pancreas. He's basically spreading throughout my body. I've not been feeling 'right' for a little while, but just put it down to how busy things have been around here lately.

I found out for certain six weeks ago! Six weeks ago, I was told I'd got six weeks to live, that's how advanced it was (is).

I really did try to find a way to tell you what was happening, I struggled to find the right words to convey that I would be leaving you. I tried every day, but the words just got stuck in my throat. I managed to talk myself into telling you when you came home from Berlin, but unfortunately you had other ideas, telling me you wanted a divorce which, if I'm being truthful, hurt more than being told my days were literally numbered.

Please know that I take full responsibility for the decline in our relationship over the past few months. I've felt so poorly at times, I've simply not been able to fulfil my obligation to you, no, my promise to be your wife, in all senses of the word. Therefore, I do not in any way blame you for looking elsewhere.

I'm not angry at you, Lawson. When you asked me for a divorce, I wasn't surprised. I was just deeply sorrowful, as I knew eventually it would come. That's why I agreed to your request, but with the addition of my condition.

Why? I know, I can hear your voice even now!

I asked you to wait 30 days before making anything official. Well, the reason I asked for that is because, deep in my heart, I knew I'd never make it to 30 days. I knew you'd never need to file for a divorce. I knew you'd never need to leave our home. Because I knew I would be gone before those 30 days ended, and it would solve the problem. While I considered how to stop you leaving our family, I realised that I needed to ensure I could spend as much time with you as possible. I knew my time was precious, and I wanted as much of it as possible to be with you all.

I'm not melancholy or even remorseful. I am simply full of regret. Regret that I couldn't be the person you needed me to be, I couldn't be the Momma our two monsters deserve. I feel that

I have let you all down, and for that, I'm truly sorry. I'm sorry I'm not able to be with you as you walk through this wondrous thing called life. I'm sorry I'm not able to watch the kids become the people they are meant to be. I'm sorry I couldn't be the wife you were always meant to have.

If I had a choice, of course, I wouldn't want to divorce you or leave you. I love you. I always have loved you and I always will. But I'd like to think that I'm not a selfish person, and if my choices were making you in any way unhappy, I would never stand in your way.

I have said goodbye to the kids individually over the past few days. I have also written each of them a letter that's inside this big envelope. There is also a big box in the bottom of my wardrobe that has letters and cards for each of them for important moments in their lives. In the bottom of our main wardrobe, you will find two big boxes containing wrapped presents for all of you from me, again for important moments in yours and their lives. I may not be able to be there in person, but everyone should have a present from their momma on their 18th birthday.

Mum, Dad and Andy know that I'm sick. I'm not sure they understand the ins and outs of it, but they know I won't be around for much longer and, without even taking a breath, they told me that they will be there for you, in whatever way you need them to be. You will not be on your own.

Please don't be mad at them. They have abided by my wishes that you three were not to know.

I have had a happy life, Lawson. Our life together has been everything I'd hoped when I envisioned being married as a little girl. We created two amazing little mess creators, and I'm so proud of you all. So proud to call you my life.

My biggest regret about leaving is that I have to leave without making you happy. Lawson, I made a vow, a promise to make you happy for the rest of your life – a colourful marriage – and I haven't, and I'm truly sorry, but please know how truly happy you have made me.

Love always
Your Ann

Words failed me. I was unable to make any verbal (understandable) sounds as I moved the letter away from my body, fearful of smudging the ink as more tears fell. But, in my head, I was repeating the same phrase over and over again:

"You did make me happy."

Seventeen

The Aftermath…

Scattered all over my legs and the floor in front of me and Beau were leaflets, pamphlets and letters. I could see:

- Ultrasound appointment letters and results

- MRI scan appointment letters, including a leaflet about what to expect

- Endoscopic ultrasound results (What the hell is that anyway?)

- Magnetic Resonance Cholangiopancreatography (that's wasn't even a real word – surely?)

- An A5 purple notebook

How the hell did Annie do all of this without me even knowing? How the hell did she do it on her own? Oh God, ANNIE.

My phone started to ring on Annie's bedside table, where I'd left it while I was talking the lady at emergency services. Dragging myself to my feet, I stumbled around the bottom of the bed, feeling the sheets where her body lay not half an hour ago.

ANNIE...

I didn't even look at the screen, just swiped to answer.

"Rob? Hello?"

It was May.

"Rob? Can you hear me? Zak just called. My baby girl, is it true?"

A massive sob escaped me.

"OH nooooooo, my darling girl." I heard her voice breaking.

I needed to tell her. I needed to make my body work with me, not against me.

I moved my mouth, but no sound coming out. I pulled the phone away from my face, and rubbed my face with my free hand. My face wet with tears. Smacking my cheeks. Come on ROB!

Putting the phone back to my ear, "May..." It came out more like a cough. "May, she was gone by the time I got home."

I heard a wail. What sounded like the phone falling to the floor.

I heard another wail. This time it came from me. I was stroking the sheet. I could smell Annie's perfume on the sheet. I could see the imprint of her head on the pillow.

"Rob? Hello?"

All I could do in response was make a grunting noise.

"Rob, it's Malc. Rob, it's ok." I could hear his voice wobbling, "Rob, son, can you hear me? The kids are fine with us, ok? As long as you need us to have them, we will. We won't say anything to them, ok son? What do you need us to do?"

I heard everything he said. I considered his question. The only answer I could come up with was, "Bring her back, Malc. Bring her back." I sobbed uncontrollably.

"Oh son. Now you listen to me. We need you. Do you hear me? We all need you, so you allow yourself to break before our beautiful babies come home to you. We need to grieve our Annie, but we all need to be ready for when they find out that they've lost their mommy."

Sniffing, wiping away my tears with my free hand, I said, "You're right, Malc. Oh God, what am I going to tell them? What are we going to do without her?"

"You tell them the truth, that their mommy loved them more than the moon and stars, that she will always love them and that we will love them hard until they tell us to love them a little less."

"Malc... I love her so much."

"Me too son. Me too."

We both just stayed silent, both struggling to control our breathing.

"Can you look after the kids, Malc? I... I... I... I need to not be their daddy, just for a bit, just so I can understand."

"As long as you need, Rob. We love you son, so much."

"I love you. Please tell the kids how much I love them..." More tears.

I slouched back down the wall where the leaflets were still scattered across the floor, Beau still looking at me with giant sad eyes.

I put the phone on the floor and rubbed her ears.

"She's gone, girl. Momma's gone." She started to whine.

"What are we going to do, girl?" Her whole body beginning to shake.

"I know, girl. I know." And I put my head against her body and cried into her fur. "Momma's gone."

I just stayed there with Beau, repeating this statement over and over, until her body stopped shaking, and my tears stopped.

I began leafing through all the flyers, letters, information guides that had fallen out of Annie's envelope.

Page after page, words, so many words, appointments for this, test results for that...

"What?" I asked, picking up the last sheet. Annie's handwriting was on the bottom of the page.

"Lawson, call this number and ask for Tanya."

144

I picked up my phone and keyed in the number. Who the heck is Tanya? I've never heard Annie talk about anyone called Tanya. God, what else didn't I not know?

"Hello?"

"Umm…" Trying to steady my voice, "Hello, I've been told to call this number and ask to speak to Tanya?"

"I'm Tanya."

"Tanya, my name is Rob Lawson. My wife Ann…" the shaking in my voice was returning, "Annie told me to ring this number."

"Mr Lawson, I'm Dr Tanya Prescott. I'm Annie's consultant. Was Annie's consultant. I'm so sorry for your loss."

I could feel my breathing getting quicker. I tried to stifle a sob. I wasn't sure if I was supposed to talk.

"Annie wanted you to have a better understanding of what has happened to her body, so you can understand and hopefully accept the difficult decisions she made."

"Dr…?"

"Prescott, but call me Tanya. Rob, I need to start this conversation by saying what a truly remarkable woman Annie was. She just lit up a room, didn't she? She struggled with not telling you about her illness. She was consumed with guilt. She told me that she has never lied to you. However, she felt deeply that she just couldn't watch your face as she left you, knowing that she'd cause that pain. She loved you all too dearly."

"I… I didn't…know."

"No, Rob. It's what she wanted, above everything else. She was very adamant about that. However, she was also adamant that you must understand, once she had gone. Annie had a very rare form of pancreatic cancer; it was extremely aggressive. When we realised the severity of Annie's illness, it was already too late." There was a small silence and I could hear papers shuffling at the other end of the line.

"Ughhh. I just…"

"It's ok, Rob, would you prefer if I just talk?"

"Yes."

"Ok, well, Annie's cancer was classified as T4b, N2 and M1.

Now that's medical jargon. Here's how I explained it to Annie. T4 means, in essence, the sizing guide we use for measuring the initial tumour. T4 is large, and the b means that it's spread beyond its initial site within the body. Does that make sense?"

"Yes." My breathing was slowing as I absorbed what the doctor was telling me.

"Ok. N2 means has it spread to the body's lymph nodes? In Annie's case, it had. Which in terms of prognoses and recovery is tricky. Again, does that make sense?"

"Yes. I think so."

"M1 is the worst possible reading we could have received back. It means that the cancer has spread away from the initial site within the body. In Annie's case, the cancer was not localised to her pancreas. Now that is simply because of the nature of the cancer and how aggressive it was. By the time Annie had gone to Dr Pacey when her symptoms had become unmanageable, it was too late. I estimate that she had been living with the cancer for as long as six months prior to her initial blood test."

"So, she stood no chance?"

"Honestly, Rob? That's a really difficult one to answer. No one can say with certainty. However, the odds were not in her favour. She could have chosen to lean towards extreme forms of intervention to help prolong her life. But, as I explained to her, each of those come with their own plethora of side effects and, once Annie had learned this, she dismissed this course of action. She didn't want what little time she had left with you to be marred with even more sickness or debilitating pain."

I heard the front door slam.

"Lawson?" Zak, shouting from downstairs.

Covering the phone speaker with my hand, I shouted, "Here," as Zak bounded up the stairs two at a time. He saw me slumped on the landing surrounded by paper, Beau's head on my lap and the phone to my ear. In the months since that moment, Zak has told me that I didn't actually look like the man he'd known for twenty-five-plus years. I looked empty.

"Beau," he called to her, and she lifted her head, rose and trotted over to her mate. She loved Zak; he teased her so much. He took her by her collar and led her downstairs. This simple act mattered to me. He was occupying the only other member of my family who was here, and giving me some privacy while I listened to Dr Prescott.

"We discussed in depth the options available to Annie. Medication was never on the table. We spoke about palliative care, which she would have needed towards the end of her life. I gave her some leaflets about local hospices that would be able to help. It was strange because she smiled at me and simply said 'I won't be needing those,' and slid them back across the desk to me. It was as if she knew she'd simply take her final breath in her own surroundings."

"She did," I whispered.

"Rob, even if you knew, there simply wouldn't have been anything you could have done to help Annie, or ease what was happening within her body. No one could. I've been specialising in cancer for the past fourteen years and there was nothing I could do, other than offer reassurance and answer as many questions as she needed answering."

She was trying to help ease the all-consuming pain that was radiating throughout my body at that precise moment.

"Personally, my own opinion on Annie's choice is that she made a decision knowing how limited her time was. There wasn't enough time for everyone to adjust to the news that she would be leaving and, therefore, she didn't want what time was left consumed with grief. She wanted that time filled with laughter, love, memories. She didn't want your lasting memories of her to be of someone who was 'sick'. Does that make sense?"

"I...ughhh... Yes, I think so. She did it to protect us?"

"That is exactly what she did, Rob. She did it all by herself to ensure you guys had nothing but...what did she say? 'Magically colour-filled lives.'"

That was enough. My tears were flowing. I just couldn't believe how brave my Annie had been, and how blind I'd been.

"Rob, what I will do is send all this to you in an email. I'm pretty sure you won't remember half of what I've told you. Annie has already given me your email address. It will be with you by the end of the day. I can't even begin to imagine the pain you must be experiencing right now, but please know you're not alone. We're all happy to support you and the children. When you're ready. If you would like to, at some point in the future, please know you're welcome to come to my office and sit and chat with me. Annie has given written consent to enable you to look at any of her medical records, scans, anything. She wanted nothing hidden from you."

"Thank you, that's…kind. Thank you for your time. I realise it's a Saturday. It is Saturday, isn't it?" I was confused.

"Yes Rob, it's Saturday, 7th of May."

A date I will never EVER forget.

"Don't forget, we're here if you need us. I'm truly sorry again. Bye Rob."

The line went dead. I pulled my phone from my ear and stared at the screen.

Eighteen

The Cold Light of Day...

I dropped the phone back on the floor, in among the papers. Running my hand through my hair and down across my face, I simply didn't know where to begin.

What should I be doing?

Should I be talking to people?

Undertakers?

Florists?

Then it hit me like a brick wall. I couldn't remember what Dr Pacey had said, I couldn't remember where those people were taking Annie. I couldn't talk to anyone if I didn't know the simple fact of where my wife's body was!

Then...

Why do they want her? What will they do to her?

Will they cut her open?

Will they hurt her?

She's on her own...

Of course, they can't hurt her, she's not her anymore.

All these jumbled thoughts all in the space of about ten seconds. Smacking my forehead, trying to make those thoughts regain some sort of order.

I hadn't heard Zak coming back upstairs.

"Mate...?"

I turned and stared at him. Someone who wasn't a stranger. Someone who knew me. Someone who knew Annie. Someone who would catch me. I'm falling.

He was on his knees next to me as the tears came again. I sobbed. I wailed. I shouted. I screamed. I begged. I pleaded. I prayed. I hoped. I wished. I broke.

She was gone.

An amount of time passed. I only know it was about an hour because Zak told me a few months later. An hour, could have been ten minutes, could have been ten hours.

I was spent. I was hoarse. I was aching. I was damp from my tears, as was Zak's jumper. We both sat with our backs against the bannister. In front of him was a case of bottled beer. He cracked one open and simply said, "I won't leave you. Tell me what you need me to do."

Just as he finished speaking, my phone buzzed to life, "Mum calling" displayed across the screen.

I knew May and Malc must have spoken to her.

Nodding my head, I asked Zak, "Can you?"

"Of course." He reached across and answered the phone. "Janie? Hi, yeah it's me." He stood up and walked back across the landing, moving into Lexie's bedroom. "Yeah, I'm with him."

Beau came bounding back up the stairs and deposited herself on my lap. I realised that she needed me as much as I needed her.

"Will do, and thanks. Bye." He handed me my phone.

"Your mum says she loves you. I put her off coming over, figured you'd need a bit of space before everyone descends, so she's going to go over to May and Malc's to help them with the kids."

I could only smile to show my appreciation. It hadn't even crossed my mind that people would want to come here, to come together at this time. I definitely wouldn't have been able to handle that!

Zak sank back onto his knees next to me and Beau. "Mate, I am so so sorry. I don't even know what to say." Tears were filling his eyes. "I loved her like a baby sister. I... I can't believe she's gone." His tears fell. My best friend in the whole world was breaking in front of me, and all I could think about was the food I'd bought for the make-or-break dinner that I should have been cooking.

"Lawson, we need to start making phone calls. Where's your charger? Your phone doesn't have much battery." He'd pulled himself together. Zak has always been the same. He's very practical, good to have around in a crisis. This is the biggest crisis I've ever known.

I pointed into our bedroom. "Top drawer, this side of the bed."

He walked into our room and looked at the ruffled bedsheets. Grabbed the charger and then walked out. Bending over, he started to gather up all the contents of the envelope. "Come on, we're decamping to the lounge. Come on Beau."

Unbelievably, my dog obeyed his command. She rarely obeyed me, and I'm her bloody owner!

Nothing. Physically, nothing was in front of me. Emotionally, nothing was inside of me. Mentally, nothing was inside of me. I was spent. I rose and descended the stairs, for the first time since my wife had died. My wife was dead. How was that even something that I was thinking? I couldn't understand.

I'd read about brain fog before. I always assumed, rather innocently or ignorantly, that it was a hippy phrase that didn't actually mean anything. But, my God, is it true. I couldn't form coherent thought patterns, let alone make rational decisions. Nothing!

When I walked into the lounge, Zak was pulling out one of the occasional tables and putting it in front of the sofa.

"SIT," he ordered.

I did as instructed. He placed my beer in front of me.

"Right, the doctor that phoned me said there is a letter for me in an envelope? I assume it's this envelope?"

"Annie left a letter for you?" I was genuinely surprised. Why would Annie leave a letter for Zak?

"Ahhhh, here it is. Shall I read it aloud to you?" I just nodded.

Thursday 5 May

Dear Zak

First things first, bring beer! He'll need beer.

Secondly, I'm sorry I'm not there to share said beer with you guys.

So, my time is done, and I've shuffled off. Possibly to float on a cloud somewhere! JOKE! Nothing like breaking the tension with a good death joke!

Ok serious faces now…

My time has come to an end, and now I need you. For the past…years (more than I'd like to commit to paper) you have been like another brother to me. You've listened to me moan about Lawson; you've moaned about Lawson to me. You've made the best godfather to our two terrors. You made an excellent bedfellow during that camping trip to Lyme Regis (take that look of horror off your face, Lawson – he simply shared the tent with me when you were too drunk to be trusted inside the canvas!).

I need you to love him hard. Catch him when he falls. Shove him when he stumbles. Be practical you, and help organise him in the coming days. Mostly, I just need you to be wonderful, amazing, caring, compassionate, kind and generous you.

I will miss all of you terribly. But please know what a wonderful life I have led, and how truly blessed I have been to have you all fill it with colour and magic.

Annie xxx

PS you're going to need my diary – it's in the top drawer of my bedside table. It contains passwords to all my accounts. It also has all the numbers and addresses of my friends. My phone – I'm not sure where exactly it will be when the time comes, but my password is our anniversary 2310. Lawson will be useless at telling people; this is where he'll need you.

Thank you for being one of my most treasured friends. Thank you for being Lawson's best friend. I love you.

Tears are streaming down both our faces. Her words acted like a catalyst. She could have been in the room with us, it could have been her voice vocalising the pleas for help once she'd gone. Instead, it was not, and it never would be.

Zak bounded back up the stairs to retrieve Annie's diary and find her phone. I walked from the living room, through the dining room and into the conservatory. It was starting to move towards twilight. My favourite time of day. Animals were starting to make their final noises of the day. I sat in my chair as I stroked Beau's ears. She seemed more comfortable with venturing outside knowing she could see me.

I listened as Zak began the arduous task of phoning people and informing them that Annie had passed away.

"Hello, is that Jennifer Andrews?" A pause. "Hi, my name is Zak Matthews. I'm Rob Lawson's best friend. I'm calling about Annie." Another pause. "I got your number from her diary. I'm sorry, Jennifer, I'm calling to tell you that Annie has passed away." Another pause. It was then that I realised I'd been holding my breath. "At the moment, we're not sure. As soon as we have any details, we'll let everyone know." A single tear fell from my right eye, but I didn't even feel like I was crying. "You are on her Facebook page?" Perhaps it was my heart crying? "Yes ok, that's probably a good idea. When we know more, we'll post to her Facebook wall." I felt hollow inside. I wasn't thirsty. I wasn't hungry. I didn't need to use the bathroom. I wasn't even sure I needed to breathe. "Yes, thank you so much, I will pass it on. Take care. Bye."

One down, probably hundreds more to go. Annie knew a lot of people!!

I stared out at the ever-changing sky, moving from reds and oranges to inky blues and black. I realised that Zak hadn't uttered a word about Annie's illness. Jennifer Andrews obviously hadn't asked.

I suspect that the chair took on the imprint of my body because I know I felt numb, very heavy and unable to really move myself after what felt like the millionth phone call.

Somewhere in between the calls, Zak had phoned and ordered a pizza delivery, which arrived around 11.30pm. He brought the food through to the conservatory and we sat in relative darkness. Another beer placed on the table next to my chair, and I was again ordered by my best mate, "EAT!"

The cheesy mushroomy chickeny goodness actually did help! While I ate, Zak took Beau for a trot around the close. Poor Beau. No way of understanding properly what was going on, only that one of her constants had gone.

When he came back, Zak was firm but gentle with me again, "Come on mate, it's well past midnight, it's time to get to bed." He pretty much frogmarched me upstairs. As we reached the top of the stairs, I noticed the door to our bedroom was closed.

I must have looked confused, because Zak said, "I closed the door, mate. Come on, into the spare room with you." He pushed open the door, and flicked on the overhead light. As always, the bed was made up with fresh sheets – Annie's doing.

"I won't leave, ok? Liv knows where I am, and doesn't expect me home any time soon. Ok?"

All I could do was nod in agreement. He filled the empty glass that sat beside the bed with water from the bathroom. I sat on the edge of the bed, unsure what to do. I'd never slept in this room before. It is ridiculous the things you realise at the most obscure moments!

"Do you want me to sleep downstairs? Or shall I bring a blanket and bunk down on the landing? Or I can go on the floor in here?" Zak suggested.

I know I heard every word he said. I know I did. I just didn't know how to process them, and then formulate an appropriate response. All I could manage was, "Ummm…"

"I'll grab a blanket and pillow and sleep on the landing, mate. We can pull this door a bit to, and then if you need me, I'll be right outside, ok?"

I nodded.

"Alright mate. Listen, try and get some sleep, you're going to need all the rest you can get for the next few days to come. If anything happens, anyone phones, or anything, I promise to wake you."

Again, I nodded and Zak left, flicking off the light and pulling the door slightly closed.

I was left in semi-darkness, light from the landing spilling into the room, illuminating the furthest corner that housed an old bookcase containing DVDs and some of Annie's old art books.

I climbed under the bedcovers and rested my head against the cold pillow. Everything felt distanced, like I was watching, like I was watching everything happening around me, but not actually being involved.

I don't know how long I'd lain in the bed before I heard shuffling outside the door. At first, I thought it was Zak making up some sort of bed on the landing, but it went on for quite a while.

I got up and opened the door, the light flooding the whole room this time. Immediately in front of me, the door to our bedroom stood open, and my best friend was knee-deep in bedding. He was stripping the bed. Looking up from wrestling with a pillowcase, he said, "This is something you don't need to do, Rob. Unless you want me to stop?" He looked worried.

I stared at the now bare mattress, the spot where Annie's body had lain. I spoke for the first time in a good couple of hours. My voice was hoarse, my throat dry, but my words utterly sincere, "Thank you, Zak, for everything." I turned back to the spare room, shut the door and climbed back into bed.

Sleep didn't come easy. I know I flipped from one position to another. The shuffling stopped, the landing light went off, and I could hear Beau and Zak's combined snoring. I must have dropped off at points throughout the night. But I was most definitely awake to see the sun rise on the very first day of a world that no longer contained Annie.

I felt all cried out as I lay in the bed watching the changing shadows on the ceiling. I felt drained. Exhausted. Confused. Angry. Frustrated. Hollow. Alone. Overwhelmed. Guilty. Tired. Thirsty. In need of a wee! I acknowledged each and every one of those things in turn. It felt important, like I needed to know that I was feeling something.

Around 4.45am, I gave in and got up. Zak was still asleep on the landing under Lexie's unicorn duvet, Beau snuggled up to him. Our bedroom door was closed again. I locked the bathroom door and recognised it would probably be a good idea to have a shower.

The warmth of the running water penetrating into my skin felt…soothing.

When I emerged from the shower, I knew I would be facing my next problem, or stepping stone, as Zak would go on to name them. All my clean clothes were in our bedroom.

I gently unlocked the bathroom door and was stunned to see a pile of neatly folded clothes waiting for me on the carpet just outside the door. The jumbled mess that was Lexie's duvet had gone and the landing was empty. I could hear movement downstairs, and knew that Zak was in the kitchen.

After getting dressed I walked downstairs, expecting to be mobbed by Beau, but she was very busy investigating the garden.

"Tea?"

"Thanks."

Zak put the steaming cup on the dining table and pulled out a chair next to it.

"How you doing?"

"I don't know. I can't get my head around it. How can she be gone?"

Zak simply shook his head, seemingly as confused as I was.

"How did I not notice that she was poorly? Your wife being ill, that's the sort of thing a husband should notice! If I hadn't been so bloody selfish, I might have noticed. She wouldn't have had to do this by herself."

"I don't think Annie wanted you to notice, mate. She was clearly very sure that you weren't to know. She didn't want to feel like a patient in her last days with you guys. She wanted to be her; to be free."

"You know all I keep thinking about is the pain she must have been in, the pain she suffered in silence. What hurt her, Zak? Where did it hurt? She never uttered a word. I saw her poorly two weeks ago and I thought it was food poisoning. It wasn't though, was it?"

"That's hard to answer, Rob. I don't know. I'm not sure you'll ever know for sure."

"What's going to happen now? What are they doing to her body? Where is she? Who should I ring? Should I talk to someone? What if they don't know who she is? You hear of it, don't you, bodies being lost? Should I go out and get a coffin? Where do you buy a coffin? Has she been left on her own? I don't want her to be on her own…"

Zak grabbed me by the shoulders and stared me in the face. I knew I'd gone into a slight meltdown. "Rob. Annie's body is at the hospital. They have to perform an autopsy on her so they can establish exactly what caused her to pass away. Dr Pacey already recommended a local funeral director, Thompson and Morgan. I'm going to give them a call in a little bit. They will sort everything. Annie is safe. They know who she is. You don't have to ring anyone, or speak to anyone unless you want to. Rob, Annie isn't here anymore, just her body. Worrying about if she's on her own isn't something you need to be thinking about anymore."

He wasn't rude, he wasn't forceful. He was calm, he was collected, he was rational. Everything I wasn't.

"As for how Ann was feeling? Again, I can't answer that. But maybe the consultant you spoke to last night will be able to help?"

"That's right. She said if I had any questions, I was to just ask her. She also said she was going to email me last night. I could go and respond?"

"That sounds like a great idea. It's a start to getting the answers you need. Why don't you take your tea into the study, fire up your laptop and send her an email?"

"Yeah, I will. I also need to think about what I'm going to do with work." The suddenness of the weight of responsibility dropped back on my shoulders. "Oh God, Zak, what am I going to do?" I dropped my head into my hands. "The kids need me. Work needs me. The house needs me. Everyone needs me." I looked up through my hands at him. "All I need is Ann." I didn't cry though. I was dry.

"No, mate. All you need to do is take each day at a time, even each hour at a time. Work will understand. But you have to communicate with them. The house will remain your home. Nothing needs doing, you know Annie was a clean freak – be thankful for that! I've already mooched in your chest freezer, it's full of meals she'd obviously been batch cooking. The kids...those kids are your priority now. When you tell them, they will need you, every hour of every day, for as long as it takes. You are their world, mate. Annie needs you to become their stability in a very rough sea."

I knew he was right. I also recognised that the weight of responsibility I suddenly felt had nothing to do with work and everything to do with my two beautiful babies. How on earth was I going to tell them that their momma was never coming home, never going to hold them tight, kiss them goodnight, or whisper that she loved them?

"Take the tea, mate. Let's start taking some steps with things that we can do. Come on, you'll feel better for doing it. I'll phone the funeral director for you."

Picking up my tea, I grasped Zak's shoulder as I walked past him. "Thanks, mate. It's ok – that's a phone call I need to make."

"You sure, dude?"

"Yeah, I think so."

"Ok. Mind if I hop in your shower?"

"Don't even need to ask. Thank you again, for everything."

Placing his hand on top of mine, "No thanks needed, mate. I'm here till you tell me to bugger off!"

"Bugger off and de-smell!"

Beau followed me to the study. As I opened the door, I was hit with a wall of Annie's perfume. I took a step back, as if the smell had physically hit me in the stomach. The pain in my heart felt that it was growing with each passing moment.

I moved around and sat at the desk, putting my tea on the USB warmer that Annie had given me last Christmas. At the time, I'd thought it the most ridiculous present. Now, I thought it the most wonderfully thoughtful thing anyone could have ever bought me. It did the one thing I needed while I was working – it kept my drink warm. But that was Annie, so thoughtful with her gift-giving.

I entered the password and looked at the time. 5.47am. Could I get anything productive done? I couldn't ring anyone at this time on a Sunday, could I?

Sticking with Zak's rational plan, I opened my personal emails and, sure enough, sitting under five junk emails, one of which was trying to sell me hair transplant surgery, was the email from Dr Prescott.

From: TAPrescott@mids.nhs.co.uk
To: rlawson1978@imail.com
CC: MCPacey@mids.nhs.co.uk
Date: 7 May 22.17pm
Re: Annie Lawson

Good evening Rob

Further to our conversation earlier this evening, I hope this email will offer some clarification to you and your family.

Firstly, may I take this opportunity to express my deepest condolences to you on the loss of Annie. She was a truly remarkable lady, who had a natural ability to simply light up any room she walked into. Her infectious personality had me and my staff in stitches at times. I know I will treasure the moments we shared that were filled with humour.

As we discussed, hopefully an email in simpler terms will help you understand what we know of Annie's condition.

She was suffering from a very aggressive, fast-moving form of pancreatic cancer, medically classified as:

T4b, N2 and M1

T4 refers to the size of the initial tumour. T4 is large, and the b means that it's spread beyond its initial site within the body and the spread could be localised or extensive. In Annie's case, it was extensive.

N2 examines whether it has it spread to the body's lymph nodes. In Annie's case, it had. In terms of prognoses and recovery, this is not positive if the patient's cancer spreads to the lymphatic system. Due to the nature of the system within the body, there simply isn't an area that the lymph nodes don't, in some way, have access to.

M1 is the worst possible reading that can come back with the blood tests. It means that the cancer has spread away from the initial site within the body. In Annie's case, the cancer was not localised to her pancreas. Unfortunately, cancer was ravaging her body.

This isn't because of anything Annie had done wrong, or a bad decision she made within her life; it is simply because of the nature of the cancer and how aggressive it was. By the time Annie had gone to Dr Pacey when her symptoms had become unmanageable, it was simply too late. I guesstimated that she had been living with the cancer for as long as six months prior to her initial blood test.

One of the first indicators of an issue with the pancreas is normally a yellowing of the skin. However, in Annie's case, that didn't happen. Which, given her eventual decision to not tell her closest loved ones of her illness, made it an easier process for her to handle.

You asked me on the phone if Annie stood a chance of surviving. I think I said that's tricky. I have given your question some more thought, and it is very difficult to answer. No one can say with any certainty. The odds were not in her favour, everything was stacked against her. I never actually gave her a percentage chance of survival, simply because I knew there was no chance of her ultimately surviving. The question was – how long would she get? She could have chosen to lean towards extreme forms of medication to help prolong her life. But, as I explained to her, each of those come with their own plethora of side effects and, once Annie had learned about these, she dismissed this course of action. She didn't want what little time she had left with you to be marred with even more sickness or pain. Therefore, the discussion about how much longer the drugs would have given her simply didn't take place. If you are asking me now? I'd have told her that the drugs would have given her around another 8 weeks, so she could have had as long as 14 weeks.

What I discussed in depth with Annie was every option available to her, from home support and occupational health (grab rails, etc.) to medication (as I've mentioned), physiotherapy, hydrotherapy (to help with the pain), speech therapy (if her speech were to become slurred), palliative care, which she would have needed towards the end of her life. I gave her some leaflets on local hospices that would be able to help. However, she simply slid them back across the desk to me. She knew she'd pass away in her own home.

In the final weeks of her life, Annie maintained her regular appointments with myself and Dr Pacey. We ensured that we managed her symptoms as best we could, with the underlying motto always being that she must be kept out of hospital, and functioning as normally as possible.

I think I mentioned I've been specialising in cancer for the past 14 years and, in all that time, I can honestly say, with my hand on my heart, that I have never, EVER, encountered anyone like Annie. To put it simply, she was remarkable. She seemed to emanate light, colour, life, and there was nothing I could do to help her, to make her better, to allow her to continue to shine. This is the part of my job that I absolutely hate. Knowing that there are some people who I simply can't fix.

Annie's decision, as she explained to me at one of our appointments, to keep her illness from you was based purely on love. She simply didn't want to see you hurting. She wanted whatever time she had left with you all to be filled with laughter, not sorrow. "Mourning is for the dead, not the living," is what she told me. She loved you all with a passion, that was clear to see. She never meant for her choice to be interpreted as malicious or self-centred. She was being the brave one, one last time.

I hope this helps, Rob. Please do feel free to contact me if you require any more information.

Kind Regards
Tanya

Dr Tanya Prescott
Medical Oncologist (Pancreatic Specialist)
Driftwood Unit
email: TAPrescott@mids.nhs.co.uk

I sat back in my chair, staring at the screen. Dr Prescott summed this whole situation up perfectly. Annie was being the brave one, one last time.

Turning my head, I looked out through the window that faces onto the front lawn. Two pigeons scuttled around on the grass looking for food.

I knew she was brave, of course I did. I didn't know she was this brave, this capable.

It hadn't even been twenty-four hours since Annie left us, and yet I felt as if I'd learned more about my wife from a stranger than the whole time we were together. I felt...ashamed, humbled, proud and, most of all, guilty.

Turning back to the screen, I knew I needed to respond to this doctor who had supported Annie, and I needed to articulate my thanks. But I needed a while to collect my thoughts, absorb what she'd told me.

I also needed to think practically. I needed to think about work.

Pulling out my mobile phone, I scrolled through the contacts until I came to G. I touched the screen and two numbers appeared. I pressed onto the mobile number and put the phone to my ear as it began to ring. I was surprised to hear the ring tone, given the time of day. A very sleepy voice answered.

"Hello?"

I know I coughed. I know I did. "Glenda? It's Rob."

"Rob?" I could tell I'd woken her. She was confused.

"Glenda, I'm so sorry to wake you and disturb you at home." I could hear shuffling at the other end of the line.

"Rob? What's the matter? Are you ok?"

She knew. This woman who would, given time, become like my work wife. Knowing me, my strengths, weaknesses, faults, facial expressions. She'd know me. She already knew something was wrong.

"I... I..." coughing again, I was struggling to say the words, to vocalise to someone my absolute worst fears, "Annie. It's Annie."

"Annie? Is she ok? Are the kids ok?"

"Glenda, she's gone." The final words barely came out before my voice broke.

"Gone? What do you mean? Gone?"

Confusion again. I was confused too.

"Glenda, she's...," big breath, "dead."

I heard the gasp. I heard the phone drop. I heard the sob. I heard the "NO!" I heard it all. However, I felt detached from it. I simply didn't have space within me to absorb someone else's grief, not at that moment.

"Rob?" It was Glenda's husband, Danny. "Rob, please tell me what we can do, son?"

"Honestly, Danny? Nothing. But thank you. I needed to tell Glenda personally. I know how fond she is of Annie. I'm not going to be in the office, Danny. I'm not sure for how long."

"I should bloody well hope not! You look after them nippers, you hear me? That bloody factory can wait. You don't go nowhere near it, you hear me? Now, don't you worry about nothing. I'll make sure that Glenda is sorted, and she'll be there tomorrow to sort everything. Ok?"

"Thank you, Danny."

"Right you are, son. Our condolences," and the line went dead.

I couldn't help but think later about that last comment. "Our condolences." What on earth did that mean? Really? It's such an odd turn of phrase.

I opened my work email icon and clicked 'new message'. It took me quite some time to compose it. I wrote a bit, deleted a bit, wrote a bit more, then deleted it again. I couldn't seem to find the right words to articulate what I wanted to say. Then I realised that was because there were no words in the English language that could allow me express that my wife had died.

To: managementteam@morrisandco.co.uk; glenda.willis@
     morrisandco.co.uk
From: robert.lawson@morrisandco.co.uk
Date: 8 May 05.58am

I am writing to inform you all that after a brief illness, my wife Annie passed away yesterday.

As I'm sure you can understand, I won't be in work for the foreseeable future. Therefore, I am asking that we implement emergency Management Team Protocol Number 1 – incapacity of MD.

My priority right now is and has to be my children.

I will liaise with Glenda, so anything major that requires my input please leave with her.

Please, can you all work with Glenda to put together a statement for the Team – they need to know why I'm not around. Similarly, please put together a statement for our Clients.

Thank you for your understanding.
Rob

Managing Director
Morris and Co
Tel: 01905 769769
Email: robert.lawson@morrisandco.co.uk
"No project too big, we'll always deliver your vision."

I hit send.

I breathed a sigh of relief. One thing off my shoulders, for now at least.

Next, on what felt like my ever-growing list of things to do, I took the house phone from its cradle and dialled the number on the piece of paper that Zak had given me.

"Thompson and Morgan, how may I help you?" a disguised-sleepy voice answered within four rings.

Again, as with Glenda, I struggled to find the words, almost as if when I spoke them everything would become very real. "I'm sorry to call so early... I... We...my wife... My wife has died suddenly, yesterday. I've... I've no idea what I'm meant to do?" Raw honesty. It was all I had. I literally and figuratively threw myself at this stranger's feet, hoping that he was awake enough to be able to help me.

"I'm so sorry for your loss. My name is Richard Morgan. Can I ask your name?" He was so softly spoken. His questioning didn't seem intrusive in any way.

"Rob, Robert Lawson. My wife is Annie, was Annie," I corrected myself. It slashed across my body like a knife.

"Thank you, Mr Lawson. I'll just get a few things together and I'll come and see you if that's ok? Can you confirm your address?" he enquired.

"Sixteen Chestnut Grove, Bromsgrove."

"That's not too far from me. I would hope to be with you within forty-five minutes, if that is ok?"

"Thank you, yes."

"Mr Lawson, please try not to worry. We will sort everything out. I'll see you soon. Bye-bye."

The line went dead again.

How could I not worry? How could anything ever be the same again? I couldn't get my head around it.

Annie was young, for God's sake. She never smoked. Never drank to excess. The most reckless thing she did was eat two portions of ice cream once! How could she be gone? Who gets to pick who's going to pop off? Because I want a word with them!

When I came out of the office, I found Zak asleep on the sofa in the conservatory, Beau wrapped around his feet. I know how lucky I was to have a friend like Zak. I don't think there is anything I could say to him that would warrant our friendship ending. We are together for the rest of our lives, and I'm very grateful of that.

Putting the half-drunk cup of tea by the sink, I unlocked and opened the front door, and sat on the porch step waiting for Richard Morgan to arrive.

I pulled out my mobile again and composed a message to May.

Morning. How are the kids? How are you?

She read the message almost immediately. It was, after all, almost 6.30am. Of course, the kids would have them up!

Hi. They're just deciding what to have for breakfast. It's a big decision, so Lou is telling us. How are you? We're...ok.

:-) he's such a character. I'm...honestly? Numb! I'm sat on the front step waiting for the funeral director to come. It is all surreal, May. How can she be gone?

I know. It all seems like some terrible mistake. That she's going to come bursting through the door and shout 'surprise'. Malc is broken, as am I.

"I'm so sorry May. I wish I'd gotten home sooner. Maybe I could have done something."

"There's nothing you could have done, son. She knew she was going, and she'd

167

made peace with that. She just wanted to make sure that you three were surrounded with love and magic."

"We were, May. I think I'd like them home with me if that's ok?"

"Yes, of course. When shall we bring them back?"

"Can I meet with the funeral director and then ring you, once I know a bit more of what's going on?"

"Of course, son. We love you."

"Love you too."

As I hit 'send' on the last message, an immaculate BMW pulled into the close and moved slowly towards our house. I stood and waved as the car pulled onto the drive behind Zak's car.

A middle-aged, well-kept man – Richard Morgan – got out, carrying a briefcase. I wiped my face, making sure the fresh tears I'd cried were gone, although I was sure he'd seen plenty of tears shed with his job.

I walked over and extended my hand. "Hi, I'm Rob Lawson."

I'd not even known this man existed twenty-four hours ago, and now I was about to hand over to him responsibility for one of the three most precious things in my life.

Nineteen

The Hardest Decisions I Didn't Have to Make…

I led Richard Morgan into the lounge and left him to unpack his papers as I made a pot of coffee. Zak appeared from the conservatory as the kettle came to the boil.

"You ok, mate?" he asked.

"The funeral director is here." I motioned to the living room. "Do you want a cup of coffee?"

"How about a travel mug? I can take Beau out for a long walk while you talk, unless you want me to stay?" He sat at the dining room table and began pulling on his shoes.

"Thank you, mate, that's kind. If you could take Beau, that would be a big help. Poor girl, she needs normality." I pulled a travel cup from the cupboard and began filling it with boiling water.

"You go and sit with him. I'll bring this through." Zak gestured to the cups that kept shaking in my grip.

Returning to the lounge, I found that Richard was ready for me, a raft of papers and folders on his lap.

Sitting on the sofa opposite him, I knew, in that moment, that

I actually didn't have a clue what to say to this man. What did he do? What should I ask him? What decisions was I meant to make? Like a wave crashing over the top of my head, I very quickly became overwhelmed by his very presence in my home.

"Mr Lawson, I can see how truly devastating your loss is, and I offer my deepest condolences. There are a few things I need to confirm with you, if that's ok?" Richard pushed on a pair of reading glasses and clicked on his black ballpoint pen.

"Rob, please. Yes, go ahead," I said.

"Can you confirm your wife's name, the date and month of her birth and full address to me?"

"Annie Clarice Lawson. Her date of birth is 17 May 1982. Her address is here, 16 Chestnut Grove."

Zak came in, with Beau at his heel, carrying a large tray loaded with the big pot of steaming coffee and a plate of shortbreads. Introducing himself and then excusing himself, he shut the front door behind him and ventured off.

"Thank you. Finally, for data protection reasons, can you tell me the memorable word that has been placed on our records?"

"Memorable word? What?" I must have looked like I'd been slapped in the face with a wet fish; confused didn't even come close to how I felt.

"Yes, Rob, the memorable word associated with our files?"

"I'm sorry Richard, I've no idea what you're talking about. There can't possibly be any 'memorable words', there can't even be a file, I just phoned you to tell you Annie has… Annie is… Gone."

Pulling his glasses off and resting them on top of the papers on his lap, Richard looked me in the eye. "Rob, Annie has already organised the whole funeral, coffin, service, flowers, even the order of service," he ticked each off on his fingers. "I met with her some weeks ago. She made all the decisions herself, knowing, rightly, that you'd be in no fit state to even begin thinking about what colour handles should be placed on her coffin. I'm so sorry, I assumed you knew of this?"

I fell back against the cushions, staring at this man. How could I not know that my wife had planned her own funeral? Was

I so blind to everything around me that I simply didn't see all the pain she was in, all the trauma she was experiencing all by herself? Holding my head in my hands, I let my breath leave my body slowly, as I fought to keep control of myself.

"No, I... I...no. I didn't know." Slowing my breathing down.

"Annie placed a memorable word on the file. Simply by telling me this memorable word, we can begin to discuss her decisions." He pulled his specs back on, and gestured to the tray of coffee. "Shall I pour?"

Absently nodding, I sat in silence and tried to think of a memorable word. Stupidly I asked, "How many goes have I got to get the right answer?" I realise now just how stupid that question must have sounded. It wasn't as if her file was going to blow up after three incorrect attempts!

"As many as is necessary. I will try to steer you in the right direction, but I'm not allowed to simply tell you!" He bit into a shortbread.

So, I simply started saying random things that I thought might be it:

"Worcester

Chestnut

Beau

Lexie

Rob

Annie

Louis

Lawson

Painting

Jumper

Petal"

All the while, the funeral director simply sat there and shook his head. Then it dawned on me. I knew the memorable word.

"It's Watermouth, isn't it?"

A small smile spread across the man's face. "Yes, it is."

Of course, it was!

"This folder contains the details of everything that was decided between Annie and myself. But I'll summarise for you. By deciding herself, Annie hoped to be able to take the pressure off you, so nothing is set in stone. She was very firm that you must have the final word on all decisions that are made. She has chosen a Water Hyacinth coffin, a very natural coffin, fabric-lined inside, simple rope handles. She has already left the clothes she'd like to be dressed in; they are at our office, waiting for her. She is happy to be seen in the chapel of rest; however, she explicitly requested not to be embalmed, unless absolutely essential. We won't know if it will be required until after the autopsy. A Home Office pathologist will perform an extensive investigation to establish the exact cause of Annie's death. Does that all make sense?"

Did it? Truthfully no! But, of course, I had to respond, "Yes."

"Good. Once the autopsy has been concluded and, assuming the pathologist is happy, he will get in contact with my office to inform me that he is releasing Annie's body. At this time, one of our private ambulances will transfer Annie from the hospital to our chapel of rest. Upon arrival, Annie's body will be prepared in accordance with her wishes. This will include dressing her, and placing her inside her coffin."

Control my breathing, that's all I could focus on. In and out…

"Once Annie is ready, I will contact you and advise that she is ready to be viewed by family and friends in the chapel. We will need around thirty minutes' notice of arrival, but the chapel is open twenty-four hours a day, so if you need to see her at 2am, then you can."

In and out…in and out…

"Annie has chosen a cremation ceremony, with the request that her ashes be taken back to Watermouth and scattered around the bench you sat at on your honeymoon in the harbour."

In and out…In and out…In and out…

"The hymns and order of service have already been agreed, but I'll leave this for you to look over once I've gone. She has asked that there be one reading, and she'd like her brother…" he looked down at his notes, "Andrew to read it. All music has been chosen, and Annie provided me with a CD. She wasn't sure about cars, so that is a decision you'll have to make. Traditionally, there is one family vehicle that follows the hearse, but again, it's up to you. She made a specific request that any flowers are to be passed on to a local hospice or care home after the funeral. She said that flowers are too beautiful to waste on those who have gone, and should be enjoyed by the living."

In... In... In...don't forget to exhale! Knob! Out... In and out...

"We spoke at length about Annie's wishes regarding your children, and she felt it important that I be able to speak on her behalf. She said that she felt they were too young to visit her in the chapel of rest and that, particularly, Louis wouldn't understand why she wouldn't be able to 'wake up', but it is also vitally important that they be involved as much as possible in the funeral. It will enable them to feel like they are part of what is happening."

In...and out... STOP...

It pulled me up short. He was right, she was right. "You're right. I mean, Annie's right. I wouldn't want them to go and see her. It would destroy Lexie, she is so close to her mommy. And she's nailed Lou to a tee, he would be shaking her, trying to wake her. No, they can't go. But be involved? I don't know what they could do?"

"Annie had a couple of suggestions. One being the flowers for the top of her coffin, allowing them to decide. She also suggested that perhaps they'd like to write letters, or notes, or do drawings for her? We can put whatever you like inside the coffin, prior to it being sealed."

"The flowers? That seems like a good idea, doesn't it? Then they'd see their efforts. Ok, we'll do both. They will be coming home later today, so I'll talk to them about it."

"Rob, as I mentioned earlier, none of this is set in stone, so if you change your mind and you'd like to bring your children to see their mum, that is absolutely fine." He put his coffee cup down and slid some more forms across to me.

"All I need you to do is sign these two forms, and I can officially begin the process of Annie's final journey."

Looking down at the forms, giving my consent for the funeral director to take possession of Annie's body once released, I felt such sadness deep within my soul.

"Richard, what about cost? I've just realised I'll need to talk to the bank."

"All costs have already been agreed. On the second page you'll see that Annie paid the full cost when she visited me. I believe that the money came from her parents, and that she said once her life insurance came through, she hoped you'd pass the cost back to her mother and father."

Annie had already paid for her own funeral! Fuck me! That woman was simply...incredible. I took her for granted, and I'd never be able to make up for my mistakes.

I signed the two release forms, and effectively handed Annie over to him.

"I'm hoping that the Home Office pathologist will perform the autopsy today; however, it may be tomorrow. I'd hope the latest we'd have Annie with us is tomorrow evening. But as soon as she's back, I'll give you a call. Once they release her, I can begin to make arrangements. For instance, I can't book the crematorium date and time until I know for certain that they will release Annie. So, once she's with us, things will start to happen and quickly, but I'll keep in touch." He slid the release forms back into his briefcase, leaving a Thompson and Morgan branded folder on the coffee table, and rose from the sofa.

Reaching across, he shook my hand again, and walked towards the front door.

"Annie was a remarkable woman, Rob, so much strength and drive to ensure that her family was looked after even after she'd gone. It was a pleasure to work with her. I'll be in touch." And, with that, he was out the door and striding down the drive.

I walked back into the empty lounge and lifted up the folder, the brand a beautiful blooming stem of lilies with Thompson and Morgan's logo sitting behind them.

Opening the folder, I sat back down and rested it on my lap. On the left side was Richard Morgan's business card and from the right I pulled out sheet after sheet of paper. Annie's name was printed at the top of each page, along with a reference number, LAW096a. Annie had become a reference number. God, I hadn't ever even considered death requiring administering!

The top sheet had a Post-it with a handwritten note from Richard,

"Mr Lawson, this is the only element that needs finalising. Please let me know if you would like to have family cars to and from the service and, if so, for how many people.

Of course, you have the final say over all of Annie's pre-made decisions."

Request for Family Vehicles to place of Service and Return. Again, this form had Annie's "reference number" printed on the top. It all seemed so...formal? So clinical? I suppose it has to be. No matter what happened, or what I decided or didn't decide, they were a business, and clearly a very organised one at that!

The next sheet of paper set out Annie's plans for her body, including the coffin she'd chosen. There was a picture included on the sheet. The image really caught me off guard. I couldn't imagine my Ann being inside that! She was Annie. She would be coming home soon and would potter about the house before making us all Sunday lunch.

She wouldn't though, would she?

She was going to be inside this natural-coloured woven coffin. She was never coming home again.

I couldn't look at more of the paperwork. I needed my children, our children. I needed them home.

I pulled out my phone while simultaneously choking back tears that threatened to overpower me, and hit 'call' on May and Malc's home phone.

"Daddy!"

My beautiful Lexie was being all grown up.

"Baby girl, good morning. Did you have a nice sleep?"

"Yep! I even got myself out for a wee, all by myself. Nanny came to make sure I hadn't fallen down the toilet though!"

"You didn't fall down, did you?"

"Oh Daddy! No, of course, I didn't! That would be silly!" she laughed. Hearing her laugh almost broke my heart, because I knew in a few hours' time, I was going to have to break the news to her that her beloved mommy was gone, and that laugh wouldn't return for a long time.

"How's your brother?" I asked her.

"Oh, he's ok. He's had three breakfasts. Can you believe it! Now he's sitting in the front room, watching the car racing on the telly with Gag. Seems like a load of rubbish to me!" She was always bored with any form of sport. "Do you want to talk to Nanny?"

"Yes please, sweetheart. Lexie... I love you darling, so very much." I held my voice, hoping that the pain I was feeling inside wouldn't come through to my beautiful baby girl.

"Love you too Daddy, bye-bye."

"Hello Rob."

"Oh May. You knew, didn't you?"

"About my baby being poorly? Yes. About her taking control of the final aspects of her life? Yes. That she loved you three so fiercely that she'd have done anything and everything she possibly could to protect you from what was happening to her? Yes." May sounded almost resigned to the bollocking she thought I was going to unleash upon her.

"Thank you. Thank you for being the best parents she, and I, could ever wish for. I love you both as if you were my own parents. I think... I think I'm going to need help, May. I don't know how to do any of this – life, the kids, the house – I don't know how to do any of it without Annie."

"Oh darling, you don't have to. We're here, Andrew as well. Your mum is waiting for you to ask, she's probably even sat, as we speak, engine running, at the bottom of your road. We're all here to help each other get through this. You know the most remarkable thing I've realised over the past few hours? Annie's gone, and this massive void will always form a structure of our lives, but the void isn't black. It's purple, and bright red, mixed in with orange and splashes of green, and..."

"Marshmallow," we said together, a small laugh escaping my mouth.

"She was colour Rob, she was vibrant, she was laughter, she was music, she was happiness, she was magic. Aren't we the lucky ones?"

She was bang on. I realise that now. She was so bloody right.

"Can you bring them home, May? I need to tell them. It's going to break their worlds forever, and I don't even know where to begin," I whispered.

"You start by making sure that these two adorable little mess makers know how loved they are, then go from there. We'll stay if you want us to. I can call Janie too, if you think it'll help?"

"I don't know anything, May. Other than I want my babies with me."

"I'll get them washed and dressed and we'll be on the road. Be with you in the hour."

"Thank you, May. Thank you for allowing Annie the opportunity to regain control. I'm seeing now just how important it was for her to be able to keep control, organise, and have her stamp on the final aspects of her life."

"She's our baby, Rob. There's nothing we wouldn't do for that girl, or you three for that matter. You are our world, and always will be. Love you."

"I love you. I love her, May. I love her so much. I ache inside, the pain inside, it doesn't stop."

"We know, son. We know." The line went dead.

Twenty

Four Become Three…

Zak came back with Beau and I sat in the garden, fresh cup of coffee steaming beside me and a piece of blank paper and a pen in front of me. I ruffled the fur baby's head and she trotted off to get a drink from her bowl.

"Alright mate?" Zak slid into the chair opposite me.

"Annie organised the whole funeral! I mean everything!"

"Really?" He sat stunned. "Bloody hell, Lawson!"

Staring down at the table, the weight of Annie's loss consumed me again, it was like waves crashing to land.

"I need to make a list of people who I need to contact to tell them that…that…tell them."

Zak pulled the paper across the table and clicked the pen on and wrote the number '1' at the top.

"Fire away then."

"The bank, I guess. Will they be open on a Sunday?" Anxiety filling my voice.

"Yes, mate. The bereavement department will be open, I'm

sure. We'll Google it and find out?"

"Yeah, ok. Umm... I don't know, all her bills? Mobile phone? Where is her mobile phone?" I started to panic.

"Beside the bed," Zak reassured me.

Slowing my breathing down, I loosened my grip on the edge of the table.

"Sorry." I felt shame. Shame that I wasn't coping. Should I have been coping?

"Sorry? What for?" Zak looked so confused.

Looking my oldest friend in the eye, I struggled to find the words to express what I was feeling. "I'm not coping, mate. How am I meant to cope? The kids will be here in a minute, and I've no idea what I'm going to tell them. How can I be strong for them, when I can't even be strong for myself?"

Putting the pen down, Zak looked me in the face, took a breath, obviously considering what he was going to say to me. "Rob, maybe it's not about having to be strong for yourself at the moment. Maybe it's just about being strong for them?"

"What do you mean?"

"That my godchildren are going to need you. Therefore, you need to summon all your strength to become their stability, their lighthouse in this storm. You have me and Liv, your mum, May, Malc and Andy. The kids have us all too, but they are going to want you close to them. We are all here for all of you, but the babies will need you more. Does that make sense?"

"You mean I need to just focus on the kids, and forget myself?" I was still confused.

"Not at all. Mate, this is going to change you all, forever. Just for the time being, let's focus on the kids. Try not to become overwhelmed with it all, take everything a bit at a time," he clarified.

He was right. I was an adult and I still didn't understand what was going, what chance did two under-seven-year-olds have? I needed to be stable, I needed to be calm, I needed to be there for them.

"You're right, mate—"

"DADDDDDDDDDDD!" interrupted our conversation as the sound of running feet came from inside the house.

"Oh God." My insides contracted.

"We're here for you mate," Zak rested his hand on my arm, offering reassurance.

"DADDDDDDDDDY!" Lexie came running into the garden and launched herself onto my lap. "Uncle Zak!"

"Yo, Daddy-O." Louis sauntered into the garden, carrying what looked like a new tractor, probably from May and Malc.

"Aghhhh, you both scared me!" I feigned shock, hoping to cover the all-consuming sadness.

"We had such a great time at the sleepover, I even got to have a midnight snack at widdle time!" said Lexie proudly.

"You did? What?"

"Gag went and got us all biscuits, and we sat on the stairs in the dark and ate them! It was so exciting!" She laughed.

"WOW! Well, I didn't know you could have midnight feasts! No one brought me biscuits!" Zak intervened, lightening the mood, and she laughed even harder.

"Lou darling, come here and sit on my other knee. I need to speak to you both." I motioned my boy over to me.

"Remember, we're all here for you," Zak motioned with his head back towards the house, and I could see May, Malc and my mum standing in the conservatory, waiting, waiting to catch their grandchildren, waiting to catch me.

"I'm going to go and make hot chocolates. Who wants one?" Zak said, as he headed back towards the house, and began hugging my mum and Annie's parents.

I told myself in that moment that I needed to find every ounce of strength I had, just to get through the next few minutes, just to be able to spit out the words that would break their worlds for ever.

"Now, I need you both to listen to me, ok?" I said, making sure I had eye contact with them both.

"Put the tractor down for a minute, Louis..." Lexie instructed. Her obedient brother did as he was instructed.

"I have some news to tell you. But before I do, I need you both to know that I love you so very much." The final word caught in my throat. Big breath, "Mommy has been poorly. Very poorly."

Lexie's face clouded with concern. "Oh no. I can get my nurse's outfit, and help take care of her."

Smoothing her hair around her face, I said, "That's so kind, Piggy. The doctors tried to make Mommy better, but they couldn't. Mommy fought so hard to get better, but she couldn't. She wanted to get better, but she couldn't. Mommy died yesterday. She has gone to live with the angels now. She will watch over all of us always." Tears were falling, I couldn't stop them, they splashed on Louis's tiny hands.

Utter confusion was etched across Lexie's face. She pushed herself off my lap and started to back away slightly from me.

"No, you're wrong, Daddy. Mommy wouldn't leave me, she wouldn't!" She turned around and began to run back towards the house, shouting "Momma! Momma! We're home!" She ran straight into her grandparents and godfather, who scooped her up and cocooned around her as her uncontrollable crying started, a gut-wrenching noise emanating from my daughter's very core.

"Lou, do you understand what I'm saying?" I looked down at my tiny son, still on my lap, twiddling with his tractor wheel.

"Momma is poorly? Is she in the hospital?" His big eyes searching my face for something.

"No, mate, she's not in the hospital…"

"Oh, she's in bed like last week. I'll go and kiss her better!" he interrupted, and jumped down and started off towards the house.

"Louis, Momma isn't upstairs." He turned back to face me. "Momma isn't here anymore. She died. She didn't want to leave you. She loves you so much. It's just us three now mate. But Momma will always be with us, in our hearts, because we love her."

Seeming to hear his sister's wails, he switched between looking at her, and then me, and then her.

"Why is Nan Nan, Nanny, Gag and Uncle Zak here?"

"Because we are all so upset that Mommy isn't here anymore.

We all want to be together to help each other, and to hold each other, and remind each other just how much we love each other."

"But I want my mommy." His lower lip began to tremble.

"So do I dude." I got down on one knee, so I was level with his now tear-filled eyes. "I miss her so much, my insides hurt. Do yours?"

He nodded, and the tears flowed over. I grabbed him and picked him up off the floor and held him as his little body began to shake, my body began to shake. How was I meant to be strong with this tiny human being, when I couldn't be strong for myself?

My mum came out into the garden, and reached for Louis and cradled him close to her chest.

"Nannnnnnnnnnnnnnnnnn. Mommmmmmmaaaaaa," he wailed, as Lexie's cries became more breathless.

I knew she needed me.

"Baby it's ok. Daddy's here." I lifted her from Malc's arms into my chest and held her as she trembled and sobbed.

I sank to the cool tiled floor of the conservatory as May and Malc crouched down next to us, engulfing us with their arms.

Zak has since told me that he went to my mum and held onto her as she held onto Louis. Everyone crying, everyone broken, everyone needing everyone else.

Looking back at these moments (and I have done many times), it has become very clear to me that Annie was actually the glue that held all of us together. She was the organiser, the motivator, the challenger, the adventurer, the strong rock that we all needed without even knowing it.

What I don't know, none of us know, is how long we all stayed together in the garden and conservatory that morning. Perhaps it was a few minutes. Or maybe hours. We stayed until we were ready to move slowly apart.

We all moved into the living room, Lexie and Louis both sitting either side of me, while May and Malc took one sofa, Zak the floor and my mum busied herself in the kitchen making drinks for everyone.

"If there's anything you want to ask, or want to know, you just have to ask, ok? No question isn't worth asking, ever!" May told Lexie and Lou. I see Annie in May – sensible, thoughtful, so kind and compassionate. Just like her daughter.

"Is my mommy hurting?" Lexie's big eyes looked up to mine.

"Oh sweetie, no. Mommy has no pain anymore. She's absolutely fine. We just can't see her anymore," I answered, smiling at my beautiful daughter, my daughter who looks so much like her mom.

Mum's arrival with drinks helped, and the kids thankfully both gulped down their hot chocolates.

"We're going to head off now, if that's ok?" Malc asked the kids directly. They are both so mindful of the children.

"Will you come back?" Louis asked with worry reverberating through each word.

"Come 'ere, champ!" Malc grabbed Louis and plonked him on his lap. "I need you to know that your Gag isn't going anywhere – except home to have a shower, in peace!" Louis smiled. Obviously, a story for another time. "I love you more than I could ever tell you, and I promise that when Nan and I get home, we will video call you. How does that sound?"

Louis thought about it for a few seconds and nodded in agreement, before burying his head in Malc's neck, catching hold of his shirt in a death grip.

"Mate, I'll head off if you want to be just the three of you?" Zak said to me. "Or I can stay? But I'd need to nip home and get some clean clothes."

"No mate, you head on back home. I couldn't have done the past few hours without you. I mean it. You have helped me so much. I'll never be able to thank you."

"Anytime you need me, just shout, ok? Even in the middle of the night. I'll leave my mobile on. Ok? Oi, you two mess makers, I want you to ring me before bed please, I need to know that you have successfully managed to get your old dad to brush his teeth." He brandished his teeth at Lou and Lex and they both started giggling. "Right. You pair, come here. Time for kisses and tickles, I mean hugs!"

He grabbed each of them as they ran over to him on the floor, and proceeded to blow raspberries on any exposed skin. The living room was filled with the sound of squealing and laughter. It was...nice.

My mum headed off not long after Zak. For the first time, it was just the three of us. We closed the porch door, Lexie holding on tight to my hand, Louis to his tractor.

"Right. You pair, who's hungry?" I wasn't hungry, but they were still children, and kids are always hungry! "We have left-over pizza?"

"Pizzaaaaaaaaa!" Louis ran off and was already seated at the table by the time Lex and I arrived!

"Can I stay with you while you make the food, Daddy?"

"Of course, Piggy. How about you help me? Can you get the plates out?"

"Can I still hold onto GG while I do it?" she asked nervously.

"Well, I don't see why not. Aren't giraffes known for their plate-carrying abilities?"

"Don't be daft Dad!"

Dinner was a sombre affair, although both kids ate well. I just pushed my slice of pizza around the plate. Loading everything into the dishwasher, I clicked it on to wash, and called Beau back into the house; she was tormenting a squirrel in the garden again.

"Come on then, you two, we need to have showers before bed." As I ushered them up the stairs, I couldn't help but be pulled up short as I recognised the normality that came with having the kids at home. Children have a remarkable way of bringing everything back to the 'now'; they have wants that need to be met instantly, there's no time to ponder, or slump.

"Can I go in first please, Dada?" Louis asked as he stripped off his clothes and put them in the clothes hamper in the family bathroom.

"Sure dude. Although you've got to use bubbles, ok?" I answered as I turned the shower onto warm. As I looked back at him, I could see he was looking back across the landing at the closed door to my and Annie's bedroom. I knew he was crying.

"Mate, you ok?"

"I want my mommy." He turned and ran to me and buried his head in my legs.

Lexie came into the bathroom, her chin wobbling, "I want Mommy too. I've never gone to sleep without a goodnight kiss from her. How will I sleep, Daddy?" and she buried her head in my other side.

I pulled them off me slightly as I sat on the floor, and allowed both of them to hold my chest, tears falling, emptiness surrounding their very beings.

I stroked both of their heads as I watched the water cascading down the shower screen. I didn't know what to say to them. I didn't know what words would comfort them. So, I didn't say anything. I just held them, so they knew I was there. I wasn't going anywhere.

After a couple of minutes, Louis sat up, face blotchy from crying, "I need to go in the shower. Momma never lets me go to bed without having a shower," he managed to say.

"Ok mate, we'll get you washed, and then your sister can go in while I dry you, ok?" They both nodded in agreement.

I sat up, Lexie releasing her death grip on me, and checked the temperature of the water. Louis climbed in and immediately sat down under the stream. I closed the door as he began to pump his 'big boy' soap and lather up.

"Has Mommy really gone?" Lexie suddenly asked.

I turned to face her sweet innocent face. "Oh, my precious, precious girl. Yes, she has. I'm so very sorry. I wish I could take the pain away. I want to take the pain away and carry it for you. Mommy wanted to stay so very badly." I tried to keep my voice from breaking.

"What's going to happen, Daddy?"

I didn't know, I didn't have the answer she wanted, I didn't have any answers, so I did the only thing I could – I didn't lie. "I don't know, sweetie. I have no idea. I don't know how we're going to live without her, I don't even know how we're going to get through tomorrow, or even tonight. But I do know something..."

"What?"

"I know that I love you and Lou more than life itself, and we will get through everything together, just us three, ok? OH, and Beau of course!"

"Ok Daddy. But… I'm scared."

"You're scared?"

"What if you leave as well, and it's just Louis and me? I don't think I'm old enough to look after him by myself!"

I pulled her into my chest. "Oh darling, I'm not going anywhere. I promise! Even if I did, you have Nan and Gag, and Nan Nan and Uncle Zak and Auntie Liv and Uncle Andy. None of us are on our own. They are all there to help us, to protect us, to love us. No one is going anywhere, ok?"

"Ok Daddy. I love you."

"I love you my baby, so very much. Right then, let's attempt to extract your brother from whatever mess he's made inside that shower. Then it's your turn, so clothes off!"

Bedtime went better than I'd hoped, both kids falling asleep in their beds quickly. I went downstairs, locked up the house and broke the first rule of dog ownership – I brought Beau back upstairs with me. I felt like I needed all of us close together, and she was very happy with the arrangement.

I'd explained to the kids that I would be sleeping in the spare room for a while. I wouldn't be venturing back into our bedroom anytime soon. Zak had kindly brought through my clothes and put them on the bed, so I dumped them in the corner of the room, and collapsed on the mattress.

I hadn't been there for more than a few minutes when Beau's ears pricked up, and I caught the sound of whimpering coming from Louis's room.

I walked down the landing and into his room.

"Alright mate?"

"I can't sleep, Daddy. I need my Momma cuddles before I go to sleep. She always cuddles me till I pop."

I walked over to the little bed that was once his cot and knelt on the floor.

"Daddy cuddles just aren't the same, are they?"

"No, they don't smell right!"

His response took me by surprise and I couldn't help but smile at him. Kids are so honest, aren't they!

"What can we do to make it feel better? Shall I come and sleep on your floor?" An emphatic shake of his head.

"Shall we go down and get some warm milk?" Again, he shook his head frantically.

"Want to come and sleep with me and Beau?" A nod this time. There we go! We got there in the end.

"Can Mr Hefalump come?"

"Of course, he can, so long as he doesn't wriggle!" I picked up my darling boy and started back towards the spare room.

"Will there be room for me and GG, Daddy?" came a little voice from the darkness of Lexie's room.

"Well…hmmmmm… There might be as long as GG doesn't wriggle either! Any wriggling and they're both out!"

I walked back into the spare room and deposited Louis, then lifted Lexie up and under the duvet. I climbed in and, once everyone was settled (dog included), clicked the bedside light off.

"Night night, Daddy."

"Night night, mate. I love you."

"Night night, Dadda."

"Night night Piggy. I love you."

"Night night, Momma. I love you," added Lexie.

"Night night, Momma. Please come back soon, I miss you," whispered Louis.

"Night night, Ann. I love you."

Twenty-One

Saying Goodbye...

Monday dawned quickly. Thankfully, I had managed to drop off to sleep, holding my children close each side of me. Cocooned for just a few hours of stillness. Beau slept across the threshold of the doorway, always keeping one eye on the closed master bedroom door.

The children woke and for a few moments their inner sadness and torment were forgotten. Then they came the realisation that their mommy wasn't there.

I managed to get them to eat some breakfast, with the compromise that it contained chocolate! So, chocolate toast and cereal were served up.

While the children ate, I took my mobile to the conservatory and, with a deep breath, pressed 'call'. After a couple of rings, "Good morning, Bromsgrove First School. Mrs Smith speaking."

"Hi. It's Rob Lawson, Lexie and Louis's father."

"Morning, Mr Lawson. How can I help you?"

"I'm ringing... I'm... I..." I coughed, mentally trying to pull myself together, just for this call. I knew if I could get through this call, I could get through all the calls that were to come. "I…we… It's Annie, my wife… Annie passed away on Saturday."

I heard the intake of breath. "Oh, Mr Lawson, I'm so terribly sorry. Please just hold the line."

As the line went silent, I watched the kids, Lexie pulling apart Louis's toast. She was looking after him. My girl is so caring.

"Mr Lawson?"

"Yes?"

"Mr Lawson, it's Mrs Lycett, I'm so sorry to hear the news of Annie's passing." The head teacher's words were heartfelt and sincere. "Please don't worry about school. We are here if you need anything, at all. If there is anything you need, please don't hesitate to ask."

"Thank you, that's so kind."

"How are Louis and Lexie?" she asked.

How are they? "Functioning" was the only word that I could think of that summed up all of us.

"They're ok. Eating breakfast. It's all incredibly new and raw at the moment. I'm not sure if Louis really understands what's happened."

"We have some resources in school, books about loss and bereavement, perhaps I can get them to you? They may help."

"That would be great, thank you."

"Ok. I'll bring them around later today if that's alright? If Louis or Lexie want to come into school at any time, even for an hour, that will be fine. We are all here for you all."

"Thank you, Mrs Lycett, you're so kind. I'm not sure what's going to happen. I'm just taking everything hour by hour."

"I understand. Please do keep in touch with school. I'll make sure the children's teachers are told what is happening. I'll see you this afternoon, Mr Lawson."

"Rob, please, and thank you."

After breakfast and another round of showers, I made sure we all got dressed. We needed some structure, or normality, right then. Staying in our pyjamas is reserved for Christmas Day. Plus, we needed to walk Beau, who had been amazing. Just as we were putting her lead on, the front door bell rang. It was my mum.

Seeing her smiling face as I opened the porch door just broke me. I clung to my mum as if I'd break. She just held me and told me over and over again that everything was going to be ok.

"My two favourite mess makers!" she said as she came into the house. I took a few moments to compose myself. I never tried to hide my grief from the children. I just knew that they needed me to be stronger than I felt capable of.

"Nanny!" They came running, as did Beau with her lead in her mouth.

"My beauties. Oh wow! Look at you, Lou. Don't you look smart?"

"Daddy let me choose my own clothes today!"

"Well, what a great choice, sir, you look really rather dashing!"

Lou has always loved receiving compliments. He'd chosen Spider Man trousers and his shirt and bow tie.

"How about you two take this bag through into the kitchen while I take my cardigan and shoes off?"

They willingly carried the bag for life through the house.

"I'm here as long as you need me to be. I guessed you'd need time to ring people, email? Just time to compose yourself? I've brought baking things, so me and the kids will make cakes and keep out of the way. Oh, and Zak will be here in a minute, he's going to take over walking Beau until you're ready to start walking her again."

Mum had swept in and done exactly what I needed, been organised.

"Thanks Mum."

"It's going to be ok, Rob. I'm not sure when, but it will be." She rubbed my arm as she followed the kids into the kitchen, just as there was a knock at the porch door. I turned and saw Zak smiling at me.

"Morning, mate." He pulled me into a big hug. "I've come for Beau."

I managed a smile, "I know, Mum's just arrived and told me. Thank you. It is a help."

"Is there anything else I can do?" he asked.

"I'm not sure, to be honest. I know there are calls I need to make, to the bank and others. I just need to find the energy and will to do it..." A thought hit me. "Her will! I need to call the solicitors! God! So many people!" I felt physically overwhelmed.

"One thing at a time, Lawson."

I stared open-mouthed at him. "Wh... What?"

"One thing at a time. Don't look at everything as a whole, just take one thing at a time," Zak repeated.

"That's exactly what Annie used to say to me!"

A smile spread across my best friend's face. "That's because we are both smarter than you! Beau!" he called and the dog came trotting out of the porch, lead still swinging from her mouth.

"See you later, knob!" he called as he walked back down the drive.

One thing at a time.

The first thing I needed to do was let her social media friends know, the news has spread throughout the Close, nearly everyone has knocked the door, or pushed a card of condolence through the door.

Closing the porch door, I turned back in to the hall, to find Louis standing there staring at me. "You alright, mate?" I asked.

"Just checking you're still here, Dadda," he said, as his bottom lip began to wobble.

Sweeping him up into my arms, I held him as the next wave of grief washed over my baby boy. He just needed to know that I hadn't left him as well.

"LOUIS!!!!! The spooon!" shouted Lexie, at which Louis started wriggling and wanted to be put down, and waddled off towards the spoon-licking malarky. Leaving me alone in the hall. I released that I needed to always make the children my priority, no matter what was happening. I walked into the office and fired up our family laptop.

Pulling open the folder that Richard Morgan had given me yesterday, I found the leaflet I needed.

The Lavender Trust.

The Lavender Trust works exclusively with children who lose a parent. Allowing them room to explore, express and understand their grief.

As I read the flyer properly, something was tickling the back of my mind; I was sure I'd seen something about this before. As I opened the flyer fully and saw the image of a lily lying on a rock close to a babbling stream, I knew where I'd seen it before. The search engine history on the computer. The day I was looking for property to rent. Annie had been looking at the Lavender Trust.

I reached for the house phone and called the number on the leaflet.

Talking to Benjamin at The Trust was…refreshing? Yes, refreshing. He was knowledgeable, empathetic, compassionate and considerate. He didn't rush me when I fumbled my words, he listened to my jumbled nonsense, and he was great.

Having organised support for the children, I hung up just as my mobile began to ring.

"Hello?"

"Rob? Good morning, it's Richard Morgan."

"Richard, hello. Is Annie ok?"

"Yes. I'm ringing to let you know that Annie's body has been released to our care, and she is now on her way back to our chapel of rest. She will be ready for viewing by early evening, or whenever you need to see her."

I felt like I'd been punched in my stomach. "Ohh… Ummm… ok, thank you, Richard."

"Rob, please remember what I said. You're welcome to come and see Annie, whenever you need to, ok?"

"Yes, yes, I will."

"Ok, now that Annie has been released to me, I've been able

to make contact with the crematorium. The first available date and time is Tuesday 17 May at 12pm, next Tuesday. Will that be ok?"

"So soon? Gosh, I hadn't even considered it happening so soon. Yes, I suppose it's fine. Yes, thank you."

"Ok, I'll get everything booked, and I will speak to The Boat Shack about the wake, that's where Annie wanted everyone to go after the ceremony, to enjoy drinks and a few snacks overlooking the lake."

"She loved it there," I confirmed.

"I confess I hadn't been, until I met Annie, and then I took my wife, and now we are regulars. It really is a beautiful spot. I'll be in touch, Rob," and the call ended.

I composed a group message text. Titling it "Annie", I attached the picture that I had taken of the three of them asleep in bed, just a few days ago and added May, Malc, my mum, Andy, Liv and Zak. Checking what I'd written down on the jotter while talking to Richard, I composed the message, giving them the date and time of the service.

Logging into Facebook, and waiting for my profile to load, I mentally thought about what I'd write.

I clicked on the 'new post' icon and up came the blank screen. I hit the button to tag a friend. Annie's name was top of the list, then Andy, Zak, Liv and my mum.

"DADDDDDDDDyyyyyyyyyyyyyyyy, do you want pink or blue icing?" Lexie managed to fill the whole house with her volume!

"You decide, sweetie, make it a surprise! But they've got to have lots of sprinkles, mind!" I shouted back.

It is with the heaviest of hearts that I confirm our beloved Annie passed away on Saturday after a short and bravely fought battle with cancer.

Malc, May, Andy, Lexie, Louis and I are absolutely broken, our worlds have become darker and the night sky a little brighter.

We invite you to attend a celebration of Annie's life on Tuesday 17th at 12pm at the crematorium, with drinks and food after at The Boat Shack, one of Annie's favourite places.

Donations in lieu of flowers to The Lavender Trust.

We would ask all those attending to wear a brightly coloured buttonhole.

Thank you for your support and the messages we've all received.

We are struggling to accept a world that won't be as colourful.

Rob, Lexie and Louis.

On Tuesday morning my mobile rang as it sat at the kitchen counter. It was May.

"Morning."

"Morning, Rob. How are you?"

"Tired. Not much sleep last night. The kids were in with me again, both tossing and turning."

"Oh, my darlings. My Annie is such a wonderful mother, she was always meant to be a mother."

"She sure was." Sadness filled my heart as I recognised the past tense within my answer.

"Rob, Malc and I are going to go and see her this morning." May's voice was devoid of emotion.

I didn't know how to answer. What could I say? So, I answered honestly.

"I'm not ready, May. I can't get the image of her in the bed out of my mind."

"We know, son. We feel we need to see her now. She's my baby,

Rob, and I need to hold her one last time. Andrew is going to go tomorrow."

The weight of the enormity of the situation swept over me again as I sank to the kitchen floor.

"Oh, May, how are we meant to go on? How am I meant to raise our children?" I began to cry.

"My darling. We will continue knowing how much light and love and ultimately colour Annie brought to all our lives. We are all better people because of Annie." She was so firm and certain in her response.

"How is Andy?" I enquired. "He rang me last night, but I'm just not able to talk to people yet."

"Broken, like all of us. He and Annie were so close growing up, almost best friends, for so long. He's staying with us for a few days. None of us can believe that she's gone. It's like, somehow, it's all wrong, a big mistake. The cancer, everything. And she'll come back to us with that big dazzling smile."

I smiled to myself. May was absolutely right. All of our lives were enriched because of Annie.

"Rob, when you're ready to see Annie, me or Malc are happy to come with you to see her, if you want us to?"

"Thank you May, that's really kind. I love you."

"We love you too. Do you need any shopping? I can do an online order and have it delivered to you, or to us and we'll bring it over?" May asked.

"I hadn't really given it much thought! I need to get the kids eating proper food again, can't keep having takeaways every day. I'll try to form some sort of list. It will probably just be perishables. The neighbours have been very kind, leaving large dishes of casseroles and lasagnes on the doorstep. Trouble is, there are never any notes, so I've no idea who they're from and whose dishes are whose!"

"Grief brings out the best of some folk, doesn't it?"

"It does. Also, I have been meaning to ask. I have no more room for the flowers we have received. Can you take some?"

"Yes, of course I can. How kind people have been. Our Annie really was loved, wasn't she?"

"What wasn't to love, May? She was so special," I said.

"We'll come and collect the flowers on our way home, if that's ok?"

Wednesday was not a good day. Lexie and Louis both struggled from the moment they woke. Lots of anger, lots of frustration, even resentment.

My mum came around mid-morning armed with muffins and apple juice, which seemed to calm the children for a while, but we returned to the anger as soon as Mum left. She said that she was going to the chapel of rest, and asked if I would I like her to go with me.

"Thanks Mum," I said. "May said something similar yesterday. I… I just don't think I'm ready yet. Is that bad?" I searched her face.

"Of course not, sweetheart. You must take this in your own time. Whenever you're ready, if you want me to, I'll be beside you, always," she whispered as she held me in an all-consuming hug.

May texted to say that Andy couldn't face going to the chapel of rest today; he was going to aim for tomorrow. Annie's death had rocked everyone.

Lexie asked to go into school on Thursday, but she was home again by lunchtime. It had all become too much for her.

We had become like hermits, living in a created bubble that wasn't real. I know that's what we were doing, but I felt that it was what we needed to do. The only external influences on our bubble were Zak's daily visits to walk Beau and a shopping delivery from May.

I couldn't sleep on Thursday night. It was becoming a regular occurrence, so I unlocked my mobile and sent a message to May, asking if she and Malc would sit with Lou and Lex tomorrow. I knew I needed to show my face at the office, even if only for an hour.

Of course, we will. Really looking forward to it. Andy went to see Annie today. It's definitely helped him a lot. He's going to head back to his flat tomorrow. We'll be there for 9am.

That meant they'd be here by 8.30am. Malc has a habit of being early – always.

The drive to work was quite cathartic. I'd completed it so many times, I knew every turn, every sweep of the road.

Walking into the office was great, with the buzz of multiple conversations, endless telephone calls, the hubbub of a busy business.

The sweep of silence crept across the office like a wave heading towards land, gathering pace, as faces turned and saw me standing there.

I knew exactly what they were all thinking: "What's he doing here? What do I say to him?"

It's a good question. What do you say to someone whose wife has just died? "I'm so sorry" seems quite insignificant, doesn't it? Is this how Sheila felt the first time she walked through these doors after David died?

Gosh, David's death felt like a lifetime ago, a whole other world of pain. Pain that I perceived as the worst I'd felt for a long time. How wrong was I!

Walking past the sales and admin teams, I acknowledged the greetings and head-nods as I headed towards the back of the office suite to my office, with Glenda sitting outside.

She looked up as she heard me approach, her face initially smiling; then confusion spread across it, quickly followed by sorrow, all in the space of about three seconds. Glenda stood up, came around her desk, embraced me and held on tight. A small sob escaped from her as I held on to my employee and, most importantly, friend.

"Oh Rob," she said as she pulled away from me, producing a tissue from her sleeve, "I'm so deeply sorry. I still can't believe it's true. Annie was so young. It doesn't seem fair somehow."

I didn't have any words to respond. I didn't have anything.

"Come on in." Glenda ushered me towards the double doors. "What are you doing here?" she asked as she flicked on the overhead lights.

"I... I... I needed to come. David felt I could man this ship. All I've actually done is abandon ship!" Just then, there was a knock at the door, and all of the Management Team appeared.

"We heard you were in Rob," said Louise Low, my Administration Manager, "I'm so sorry," followed by "I'm sorry" from everyone else.

After about an hour of sitting around the large oval conference table in my office, it became clear to me that the team was doing a banging job without me. I wasn't needed for now! It was agreed that I'd take more time, at least two weeks and, if I was needed during that time, Glenda would call me. After more hugs and tears I made my way out of the building and back to the car.

I rang May as I sat staring out at the fast-moving water of the river.

"Hello love, how are you getting on?" My mother-in-law's cheery voice always has a way of making me raise even half a smile.

"They don't need me! They're coping marvellously. I've agreed I'll have at least another two weeks off."

"Oh, that's grand, isn't it? Sounds like you've got great people working there."

"I really have." I could hear a lot of commotion in the background.

"Is that Daddy?" I heard Lexie ask.

"Yes, sweetheart. Do you want to talk to him?"

"No, I'm too busy. But can you ask him if we can have chip-shop chips for tea, and can you and Gag stay please?"

"Tell her 'yes', and of course you and Gag are welcome to stay," I answered.

"Sounds like a plan. Gag never turns down chippers, does he!" May chuckled.

It was now or never. I took a deep breath, "It's time May. I'm going to go and see her."

"Alright son. Do you want any company?"

"No, but thank you. I need to say goodbye alone."

"We'll be here waiting for you. We love you."

"Love you."

Ending the call, I scrolled through the phone book and called Richard Morgan.

"Hello Rob, nice to hear from you."

"Hi Richard. I'd… I'm…" I cleared my throat. "I'd like to come and see Annie, please?"

"Of course, Rob. I'll personally make sure that she's ready. When would you like to come down?"

"I'm in Worcester at the moment. Can I come straight to you?"

"Yes, of course. I'll be waiting. When you arrive, please come around to the grey building on the right. It's signposted as the Chapel of Rest. I'll be waiting. Drive safely."

What a funny thing for a funeral director to say! If I didn't drive safely, he'd have more work!

The drive back from Worcester normally takes about twenty minutes on a good day, but that Friday it seemed to take only five minutes. Before I knew it, I was pulling up in front of a tastefully decorated building with a sign that said 'Chapel of Rest'.

Annie was inside that building. A building I'd never seen before in my life, and my wife was in there.

A wave of guilt crashed over me for no reason other than to punish myself. I realised what an utter arsehole I'd been to Annie in the last few weeks of her life. I was a complete and utter selfish bastard. Annie was gone and I could never make up for that. That guilt is something that will stay with me for the rest of my days and, with all honesty, I deserve it.

The arched wooden door opened and Richard Morgan stood waiting for me. Taking a big deep breath, I got out and locked the car as I walked up the path to greet him. It's funny the things you remember, but I saw how much younger he looked compared to when I'd met him a few days earlier at home. Perceptions are warped by stressful situations.

"Hello, Rob." He smiled and shook my hand.

"Hi."

"Please come on in." He gestured to welcome me inside the building. "Can I offer you anything to drink?"

"Oh no, thank you."

"Please have a seat."

I walked into a mini waiting room of sorts, with three doors leading off it.

"Annie is through this door here." He gestured to the door on the right. "The Chapel of Rest allows you as much time as you need with Annie. There are chairs in there if you want to sit, or you can stand next to her. She is already been placed inside her coffin."

My breath caught in my throat.

"She looks very peaceful. There is the facility for you to light a candle within the room."

I just nodded.

"Whenever you're ready, Rob, go on inside. I'll be here when you are finished." He smiled at me. I know he was trying to reassure me, but no reassurance would have helped. I was about to walk into an unknown room and face my dead wife.

I stood up, rubbing my hands up and down the fronts of my thighs as I did so, trying to dry the clamminess. "Thank you."

I walked towards the door on the right and pushed down the handle.

Twenty-Two

My Ann…

My lasting memory of the room within the Chapel of Rest was the 'tinkly tankly' music, as Annie would have called it. She always loved that kind of meditation/Zen stuff. It just sounded like a load of bells being struck to me!

I've no idea what the room itself was like; I seemed to focus in on the coffin on a plinth in the middle.

I can tell you every detail of that coffin. It was stone-coloured, smooth to touch, rope handles, cotton-lined with a little pillow. The lid, propped up in the corner, had a small brass plaque detailing Annie's name and her two dates.

As I approached the coffin, I tried to control my breathing – very unsuccessfully. The first thing I saw were Annie's hands folded across her stomach. That's where I lost my control.

I'm not ashamed to admit that I became a total wreck in that room. Every single emotion was raw, painful, and real.

There she was. My Ann.

Just as Richard had said, she really did look peaceful. She

looked asleep, but not quite asleep. But there was no pain within her features. She looked – calm.

Clearly, the funeral people had tried to give her cheeks a bit of colour, but I could see how pale she was. I reached inside the coffin and placed my hand on top of hers. She was so cold, and her fingers stiff.

It was then that I noticed the bandages underneath her top. Richard told me later that this was where the autopsy had been performed. After he told me, I had a fleeting thought that it was ridiculous to bandage up a dead person! I didn't pull her top down to have a better look, I didn't want to see. She was my perfect, precious, charismatic, kind, caring, remarkable wife.

I stood there for a long time. I just stood and held her hand as tears fell freely. At times, I could barely breathe. At times, I sounded primeval. At times, I was silent. At times, I couldn't shut up.

Question after question I asked of Annie:

"How could you not tell me?"

"I'm so sorry for what I did."

"Why didn't you tell me?"

"How am I meant to do this without you?"

"Where do you keep Lexie's spare PE kit?"

"I wish I could turn the clock back. I never wanted to hurt you. I never wanted to divorce you."

"Are you in pain now? Please tell me you aren't hurting."

"Are you ok?"

"What do I tell the kids when it's 1am and they just want you?"

And on and on I went.

So many unanswered questions.

I felt raw, drained, lost and completely broken.

I reminisced:

"Do you remember our first holiday? That disastrous camping trip to Lyme Regis? You loved every minute, I was Mr Miserable!"

I touched her hair…

"Oh, Saturday takeaway night when we lived in our first place? We loved those curries even if it was only one curry to share some weeks! Money was tight at times, wasn't it?"

"Oh, Lexie being born and you laughing so much you cried, as I attempted to deal with the first dirty nappy – that was not pleasant!"

I stroked her cheek…

"Me attempting to build the kids a treehouse, only to end up in A & E with another DIY-related injury."

"Your culinary successes, no matter what the dish, and my utter failure, no matter what the dish."

"Losing each other at the music festival, but finding each other at the hot dog stand!"

Gently touching each of her fingernails…

"Staying up late to watch the meteor showers and lying under the blankets to keep warm."

"Getting up at stupid o'clock to have a day trip to the seaside, only for the bloody seagull to nick my chips! Rude!"

"Relaxing in that massive bathtub at the B&B with candles and tinkly tankly music."

Back to her cheek…

"Downing a cold beer together."

"Dancing in the kitchen at 1am to classical music."

"You waking me up at stupid o'clock again, when it had snowed, and forcing me to get dressed so we could go out exploring in the snow!"

"Your laugh. Oh, your laugh that was guaranteed to make everyone around you laugh."

"Your smile. A smile that could light up even the darkest of rooms. That smile that you've passed on to Lexie."

Gently moving across her dry cold lips…

"Our wedding day. I don't think I've ever told you, when I turned round and saw you walking towards me on Malc's arm, you took my breath away. I had to force my body to breathe again. I had never seen anyone as beautiful as you looked that day. I felt like the luckiest man alive. I was marrying my best friend and the most beautiful woman in the world."

"The night we brought Lexie home, I hardly slept. I sat up in bed and watched both of you sleep. You looked so alike even then.

You both were so peaceful. My heart felt like it was going to burst, I was so happy."

Why did I forget it all?

Holding her hand tight again…

In that room with Annie, I realised what an utter cock-up I'd made of the past few months, and how everything I'd ever want or need was right in front of me, and I had been too selfish to see it.

"I messed up, Ann. I thought the grass was greener. Turns out, I was just forgetting to water the grass our side! I need more time. I want more time. I have to make it right. I have to tell you just how much I love you. I adore you. You are my best friend. I need to know if you can forgive me. I will never stop trying to make amends for what I did to you. I'm so sorry I let you down my love. I'm so sorry." I sobbed into her chest.

Time passed. The world carried on turning outside that room. But inside it was just me and Annie. Just like all those years ago when we sat on the side of the riverbank as youngsters. We had gone full circle.

I knew the seconds were ticking away, and that I needed to say my final goodbyes to the only woman I've truly loved.

I made sure to tell my Annie everything I should have said while she was alive. I made sure to tell her how cherished she is and always will be.

"Goodbye, my angel. Watch over us. Give me a pointer or two if I go spectacularly wrong with the kids! I'll make sure that they know how fiercely you loved them, and that they talk about you every single day. You, my darling, brought love, life, magic and colour to our lives and for that I will always be thankful. I promise that our children will be raised in your likeness, to colour our world and sprinkle it with magic. Sleep well Ann, I love you."

Planting a final kiss on her forehead, I whispered "Thank you," and turned and left the room and my wife for the last time.

Twenty-Three

North Devon...

Coming home after visiting the Chapel of Rest, I held my children more tightly than I normally would. I whispered in each of their ears that I loved them. I needed them to hear it, just as much as I needed to say it.

Malc held me as I sobbed on his shoulder in the kitchen, or was I holding on to him as he sobbed on my shoulder?

As promised, they stayed with us that evening and we had chippers, with extra nuggets for Louis, because, apparently, four just isn't enough anymore! We were about to say goodbye when my mobile rang in my trouser pocket. Pulling it out, I saw it was Sheila Morris.

"Can I just get this before you go?" I asked May and Malc, who nodded.

"Hello, Sheila," I answered, as I walked into the living room.

"Oh, Rob. I'm so sorry I haven't rung sooner. I just don't know what to say." She sounded breathless.

"That's ok. Thank you for calling now. It's nice to hear from you. How are you?"

"Me? Oh, I'm fine thank you. Just taking everything a day at a time."

"Sounds like us, I can't seem to see beyond today."

"I know exactly what you mean. Everything is so raw, and very bright and loud," she said.

Bizarrely, I knew exactly what she meant. "Yes, it is. I went into the office today. Everything is fine. We seem to be busier than ever."

"You shouldn't be anywhere near that blasted building! You need to focus on those two beautiful children of yours."

"I'm trying to, Sheila, I'm trying to."

"Good. Now that's one of the reasons I'm ringing. I'm actually at our house in North Devon, and wondered if you and the children would like a few days by the sea? A bit of a change? You're welcome to stay for as long as you need."

I was gobsmacked by her gesture and responded on instinct, "Yes. Thank you, Sheila. That would be wonderful, though we'd have to come back before Monday. It's…it's Tuesday…" I fumbled for my words.

"I know, Rob, and I'm planning on being there," Sheila tried to reassure me, "Well, all the rooms are made up, so come whenever you're ready."

"Can we come tonight? I mean we'd arrive quite late."

"I'm a night owl, Rob, don't tend to turn in much before 1am."

"Ok, thank you."

"I'll send the address to your mobile. Drive safely, and see you soon."

I stood staring out the window down the drive towards the end of our road. Was a little break what we needed? A step away from the house? A move away from the madness that had descended upon us over the past six days?

Yes.

As I walked back into the hallway, many big hugs were being exchanged.

"That was Sheila Morris," I explained to May and Malc, as they disentangled themselves from Lex and Lou. "She's invited me and the kids down to her house in North Devon for a few days. I've said yes. Perhaps a short time away from the house will be just what we all need?"

"Oh, that sounds great, Rob," said May as she came up and hugged me.

"We'll pack the car up and drive down tonight. They can snooze in the back."

"Shall I come and help you pack some bags for them?" enquired May.

Looking straight into her face, I saw Annie. Why had I never seen how much alike they were? "Would you?"

"Of course, you silly horse. Come on you two, let's go pack your bags, you're off to the seaside!"

"YAY!!!!!"

"WOW!"

Thundering steps filled the hallway as the trio headed upstairs.

"Throw me your car keys, son, and I'll check all the levels in the car. Is the screen wash in the garage?" asked Malc.

"Umm yes. Thank you." Tossing him the key, I walked back into the kitchen and grabbed Beau's travel bag from the utility room. Annie, as I've said, was super organised. Even the bloody dog was organised, with a big bag for life containing travel bowls, extra toys and leads. All I had to do was add her food.

I locked the kitchen windows, ensured the side gate was locked, and closed down the conservatory. Locking the living room windows, I noticed that the bunch of flowers Annie had in her favourite vase in the living room window had died. I don't know why this opened the floodgates again, but it did! Perhaps the realisation that Annie had arranged the display? Perhaps a metaphor of what was occurring in our lives at that moment? God, the gut-wrenching pain was so consuming at times.

Sitting here now, analysing those first few days without Annie, I recognise that the pain was grief, yes, but it was mixed with guilt. Perhaps it wouldn't have been so soul-destroying if I hadn't messed up? I'll never know, and that is why I will always ensure that I am accountable for my behaviour, and how I treated Annie. I will never ever allow myself to be swept, drawn or even encouraged into that position again.

May and Malc kissed the kids' heads as we ensured they were both tucked under some thin blankets. Waving them off at 7.30pm, we followed them out of our road. The sat-nav said we should reach our destination by 10pm. I would have time to sit and talk to Sheila while the kids slept.

The journey down was hassle-free. No traffic to speak of, although I'd forgotten quite how far from the motorway Watermouth was! Thankfully, both the children fell asleep as soon as we hit the motorway. We pulled onto Sheila's drive at 9.58pm, good going.

Sheila came out to greet us, and helped me carry Louis and Lexie into the house and straight into their beds. Lex stirred and was pleased to see Sheila. After a quick toilet stop, I tucked her into bed and turned to leave.

"Daddy, how will Mommy know where we are? We have always been at home since she went to sleep." Worry resonating throughout every word.

This ripped my heart even further in two. "Oh sweetie, Momma knows where you are all the time. She's always with you, no matter what you do or where you are." I came and sat next to my beautiful daughter on the bed. "Your momma is watching you right now, we just can't see her. She's going to walk beside you throughout everything you do in your life, she's not going to miss a single moment. She's your momma and you're her girl."

"I do love her, Daddy. I just don't understand why she had to go away. Did I do something wrong?" I could see the tears beginning to form in her eyes.

"Oh God, baby, of course not! Mommy was poorly. Her body was poorly. Unfortunately, sometimes people become so poorly that the doctors aren't able to make them better. The doctors weren't able to take away Momma's poorly, and it made her very sick. You must remember, always, that if she had a choice, Momma would never have left you or Lou. She fought so very hard to stay, but her body was tired, and she needed to sleep."

"Is she hurting now, Daddy?" It was such an informed question from someone so small.

"No sweetie. She's not hurting anymore. Her body is just sleeping and resting now. But the bit that was Momma, her soul, that bit is always with you. So, in the night when you wake up and you get worried because Momma's not there, you just need to remember that she's always going to be there, she will always sit on the end of your bed every single night and watch over you and Lou while you sleep."

I could see her thinking about what I'd said. I hoped it was enough for her. In time, I know, as she grows, she'll want to know more, but for now, I just hoped it was enough.

"I think I like that, Daddy. Momma used to come and sit on the end of my bed when I had a bad dream. She always said she'd sit at the end of the bed to make sure the bad dream can't come back!"

"Did they ever come back?"

"Never. I just went to sleep listening to her humming. Will she hum now?"

"Maybe sweetie, if you listen hard enough. But you never need to worry that she doesn't know where you are. She'll always know, ok?"

Nodding her head, she scootched down under the duvet and closed her tired eyes.

"Night night, my darling girl. I love you." But it fell on deaf ears; she was already asleep. Beau jumped up and curled herself into a comfy spot on the end of Lexie's bed. Such a good dog, always protecting all of us, in her own way.

When I walked back downstairs, Sheila had a glass of white wine for me on the coffee table, and a plate of sandwiches in case I was hungry.

"You made good time," she said.

"Roads were clear all the way. Probably the first time I've ever gone all the way through without traffic, or roadworks!" I picked up a ham sandwich gladly, realising I was indeed hungry.

Taking a swig from a mug of something hot, Sheila sat across the lounge from me and pulled her feet up underneath herself. "I've a message to pass on to you, from your friend Zak."

I stopped mid-chew. How on earth did Sheila know Zak?

"He'll be here soon, but you're not to think he's here to interfere, just to be here as backup if you need him, or to have the children, or to just remind you to fill up with petrol before you set off home again!"

I swallowed the now mooshed sandwich. "Zak's coming here?"

Sheila nodded in clarification.

"But... How...? Why...? What?"

Laughing at my confusion, Sheila set down her coffee and reached for a tube of hand cream on the table next to her chair. "Your mum phoned me, not long after we'd talked. I know Janey from bridge club. She said she'd spoken to Annie's parents and she knew that you'd be with me for a few days. She is concerned for you, Rob, we all are. Losing Annie is a lot to deal with, let alone having to lose her through your children's eyes as well. So, she asked if I'd mind if she sent your best friend down after you." Putting her rings back on her fingers after smothering them in cream, she picked up her coffee back and took another sip. "Zak called a little while later. Such a nice chap. Anyway, long story short, he was going to book himself into a B&B and I wouldn't have it, so he's going to stay in the barn, the converted annexe. If you want him, he'll be there; if you don't, he'll be on the beach!"

I fell back against the soft sofa cushions, staring at Sheila in disbelief. realising I was surrounded by love, support and encouragement. No one would let me fall, so many hands were waiting to catch me if needed.

"Thank you, Sheila."

"Think nothing of it. I enjoy having guests, keeps me busy and, most importantly, occupied! It's why Dave and I bought this rambling place, to allow us to have friends down, to enjoy their company in such a beautiful part of the world." She smiled.

"It really is a beautiful part of the world. Annie and I stayed here for our honeymoon." I remembered it so fondly. We laughed so much during that week, so young, so carefree.

"Dave mentioned that. What a small world, hey! If you don't think me too rude a host, I'm going to go and have a shower," she said standing up, taking her mug with her. "There's a lovely spot just out front, a swing seat overlooking the harbour. You can see all the lights reflecting off the water. Good thinking spot, I find!" she said, tapping her nose as she walked out of the room.

Left alone, I picked up another couple of sandwiches and the glass of wine and headed out the front door, leaving it open so that I would hear the kids if they woke, though I doubted they would. Just as Sheila described, the swing seat was a perfect spot. Sitting there, all I could hear was the gentle creak of the chains as they moved me back and forth.

I sat transfixed by the rippling lights on the water, and the soundtrack of the squeak. I allowed thoughts to float across my mind – Annie, the house, Bex, the children, the future, the business, how would I cope, and so much more, but I never allowed any of those thoughts to take hold and fester; they just floated in and out again.

I was jolted from this reverie by headlights climbing the drive. Zak had arrived. He got out of his car and reached in the boot for his bag. He hadn't seen me sitting in the dark.

"You're an absolute arse for following me, but thank you for coming. Thank you for everything."

I heard him jump, I didn't see it!

"Shit a brick, Lawson! Christ, man, you nearly gave me a fucking heart attack!"

I burst out laughing! Laughing at the ridiculousness of everything!

"You're welcome, knob, I mean, Rob!" Zak went on. "I'm here if you want me, ok? I won't get in your way. I'll just do my own thing, but we just want you to know that you don't have to do anything on your own."

Standing up from the swing seat, I went over to my oldest and best friend and embraced him. I didn't cry, which afterwards surprised me. I just wanted him to know how grateful I was.

*

The kids were awake by sunrise, around 5.30am, which wasn't good given that I'd only dropped off about 1.30am. I'm sure it's not normal to have that much energy that early in the morning!

Louis was all for going to the beach immediately, and I had to explain quite a few times that the beach wasn't awake yet, and we couldn't go until after he'd eaten breakfast. Once this message was successfully received, he jumped off the bed and ran out of the bedroom, then quickly returned scratching his head.

"I don't know the way to the food room!" he said. Lexie and I couldn't help but laugh. He really is adorable.

After pulling my tired body out from under the covers, I put on the previous day's clothes and ushered the kids downstairs, with both of them talking about the importance of having strawberry jam for toast, rather than "the orange strawberry jam".

As we reached the kitchen at the back of the house, Sheila was already up and preparing what appeared to be a feast. The kitchen island looked like a continental breakfast! There were pancakes, croissants, fruit platters, massive jugs of juice and stacks of crispy toast.

"Morning you guys. Hi Lexie, hi Louis. Who's hungry?"

"MEEEEEEEEEEEEEE!" answered Louis as he scrambled up one of the chairs and grabbed a fork. "Do you have strawberry jam, Mrs Morris?"

"Of course, my darling, only the best for Mr Lawson." Sheila smiled and pushed a big pot of strawberry jam in front of Louis followed by the pile of crispy toast. "Would you like a drink, Lexie?"

"Could I have milk please, Mrs Morris? Mommy always gives us a glass with a curly straw." Lexie's face started to crumple.

Quick to spot this, Sheila replied, "Well I haven't got any curly straws darling, but I know…" she began looking through the cupboards, "that Dave had them somewhere…" moving this and that aside, "Ah HA! Here we go, how about straws that turn the milk chocolate or strawberry?" She turned round with a packet in each hand.

"OH WOW! Really?" Lexie's eyes sparkled with excitement.

"Well, you've sold me on the chocolate one, Mrs M!" came a voice from the back door.

"UNCLE ZAK! Uncle ZAK!!!!" Lou jumped down from his chair and waddled over to Zak, jammy toast in hand.

"Aggghhhhhhhh Uncle Zak!" Lexie ran over as well, and he scooped both of them up and swung them around.

"You guys didn't think you'd go to the seaside without me, did you? I mean I don't want to brag, but I make an awesome sandcastle!" he joked, kissing each of their heads.

"Morning Zak. What would you like for breakfast? I can do a full fry-up, or I have pastries in the warming oven. You too, Rob?"

"Never one to turn down bacon, Mrs M!" Zak laughed.

"I'll just stick to the fruit and pancakes, thanks Sheila." I picked at the bunch of grapes in front of me. In truth, I didn't have much of an appetite.

After four rounds of toast, ten rounds of pancakes, six rashers of bacon and four cups of strawberry and chocolate milk each, I ushered the kids upstairs and into shower and bath, respectively.

With fresh faces and clean clothes, they looked like someone actually owned them!

"We've been talking with Uncle Zak and we're going to go and spend the day on the beach and have a sandcastle-building competition. You can come if you want but, to be honest, I'm nearly a grown-up now so you don't have to come! Besides, like you said, Momma is always with us." Lexie's frankness took me somewhat by surprise.

"Oh… Ummm, ok. But don't you think I should come with you?" Both of the kids had barely left my side over the past six days.

"Nah! Anyway, being with Uncle Zak is basically being with you! You two are so similar. Well, except he lets us have extra sprinkles on our ice cream. I think Daddy what you need to do is have some time to rest. You miss Mommy too, I see it, so you need some time alone with her. Uncle Zak will look after us." She came and put her arms round my neck and sat down on my lap.

I stared into her big eyes, eyes just like Annie's. "When did you become so grown up, Missy Moo?" I asked.

"A while ago, I think? Being grown up is ok, but it doesn't mean I don't want to be tucked in at night, mind!"

"Oh no, of course it doesn't, sweetie," I chuckled. "You do know how much I love you and Louis, don't you? I know the next few days are going to be hard for all of us, but we'll get through it all together, ok?"

"Yep. My heart feels sad, Dadda, but I do believe that Momma was sitting on my bed last night, and that my made my heart feel... not so sad? She's here, but it's like I've got my eyes closed so I can't actually see her."

"Oh sweetie, I'm so sorry. I wish I could take away your sads. I wish I could take away all of our sads. I want Momma to be here with us more than anything. That's why every day we must remember her, talk about her, laugh with her and love her." I held my daughter close.

"We will, Dad, don't worry." She jumped down and ran downstairs to find Zak, leaving me alone in the bedroom, surrounded by damp towels and messy beds.

"Leave it all, Rob, go off and explore. Go off and find some space." Sheila stood leaning against the doorframe. "There's a bag of sandwiches and a flask waiting for you in the kitchen. The children will be fine. Now off you go!" She ushered me downstairs. I grabbed Beau's lead and off we went.

Beau and I must have walked miles, along the winding coast path. I've always had an affinity for the North Devon coastline – it's so rugged and battered – rather than the gentle flowing coastline of the South. We stopped somewhere along the path heading towards Ilfracombe and ate the sandwiches Sheila had made. Beau especially liked the ham!

On the way back, we came down off the coast path and walked via the harbour. It was always so pretty, so tranquil, so quaint. We walked past the harbourmaster's office and headed round the curve towards the bench where Annie and I had sat on during our honeymoon. The bench that she had specifically spoken about with Richard Morgan regarding her ashes.

As I approached the bench, I saw that an old boat had been converted into a cafe/tea room. It was quite frankly astounding. Its new blue paint job shimmered in the sun and there were lights strung all around it and tables dotted here and there with unbeatable views out across the harbour. It was…paradise.

Climbing the steps, I tied Beau's lead up and went inside the converted boat. To the left (the stern) it had been turned into a working kitchen, and directly in front of me was a lovely counter top covered in scrummy homemade cakes. To the right, stepping down into the bowels of the bow, were four tables and a small wood-burning stove. Its charm was immense; it took my breath away. The warmth just enveloped me!

"Morning. What can I get you?" A smiling lady emerged from the kitchen, rubbing her hands in her apron.

"Ummm…" Studying the array of drinks written on the board above her head. "Can I have a large tea to take out please?" I'm so boring!

"Of course." She turned to the massive and impressive coffee machine, with pipes and gizmos galore. "Can I get you anything else?"

"Can I have a piece of toast, and a slice of carrot cake, again to take out please?" I pulled my wallet out of my pocket to pay.

"No worries. Just be a few minutes for the toast. Are you here on holiday?" she asked as she pulled the cake from under the cloche.

"Oh…ugghhh…No, just until tomorrow, probably. We're staying with a friend, just over the road actually, in the big white house."

"Sheila? Oh, you must be Rob? I'm Jennie. Welcome to The Teacup."

"Wow, umm…thank you. Nice to meet you. What a beautiful spot you've got here. A slice of paradise." I took the cup and began to pour sugar in and stir the tea bag.

"It really is, isn't it? I shall miss it terribly. Do you want any jam or marmalade with your toast?"

"No thanks, it's for the dog." I gestured with my head at the ever-patient Beau sitting outside. "You're going to miss it?" I asked.

The toast popped, and Jennie slid the bread into a takeout bag and handed it over the counter. "Yes, The Teacup is up for sale. Me and my hubby are retiring. We've loved our time here. It's been the most marvellous way to end our working life. Looking out over that view every day is a blessing. It's magical."

"Yes," I turned and stared out over the view as well, "It really is." Turning back to the counter, "How much do I owe you?"

"Oh, it's already been paid for." She smiled and grabbed her cleaning cloth and began cleaning the surfaces.

"Sorry?"

"There's nothing to pay, Rob. It's already been settled." She reached behind the till and produced an envelope. "This is for you."

She handed it over to me. The word 'Rob' was written in familiar handwriting, "Ann," I whispered.

"Why don't you and your lovely dog go and have a seat outside and I'll bring these out for you?"

I just nodded, collected Beau and sat at the table closest to the harbour wall and the water. Jennie came out and put my order on the table in front of me.

A letter from Annie? What? How was this even possible?

"Umm, sorry Jennie. Umm… How? Sorry? I… How?"

"Why don't you open the letter and find out?" She smiled and walked back inside the boat.

Holding tightly to Annie's letter, I dug deep for – courage? strength? willpower? – to open it.

I tore across the seal.

8 May

Hello Lawson

216

Surprise!

Fingers crossed it's all gone to plan, I've got you a nice cup of tea and a cake! Carrot I reckon if they've got any!!

So, I suppose you're so confused and I bet your mouth is hanging open.

Well, here's the truth. I knew you'd find yourself back here one day. We loved it so much, didn't we? Sitting and looking out over the harbour, watching the sunset. We made our plans sitting there. We achieved those plans, didn't we?

We made our magic happen.

In this place, we planned, devised and concocted, didn't we!

Well, I had the most fun doing all of it, every single ridiculous thing.

So, I'm going to leave you with one final condition…

Sit here Lawson and plan, concoct and devise some new magic…

Remember, I love you all ways and always.

Your Annie

xx

Tears were trickling down my cheeks as Jennie reappeared, bringing me another hot cup of tea in a proper cup. She put it in front of me. "Look at that, Rob, it's just magic, isn't it?"

She gestured towards the harbour entrance that was framing a returning fishing boat, the seagulls following closely; a typical Devon scene.

"Yeah, magic…"

Twenty-Four

The Final Journey...

We returned from North Devon on Sunday, after Zak had filled the kids with buckets-full of sweets and oodles of sticks of rock. We followed each other until we hit the M5, then he hit the gas and was gone.

There was a time when I'd have felt jealous that he had the freedom to have a sports car while I had to trundle along in a fully loaded estate car. But not anymore. Everything I was ever going to need was inside the car, everything that was precious to me. We wound our way back up the country and got home in time for tea, which was one of those kindly delivered lasagnes, frozen garlic bread and some "leaves", as Louis christened the salad!

When the kids had gone to sleep, both asking to be in their own rooms for the first time since last Sunday, I checked my personal emails while lying on the spare bed. An email from Richard had arrived while we were away.

To: rlawson1978@imail.com

From: richard.morgan@thompson-morgan.co.uk
Date: 14 May 10.17am
Re: Annie Lawson

Good morning, Rob

This just a confirmation email clarifying all details for Tuesday. Thank you for confirming your desire to not have a family car.

The hearse will leave Thompson and Morgan premises at 11.12am on Tuesday 17 May, arriving at Chestnut Grove at 11.20am.

The convoy will then travel to the crematorium for arrival at 11.50am.

The congregation will move into the crematorium for the service to begin at 12pm.

The service is due to end at 12.45pm when the congregation will convene in the atrium.

As requested by Annie, only family flowers will be presented. I have your chosen suggestion from Lexie and Louis, they will look beautiful. I will send you a photo once I receive them on Monday afternoon.

Donations will be received in lieu of flowers for The Lavender Trust.

The order of service has been prepared and a PDF copy is attached for your approval. This will only take a few hours to print, but please let me know asap if anything needs altering. Annie compiled most of the information herself.

As agreed, The Boat has confirmed the booking of the wake. Annie asked that there be a good selection of food available, in terms of dietary requirements, as some of your family members have intolerances. The food will be simple – cakes, crisps and some savoury nibbles. Teas, coffees, hot chocolate and soft drinks. Use of the café space and the bus have been made available. The bill has already been settled, so there will be nothing to pay on the day.

The family flowers, as requested, will be divided and presented to a few local care homes, so that the residents may enjoy them.

After the service, Annie's coffin will remain within the ceremony room and staff will take over responsibility. Once the cremation has taken place, I will personally return and collect Annie's ashes, and let you know when she has returned here to us.

I hope this all meets with your approval. If at any time you need any more information or clarification, please don't hesitate to contact me.

With kind regards
Richard

Richard Morgan
Owner
Thompson and Morgan Funeral Directors
Email: richard.morgan@thompson-morgan.co.uk
Tel: 01527 789789

Attachment: A. Lawson OOS 17.05 V2

Everything was, as always, very straightforward from Richard. Almost clinical, and it helped! I read through everything he'd sent me, and responded that it all seemed fine, and thanked him (again) for all his help.

I'd brought Saturday's post upstairs with me. There was a lot of it! Forms for life insurance documents, forms from the DVLA, forms from the bank, forms from the dentist, and many, many sympathy cards. We'd even found a still-warm casserole sitting on the doorstep when we got home. I had no idea who it was from or what it was!

There was also a cheque for £10,000 from David Morris's estate. I'd clean forgotten about his additional bequest. I wasn't sure the money would go to his final wishes of a holiday or an attic conversion.

Word had spread that Annie was no longer with us, and it was becoming clearer by the day just how loved she was.

Monday was a solemn day. I mentally cleared the afternoon to ensure that the kids had their clothes ready, washed and ironed ready for the next day. I wanted them to have as much time as they needed. We took Beau for a walk around the block and both kids were quiet, so, when we got home, I sat them both down.

"So, what's up?"

Neither one would look at me. "Nothing…" they said in unison.

"I thought we'd agreed that it was us three against the world? If you don't tell me, I can't help."

"Well…" began Lexie, "We're worried about tomorrow."

"Ok, well, that's completely normal. Neither of you has attended a funeral before."

"Oh no, it's not that. We're worried about you."

"Me? What do you mean?"

"Well…" said Louis, "Mommy normally gets us ready for big events, and we're not sure that you even know how to get us ready? What if you get it wrong, and put Lexie's dress on me!"

"And Louis's hair goop on me!" pipped in Lex.

Oh, my heart. "Oh, come here you pair." I pulled them both onto my lap. "Now you listen. I know, and you know, that you ARE definitely going to have to help your old dad out. There's stuff that goes on in this house that I know nothing about. But now it's going to be my job to know – with your help. I will never EVER be as good as your momma, so I'm not even going to try. What I will be, and I promise you this, is the best Dadda I can be. And if I promise not to dress you up in a pink frock, Lou, and not put hair gloop on yer barnet, Lex, will you help me?"

Muffled replies as I was 'GOT' in a full-on bear hug. I'm sure there was agreement, but both were face first in my clothes.

Dinner was a sombre affair. As a bit of a treat, we ate in the lounge watching the kids' TV channel. None of us cleared our plates. The weight of the next day was bearing down on each of us.

Tuesday dawned and sunshine filled every room of our home. Rainbows danced as the light refracted through the hanging crystals that Annie had insisted hung from every window. As agreed, my mum, May and Malc arrived at 9.30am and, with the two nannies taking over getting the kids dressed, I focused on getting myself ready. It wasn't an easy task when I couldn't stop my hands from shaking. Malc appeared at the bathroom door to ask if I wanted tea.

"Here son, let me." He stood in front of me and tied my tie, just like my dad had done when I was eight years old. God, I missed my dad.

"You're doing good, son. Me and May are so proud of you." He smiled at me. "There you go, how's that?"

I turned and stared back in the mirror. "Perfect, thank you."

"Rob." It was my mum calling from downstairs. "Annie's here, love."

I hadn't realised it was that late. I thought I'd have plenty of time to prepare myself for when Annie came home for the last time.

The kids were waiting for me in the hall, and both held on tight to me as we all walked outside together. I was very aware that this was the first time they would have seen their mom since she left us, and the first time seeing her coffin – or any coffin come to that. But they were both troopers, so brave and grown up. I was and am so proud of them.

Getting the kids in the car was pain-free. Malc locked up the house, leaving Beau inside. She'd join us at The Boat Shack courtesy of Zak dashing back to collect her. We pulled out of our road for our final journey as a family of four.

Following behind the hearse was a strange experience. Strangers on the side of the road stopped and dipped their heads. Traffic slowed down. So much respect for the dead. Louis spent the whole journey switching between talking about how beautiful the flowers looked on the top of the coffin and waving at Momma.

Lexie hardly said a word. Thankfully, my mum had offered to sit in our car for the journey to the service, so she squeezed herself in between the two car seats and held onto each of the kids' hands and didn't let go.

I struggled to keep my eyes on the road throughout the journey; they kept moving towards the coffin. The coffin that contained our Ann.

We pulled into the crematorium at 11.49am. The hearse slowed to a stop, as did the line of cars behind us. Richard Morgan climbed out of the front of the vehicle and began to walk in front of Annie's car. We wound our way up the hill, moving at about 1mph. As we crested the hill and curved round to the left, we were all absolutely gobsmacked by the scene.

"Daddy! Look!" said Lexie, staring out of her window. "Look at all those people!"

"Good God!" I whispered. There were people everywhere. Richard told me afterwards that they took the names of 478 people in attendance.

"What they doing here, Dadda?" asked Lou.

"They've all come to say goodbye to Momma, dude. Momma was so loved." I smiled as we pulled to a stop outside the double doors leading into the crematorium.

Getting out of the cars, everyone was smiling at us, a few giving a little wave but, overall, the air was filled with sadness. Tears were already flowing for so many people. You could hear a pin drop, only fractured by the occasional nose being blown.

May, Malc, Andy and my mum came and joined us as we formed a small line and waited behind the hearse. Mum and May had agreed to walk with the kids. Richard came up to me and touched my arm. I was fixated on Annie's coffin.

Andy, Malc, Zak and I stepped forward, releasing Lexie and Louis's tiny hands. May and my mum made sure they were taken again quickly.

We each stood at one corner of the coffin. Following Richard's instructions, we took the weight of the coffin, and together turned and lifted Annie up onto our shoulders.

I could hear Lexie crying behind me, but I couldn't do anything about it. Right then and there, I had to be Annie's husband; she needed me one last time.

Slowly, we walked in unison through the double doors and into the ceremonial room, with its floor-to-ceiling window overlooking the sweeping fields down towards the old abbey.

The sounds of *Somewhere Over the Rainbow* accompanied our footsteps, Richard guiding us every step of the way. We reached the front of the room and the plinth. Waiting until we were told to, we stood and I stroked Annie's coffin, and whispered, "I love you." Turning and lowering the coffin at the same time, we sidestepped and slid Annie onto the plinth.

When I turned around to take my seat in the front row, between Louis and Lexie, I was rocked to my core to see just how many faces were staring at me. All the seats were full, people were standing down both sides of the room, and I was later told that people had to stand in the atrium and outside the building, so the speaker system was turned on. I didn't even know some of those faces; how many lives had Annie touched without me even knowing? All had come to say goodbye to our earth-bound angel.

Andy stood up and delivered the eulogy which, if I'm honest, I'd had minimum input into; I just hadn't had the brain capacity in the past few days. Zak read Annie's favourite poem – *Desiderata* – and Malc read *The Dash*, the only change to Anne's request of there being only one reading. The highlight of the service was the final song, not a hymn, but *Walking on Sunshine*. The entire congregation sang along to it! I've been told since that never had the crematorium or funeral directors staff attended a service where the congregation started singing. It was perfect. Annie had planned yet another perfect event.

We laughed, we cried, we smiled, we said our goodbyes.

As each of us rose to leave, we placed our coloured buttonhole around the base of Annie's coffin, effectively turning the plinth into a bed of flowers on which she sat.

I don't really remember much about our time greeting people in the atrium after the service. Richard stayed until the last guest left. He had a fistful of envelopes; donations were abundant.

May and Malc drove with Louis and Lexie to The Boat Shack, leaving me to journey there alone. However, I didn't leave straight away. I asked Richard if it would be possible to go back inside the service room, just for a moment, to be with Annie on my own, one final time.

I walked back into the room. Annie's coffin was awash with colour, the sun was streaming in through the massive window. The room was peaceful. It was…a perfect final moment with my wife.

I didn't walk to her coffin, I simply stood by the door, watching the scene. "Goodbye my love. I'm sorry I got it wrong, but I promise you I won't get it wrong ever again. Thank you for bringing colour into my life. I love you sweetheart. Sleep tight, my Ann."

Twenty-Five

Where Do We Go from Here…?

The first couple of days after the funeral were a blur. We didn't get much sleep on Tuesday night. Tossing and turning. Even Beau slept badly.

We spent Wednesday in PJs, watching film after film on the TV. Zak walked Beau and I was so grateful. Wednesday night came and we had another takeaway, with pizza winning the vote. As I was on the phone ordering, I heard my mobile ring and Lexie answer it, which must have meant it was someone we knew. We'd taught the children from a young age that they mustn't answer our mobile phones unless the face on the screen was someone they knew.

By the time I came off the phone, Lexie and Louis were both back under the blanket watching the next instalment of *Back to the Future*.

"Who was on the phone, Piggy?" I asked, while looking for my mobile, which she had obviously put down somewhere else.

"Nanny. She said she'll talk to you later." She returned to the film, but then: "Oh, and I told her I thought it might be a good idea if me and Lou go for a few days' sleepover. You need time not looking after us. So, Nanny said that's what she'd talk about with you later." And she was back to the TV!

When the heck did my baby girl become so observant and grown up? Nothing got past her. She noticed everything. I'd really thought I was doing well with coping, and not letting everything get on top of me.

I called May back as I went into the kitchen.

"Hello, Rob. How are you?" Malc said when he answered the phone.

"I'm ok. A bit confused, but ok."

"Oh yes, Lexie's plan! I've just been hearing all about it. We've got a smart one there, Rob, haven't we?"

"You're not kidding! She's so like her mom it's scary."

"Well, from our end, it'll be wonderful to have them for a few days. May is just on her mobile talking to your mum and she's said she'd love to have them for a few days as well. So, why don't we turn it into a bit of a holiday for them? A few days with us, a few days with Janey?" Malc suggested.

"Umm, I'm not sure. They are still very clingy at times. Night-times are tricky."

"All the more reason to break the cycle before it becomes habit, aye?"

"Yes, I suppose you're right."

"They'll be absolutely fine, Rob."

"I know. Having the free time would help as well. I still need to get back in touch with probate and the banks, et cetera."

"Well, it sounds like it'll give you a bit of quiet that you so need. Would you like us to have Beau as well?"

"Oh God, no! I can't subject you to all of them!" I chuckled.

"Ok, son. Well, how about we come and collect them tomorrow morning? Pack enough clothes for a good few days away. If it doesn't work, we will just bring them home."

"Thank you, Malc."

"Think nothing of it. We're all in this together. Love you."

"I love you."

Walking back into the living room, both of the kids had their faces in the TV. Pausing the film, I said, "Right, you pair, I need you to run upstairs and sort out some clothes. You two are off for a bit of a holiday; a few nights' sleepover with Nanny and Gag and then with Nanna. How does that sound?"

Louis jumped off the sofa. "YEEEEEEESSSSSSSSSS! Awesome! Nanna lets us have chocolate to go to bed!" he squealed, as he ran out of the room and upstairs.

"She does what?" I called after him.

Tiptoeing out of the room, "He meant she gives us milk – obviously!" Lexie tried to cover for her brother's big mouth!

As they gathered what they'd need for a few days away, I left them to it, knowing full well I'd have to repack both bags again once they were asleep. I grabbed my phone and opened the Notes app.

To get done

1. Speak to probate office and complete forms
2. Speak to bank about Annie's bills, and what to do
3. Speak to solicitor about Annie's will? My new will!!!!!!!
4. Talk to Richard Morgan
5. Speak to The Lavender Trust
6. Talk to work (Glenda)

I could have carried on typing, except I had to deal with the dilemma of whether to take Batman or Superman on the sleepover!

The pizza was demolished rather quickly by the two hungriest kids in the universe. I had one slice. Looking back, I think that I acknowledged I'd lost quite a bit of weight at that point, but I had no inclination to do anything about rectifying it. Simply sustaining myself to ensure that the kids were thriving was my goal.

Surprisingly, the kids slept very well that Wednesday night, but were up with the lark and hanging over the armchair by the bay window of the living room from 8am the next morning, waiting for Nan and Gag to arrive!

Saying goodbye to them was easier than I'd expected. I was the one who was reluctant to let them leave!

As May strapped them, in Malc came over. "Are you ok?"

"Yeah. Just taking things one bit at a time." I tried to reassure him, but I don't think I was doing a good job.

"Why don't you come and stay with us for a bit too?"

"Oh gosh, that's so kind of you, but I'm afraid I'd be gate crashing the big things those two have been planning since last night!" I smiled.

"Oh God!" Malc laughed, "Can I do anything to help? I mean practically? I'm quite handy with a lawnmower – I even know one end of a duster from the other! Or I can phone people for you?"

"I'm going to have a go at doing that after you've gone. First call is to probate and then the solicitor. There are just so many different organisations and people that need contacting, it's a bit overwhelming, and I know I've been putting it off!"

"I was the same when my mom passed away. In the end, I got so flustered with all of it that I just phoned Geoff, my solicitor, and asked him to handle everything! Cost a pretty penny, but it was worth it. Now, if you change your mind, there's always a bed at ours for you, and if anything happens, we will bring the kids straight back, ok?" He pulled me into a hug and didn't let go for a while.

The silence of the empty house was deafening. Beau was mooching around in the garden. I made myself a cup of tea and headed to the study to begin the mammoth task. I quickly realised I'd massively underestimated the length of time it was going to take to contact all the relevant people and inform them of Annie's death. One hour and twenty minutes after picking up the phone to make the first call I felt physically, emotionally and mentally drained.

Staring out the window, I realised that Malc was absolutely right. I created a new email and composed a begging letter, for want of a better phrase, to our family solicitor:

To: hannaho@johnsonsandcarter.co.uk
From: rlawson1978@imail.com
Date: 19 May 10.31am
Re: Annie Lawson

Hello Hannah

I'm writing to inform you of my wife Annie's death. I've attached a copy of her death certificate for your records.

Does your organisation take over dealing with all correspondence after a person's death? Probate? Banks? Credit cards? Bills?

I'm finding the whole situation really rather overwhelming and would appreciate it if you could take over.

Can you please let me know how much you'll charge to do this?

Also, I now need to amend my own will accordingly.

With kind regards
Rob Lawson

Pushing back the chair, I grabbed Beau's lead and locked the conservatory. I needed to get out of the house. I was glad the kids would be spending some time with their grandparents, hopefully having snippets of fun and laughter. I knew I was no fun right now, I felt like I had flatlined and they didn't deserve that!

I was…lost?

However, one thing was becoming clearer with each passing day, or even hour – I had a very big decision to make. A decision that would impact the direction of all three of our lives forever.

I let Beau off her lead in the Meadow, and I called Zak,

"Yo dude, what's up?"

"I think I'm going to sell the business," I answered.

"Mate, that's a big decision to be making right now, don't you think? Don't you think you need to let the dust settle, have time to adjust?"

He always has been and always will be a voice of reason, and that's why I called him. I needed clarity and unhindered thinking. "No mate. If I'm honest, I was considering it before. I never wanted to be the boss! I think David left me the business to enable me to do what I have always wanted to do!"

"Not be a farmer!"

I laughed out loud. He is so funny!

"What do you mean you were considering it before? You'd hardly had the business for five minutes before Annie."

Fair point! "I talked to Annie about how I wasn't coping, how I'm not made to be a boss. God, I've found it so difficult getting my head around everything involved in running a business. She told me, "one thing at a time". I set myself a goal of one month, and if I didn't feel any different after one month, then I'd need to re-evaluate. Mate, I don't. I know what's happened will be a factor in my decision, but I honestly don't think I'm meant to be the boss... of that business."

"That business? So, there's another business you want to be the boss of?"

"Possibly!" I smiled as I vocalised my plan for the first time.

"No! No, knob! No! Not that again?" I could hear he'd stopped tip-tapping on his keyboard.

"Yep! Never changed since I was seven, mate, it's what I've always wanted and it's got to be..."

We said together, "By the sea."

"Yeah, I know all this, knob, but come on! Now, more than ever, you need stability, predictability and a steady income. You can't be branching out into the unknown."

"Yep. You're absolutely right, and I totally agree with you. However, I also think you're completely wrong. I believe Annie's sent me a message. It's a sign, pointing me in the right direction."

"A sign? Knob, you do know you are completely stark staring bonkers, don't you? I mean, you've hit all the branches on the way down, mate!"

Chuckling, "I know, mate. It's bonkers, but it feels right. It doesn't feel forced, or rushed, or even hard. It feels absolutely the right thing to do."

"What about the kids? You must realise you're going to need to orbit your life around them now? School runs, clubs and all that jazz, it's going to be you." He was being Mr Practical.

"That's why I'm doing it, Zak. I need to be free of the shackles of the desk, and there for them whenever and however they need me."

"Mate, it sounds like you've done a bit of thinking already, and that's great. But I think you need to do a lot more! This is huge. Right now, you have the ability to sustain and maintain your family life. Yes, the way you work will have to change, but you know that business, you know how it operates, it's what you went to uni for. To step away from that into something unknown is a massive step."

"You're right. Thank you for your honesty. I do appreciate it. I'm going to ask for an emergency Management Team meeting this afternoon. I need to vocalise what I'm thinking. I need to be honest and say – 'actually, I'm not the man you need, but I'm not selfish enough to keep pretending'."

"You really are crazy!"

"Will you come with me to see it?"

"To see what?"

"The potential Magic Maker!"

"Of course, knob! Just tell me when and where!"

"Always a pleasure conversing with you."

"Be cool, Lawson, be cool!"

Next, I called my mum. I needed a sounding board and Zak and Mum have always been it, well, aside from Annie.

Glenda had done a fantastic job of getting the entire Management Team in at such short notice. It was comforting to see them all as I walked into the conference room.

"Good afternoon everyone. Thank you so much for coming in at such short notice, and with no indication as to why."

Eyes were following my every movement, confusion written across each face.

"As you all are aware, just under two weeks ago I lost my wife Annie. This has altered the dynamics of my family entirely. She was our heart and soul. I am now the sole carer for my two beautiful children, and they are my main priority." Taking a deep breath, I went on, "Which is why I have made the decision to step away from Morris and Co and place the business up for sale."

Gasps filled the room, low-level chatter, disbelief.

"Please let me just say that, when I inherited this company, I made no secret of the fact that I was no boss! David felt that I had potential; I, however, did not. I need to be with my children now, I need to be home for them whenever they need me, not worrying about this month's figures. I am going to instruct Glenda to contact our company accountants to come in and value the business as a going concern. My aim is to sell as quickly as possible. I hope that you can find it within yourselves to understand and appreciate that my decision hasn't been taken lightly. I will compose a statement that will be sent to the whole team this afternoon, so I'd appreciate if you can refrain from discussing this outside of this room until everyone has been told. Thank you for your time."

I walked out of the conference room and down the corridor into my office, and began to pack up my belongings, pictures of Annie and the kids, painted pictures from the kids' days at nursery. Once everything was packed, I sat for the final time at the big desk, opened up my email and composed a message to the entire team. Once it was sent, I sat back in the chair and, for the first time in nearly two weeks, felt certain that I'd made the right choice.

Kissing Glenda goodbye and promising that I wouldn't be a stranger once the business had been sold, I took my belongings and headed out to the car. Driving home, I made some practical decisions, the first being that I needed to head to the supermarket to do a shop. We had to start eating proper food, we couldn't live on takeaway food anymore, and I desperately needed to up my game in the food preparation department.

After putting all the shopping away (and still with no idea what I'd make myself for dinner!) I managed to grab Beau, who allowed me to brush her for two minutes. She hates it with a passion.

Walking upstairs, I faced my next practical decision. I stood in front of the closed door. It was time for me to face the master bedroom again. I knew in my heart I'd never sleep in there again, even if the spare bedroom mattress was like lying on boulders.

Grabbing the door handle, I took a breath and pushed the door open. Beau rushed past me and made a beeline for Annie's side of the bed.

The first thing that hit me was the smell of her perfume. It lingered in the air.

The bed was still as Zak left it nearly two weeks ago, the duvet folded on the end of the mattress with the pillows piled at the top.

Knowing the room would never again be used for its purpose kind of made it a bit redundant; however, I needed to start facing Annie's memory. Her smell was the hardest of all. *Eternity* perfume – it seemed to be everywhere, emanating from the walls. I could see her bits and bobs on her dressing table, all the whatchama things that ladies need. I pulled back the curtains and lifted the blind, allowing sunlight to flood the room.

Taking a deep breath, I walked over to the double doors on Annie's side of the wardrobe and opened them. It was like being confronted with a faceless Ann. All her most favourite clothes hung waiting for the next time they'd be worn – only they wouldn't. Pulling the hangers off the rail, I piled them on the bed. Good grief, how many clothes does a person need? Crikey! I continued to remove the clothes until finally I could see the bottom of the wardrobe. Rows of shoes, neatly arranged. Then I found what I was looking for, Annie's expanding file, which I knew had all the details of her bills, accounts and certificates. Hannah, the solicitor, had returned my email confirming that she could take over sorting out Annie's estate, but she'd need some details, and I would have to go into the office and sign some documentation.

At the back of the wardrobe was a big box with my name on it. Pulling it out, I opened the flaps and sure enough, just as she'd told me in her letter, there were wrapped presents, all labelled and with dates on them.

Putting the top present back inside the box, I looked up at the remaining clothes hanging inside the wardrobe. Right, I needed to start taking positive actions. So, pulling everything out, I made a big pile of Annie's clothing on the bed. I knew I needed to keep important items. Fluffy jumpers – they'd be good for the kids when they needed a Momma hug; her wedding dress – perhaps Lexie would like it when she grew up?

Ripped clothes (or scruffies, as Annie called them) I threw onto the floor. They'd go in the bin. All the other clothing I folded and left on the bed. I wanted May and Malc, and of course Andy, to have the option of having any of her clothing for themselves to remember her by.

Remember Annie by, that's all we could do now. I broke down and fell on the neatly piled clothing and sobbed until I was raw and aching. How could I do any of this without Annie?

Twenty-Six

Allowing the Light In…

Nearly two months had passed since had Annie left us. Lou, Lexie and I were beginning to settle into a new routine, our 'new normal'. The previous week had been a success because both had been to school all week without a meltdown and without me having to collect them early. The previous night, for the first time, Louis didn't ask for his momma at bedtime, but I was still always reminding them both that Momma would be waiting for them in their dreams, and that she'd on the end of their beds all night.

Working with The Lavender Trust helped immensely, allowing both children the opportunity to talk about Annie outside of the family unit, and to understand death and their own grief. It was especially useful for Lexie, as it quickly became apparent that she was fearful of talking about how she was feeling in front of me, for fear of upsetting me.

We raised a staggering £2,307.00 for the Trust from donations at the funeral. This money was used to part-fund another support worker, and also to add to their memorial garden. We shall all be eternally grateful to everyone at the Trust; I really don't know how we'd have gotten through the pain without them. Louis has said he'd like to work there when he grows up. I can't think of a better job for anyone to have.

It was almost a month since the sale of Morris and Co had gone through. I'd received a call from Glenda to say that the solicitors were at the office, and they'd emailed me. Opening my email account on my phone, I read the email.

To: rlawson1978@imail.com
CC: managementteam@morrisandco.co.uk
From: b.littleton@mgf.co.uk
Date: 24 May 11.32pm
Re: Valuation of Business: Morris and Co, Worcestershire
Good afternoon Mr Lawson

As instructed, over the previous two days, my team and I have carried out a detailed valuation of the business: Morris and Co, of which you are sole owner.

I can confirm that with all assets taken into consideration I am able to value the business at a total of:

5,000,000 GBP

I also confirm, as instructed, that I have copied the 'management team' email address into this email.

If you require any further information, please don't hesitate to contact me. A full and detailed report will be made available to you next week.

Kind Regards
Bernard Littleton

F-U-C-K me!!!!!

£5 million! What the actual?????

I just kept staring at the phone, shaking my head, staring at the phone, shaking my head! I couldn't believe it!

Responding to Bernard and copying the Management Team in, I indicated my thanks and to accept the email as instruction that my intention was still to sell the business.

I didn't utter a word about the valuation to anyone, not even Zak. I think I just needed time to adjust to the staggering sums of money being bandied about. Five million pounds! Annie's and my joint savings had only ever reached £20,000! Five million! God, if the business did sell for anywhere close to that, the kids and I would be financially secure for the rest of my and their lives.

The next morning, I was woken by the ping of my mobile.

To: rlawson1978@imail.com

From: managementteam@morrisandco.co.uk

Date: 25 May 05.17am

Re: Morris and Co purchase offer

Morning, Rob

We hope this email finds you well? We hope that Lexie and Louis are ok?

We, the Management Team, have formed a co-operative and have sought backing and are now in a position to place a formal offer for Morris and Co.

The value of the business has been set at 5,000,000 GBP. We, therefore, offer you 5,500,000 GBP to ensure your acceptance and with the additional funds in respect of your years of service to the organisation, and our sincerest condolences for the loss of your wife.

We hope this offer meets with your approval, and we vow to continue operating Morris and Co in the spirit of yours and David's vision.

We look forward to hearing from you.
The Management Team

I fell back against the pillows and allowed fresh tears to fall, not tears of grief, but tears of relief. I would be able to have space to breathe, space to focus on the children's and my new life.

I hit reply.

To: managementteam@morrisandco.co.uk
CC: glenda.willis@morrisandco.co.uk;
     hannaho@johnsonsandcarter.co.uk
From: rlawson1978@imail.com
Date: 25 May 05.42am
Re: Re: Morris and Co purchase offer

Morning all

Thank you for your email. Your kindness is overwhelming. I've been truly lucky to work with such amazing individuals as yourselves.

I formally accept your offer with thanks.

Glenda: Please can you inform the Morris and Co solicitor that I have copied my solicitor, Hannah Osbourne, into this email for reference.

Hannah: please can you prepare all paperwork required my end for the sale of my 100% share of Morris and Co.

With my eternal gratitude.

Saying yes was such a massive weight off my shoulders. I walked away from the business, and the money freed me of any constraints, probably some self-imposed. I could now focus on rebuilding our family.

When the sale was agreed and the money transferred to my account, the first thing I did was pay off the mortgage on the house. Then I instructed Hannah to get me the very best financial advisor, who, in turn, calculated the tax I'd need to pay on the sale. All in all, I'd been left with about £4 million.

I set up trust funds for Louis and Lexie, each with £1 million, which would continue to accrue interest and be accessible to them when they reached twenty-one.

I put £1 million into a high-interest savings account with the interest effectively paying me a very healthy £3,500 per month without touching the capital.

So, with Louis and Lexie covered for the rest of their lives, the house paid off, and my interest paying a monthly income, I felt so much lighter.

The previous week, I'd also heard from Hannah that Annie's and my joint life insurance policy had agreed to settle and £500,000 was deposited into my account.

After much protesting from May and Malc, I used this to repay the money they had loaned Annie prior to her death. I also paid off Andy's and my mum's mortgages. Our whole family was now financially secure thanks to Annie. This was her legacy to them.

About a week after the funeral, Richard Morgan called to say that Annie's ashes had been returned to him. He asked if I would like him to bring them around.

I don't want to sound cold-hearted, but I didn't want him to come to the house again. It would be too reminiscent of the day Annie left us.

You know, for all my failings throughout the past year, and I freely admit there have been a lot, I know that I must remain as level and steady as I possibly can, because I have two little people depending on me.

That's why I drove to his office and collected Annie's urn. It was a surreal experience carrying my wife's ashes out to the car. I vividly remember the inner turmoil of wondering if I should strap the urn in on the front seat, or if she'd be ok just rolling about? When I returned home, I put the urn on the mantlepiece, not really sure what I should do with it.

Death really comes with so many unknowns, doesn't it?

There have been many days when I've walked into the living room to find either Lexie or Louis sitting on the carpet in front of the fireplace, simply staring up at the urn, sitting with their mummy.

Today is Friday 5 July, almost two months since Annie's death. I have successfully got both children into school and on time – I tell you, these small achievements are like BIG wins when you're doing it all by yourself. Zak was waiting for me in the car. So, you can see it is even more of an achievement given that Uncle Zak was part of the morning madness!

"You sure you're ready to do this, mate?" he asked, as I strapped myself in.

"It was my dream, but it became a shared dream." I looked across at him as I pressed the button and the engine kicked into life, "Alright...mainly my dream! But I want to see if I can make it a reality!"

May was collecting the kids after school, and a whole weekend of sleepover madness was planned. Thankfully, for Beau's sanity, I was taking her with me.

As we travelled down the M5, past the Willow Man (or Alan, as we nicknamed him!), my chest began to grow a little tighter and I recognised that my breathing was speeding up. Utilising the breathing techniques that The Lavender Trust had taught all of us, I allowed the wave of anxiety to wash over me. Thankfully, Zak was none the wiser, as he'd been asleep since Bristol!

An hour later, I wove my way down through the beautiful town of Combe Martin and up and out the other side. Slowing as we descended the hill into Watermouth, I turned left opposite the harbour and up the hill towards our destination, a beautiful complex of wooden lodges and chalets climbing up the valley hillside and nestled in among some beautiful old growth trees.

Booking in, we unloaded our bags and crashed onto the couches. It still wasn't midday; we'd made great time! Zak was beside himself because the lodge had a hot tub. He was practically in his trunks before we'd unpacked! Although Sheila had invited us to stay at her house, I'd said I was likely to be coming and going a lot this weekend and would hate to be a burden to her, but that I wouldn't say no to a BBQ at some point. We arranged to go over Saturday afternoon for food.

I grabbed the A5 notebook from my bag and picked up my sunnies and a bottle of water. "Right mate, I'm off. Not sure how long I'll be!" I said to Zak as he began taking the lid off the massive eight-person hot tub.

"No sweat, dude. Me and this little beauty are going to get better acquainted. I'm going to video call Liv and see just how jealous I can make her!" he laughed.

"Idiot!"

Walking down the driveway, I crossed the main road into Ilfracombe and down into the harbour through the little wooden gate next to the harbourmaster's office. Rounding the boats, I headed across the front of the harbour towards The Teacup, where I grabbed a takeaway coffee and two slices of toast for Beau. We found a picnic table away from the hustle and bustle of the café. It was nearly 12.30pm and people were wanting their grub!

Placing the book down on the table in front of me, my coffee steaming away, I broke up the toast and fed Beau, who, once full, proceeded to find a nice bit of grass to curl up on and have a little snooze.

The book – the thing I'd avoided like the plague for nearly two months. I hadn't dared open the cover since it slid out of the brown envelope onto my lap all those weeks ago. I just couldn't face what was inside. I knew, deep in my heart, that it was some kind of journal or diary, but I couldn't find the strength or the courage.

I had no idea what was waiting for me inside. What would each page hold for me? All I knew was that the front cover was very 'Annie', with the words

"Shine Your Light Bright"

emblazoned across it.

Taking a sip of the scalding coffee, I took a deep breath and opened the front cover.

Journal, Diary, rambling and probably more

was written on the first page by Annie, and underneath in a different coloured pen,

Lawson

Turns out this is my Journey with Cancer, also my hopes for you and the kids should I not win this fight, but please know that I will fight till my very last breath, because I love you all so very much.

Your Ann

Tears were falling down my face, and threatening to smudge Annie's perfect handwriting, so I moved the book further along the table. I needed to preserve everything that she is and was. Thank God, practical Zak had made me pack a packet of tissues.

It was 3.10pm when I closed the journal. My wife was simply the most remarkable woman I had ever met. Selfless, kind, caring and protective till the end. I didn't deserve her, of that I was certain, I didn't deserve her love towards the end. But I had it, every ounce of it; even when I broke her heart, she simply returned that hurt with more love and compassion.

The decision to keep her illness from me was forced upon her by me and my selfishness and stupidity. She was going to tell me when I got back from Berlin, but instead she was faced with a selfish arsehole telling her he was bored and wanted a divorce. I woke her and broke her heart. She didn't want to then tell me about her illness and make me feel that I had to stay with her. She was sick and was thinking about everyone else but herself. God, that woman infuriates me! Infuriated me!

Did she make the right choice not to tell me? Maybe? But I fell in love with her all over again in those last few weeks, even though she was dying right in front of my eyes and I never saw it.

I remember staring at people as they mingled about the harbour, going about their lives, coming in and out of the little boat café, so carefree, so ignorant to the magic they weave wherever they go.

Right – tomorrow – I began to pull back from the black – tomorrow I begin to let the light back into our lives.

Twenty-Seven

Being a Grown-Up…!

Video calling the kids when I returned to the lodge really reassured me that we were heading in a good direction. They were both happy and enjoying their mini holiday with Nanny and Gag. Both were also extremely excited about today. Louis took some persuading that me and Uncle Zak weren't actually sleeping in the harbour! As promised (on pain of death), I'd taken pictures earlier of the harbour's heavy lifting equipment, which was Louis's new-found fixation. Lex just wanted pictures of the pretty flowers, and a dolphin if I saw one!

After reluctantly leaving the comfort of the hot tub, Zak and I sat on the decking as I explained what I'd read in Annie's book. He was as astounded as I was, but ultimately not surprised. He summed it up perfectly:

"That's our Annie!"

I was up with the lark on Saturday, and I sat in the hot tub watching the sun rise over the valley. It was truly spectacular.

Zak dragged himself out of bed and we were off out, arriving at our destination by 8.45am.

Getting out of the car, we both stared open-mouthed at the view straight out across Combe Martin bay, uninterrupted, absolutely stunning, breath-taking even! The photographs hadn't done it justice.

"Mr Lawson?" A voice interrupted our far-away thoughts.

Turning around: "Yes! So sorry! That view is incredible!!" I walked over to a woman standing in front of my car.

"Isn't it! Welcome, I'm Tess Jones," she said, shaking our hands.

"This is my friend, Zak Matthews," I clarified.

"Also known as moral supporter and common-sense advisor!" Zak added.

Laughing, Tess led us to the entranceway of the imposing four-bedroomed detached house. As soon as we walked through the door, I knew! It's a ridiculous thing to say now that I look back, but it's true. I absolutely knew that this was going to be our new forever family home.

How did I know, I may hear you ask! Well, as we walked in through the door, we were instantly faced with a winding staircase and a massive canvas hanging on the wall. The canvas was awash with pastel rainbow colours, and splashed across it were the words:

"Shine bright you beautiful one"

I remember nudging Zak and motioning my head to see if he could see what I saw!

"Ms Jones… Ummmm, I wonder if I could just have a moment?"

"Oh, of course, Mr Lawson. I'll be in the garden." She walked on through an open door, leaving me and Zak alone.

"This is it Zak! Look!" I pointed at the canvas.

"I agree, mate. She's here! Such an Annie thing to say!" He was as dumbfounded as me!

Following Ms Jones' path, we walked through the house and out onto the terrace, framed with that gorgeous view again!

"Ms Jones, I know I need to really see the rest of the house but, if I'm being perfectly honest with you, I don't need to."

The estate agent's face dropped; she was clearly thinking her trip had been a waste of time.

"You see, I'll give them the asking price – cash."

Her face was an absolute picture! Shock, horror, excitement, joy, happiness and confusion all in a short space of time. Stumbling from one foot to the other, Tess Jones, estate agent for twelve years, had never ever come across anything like this – ever!

"You... You want to pay cash? Ummm, ok! I'll go and talk to the vendor. They are down in the orchard – that is included in the sale. Why don't you and Mr Matthews have a good look around the house?" Walking away, she clutched her clipboard and we could see her shaking her head!

"Oh Ms Jones...," I called. She turned back around. "I'm happy to pay a holding deposit today if that helps, and I'll pay all their fees incurred through the sale of the property."

"Mr Lawson, please don't think me rude," she walked back up towards the terrace, "but this isn't a normal approach to buying a house!"

"This isn't a normal house, Ms Jones!"

Actually open-mouthed, that's how she looked. I think that if I'd walked over to her, I could have blown her over with a little puff of air!

Anyway, she continued on down the garden towards the fenced-in orchard.

As instructed, Zak and I went back inside and conducted a tour of the property. Arriving back downstairs, we heard talking from the kitchen, which had bi-folding doors to the terrace that framed the view perfectly.

Giving the kitchen door a gentle knock, we entered.

"Ahh Mr Lawson, Mr Matthews, this is Mr and Mrs Strawbridge, owners of The Wren's Nest."

After much hand-shaking and "how do you dos", Mrs Strawbridge invited us to sit down while she busied herself making a fresh pot of tea. Mr Strawbridge sat across the table from us, his hands clasped. He looked like he'd have made a great headmaster in his working life, with that fierce all-consuming stare they all have!

"Mr Lawson, Tess has told us of your proposal and offer, and of the circumstances that surround bringing you and your family to Combe Martin. My wife and I have spoken and we are both in agreement...," the pause was endless – it felt like a lifetime, "We are happy to pass The Nest on to you, but with one condition!"

As this point, I have to confess, I acted very foolishly, very selfishly and very badly. I bolted. I ran from the kitchen. I left Zak to deal with the fallout of my running.

Why did I run?

Simple.

Annie is the only person in my entire life who ever placed conditions on anything.

Conditions for going out with me...

Conditions for getting married...

Conditions for having children...

Conditions for dying...

I knew Zak would understand why I'd run and that he'd explain but, God, I was embarrassed the second I hit the fresh air. But I couldn't go back in. I needed to gather myself, dry my tears, control my breathing, become a grown-up.

This sealed it for me, that this house was sent to me by Annie. This was her way of blessing the move.

Mr Strawbridge came up behind me as I stood with my arms clasping a garden chair. "Don't hide your loss on our account. Your friend has explained quite eloquently what just happened, and for that I apologise."

I turned and faced the old man, this stranger. "You have nothing to apologise for. It's me that should be saying sorry. God, I was so rude just now! Sometimes her loss is overwhelming." I didn't justify myself, and I don't think I was trying to.

"What my wife and I would like to propose as part of the sale is that we officially rename the orchard. We've always toyed with the idea of calling it The Patch but it never seemed to sit right with us. I...we propose to dedicate it in your wife's name."

"Annie...," I whispered.

"Annie's Patch – sounds bloody perfect." This old man, who I hardly knew, smiled from ear to ear. "Welcome home, Rob. I hope you and your family are able to heal here."

Fresh tears were falling. "Thank you, Mr Strawbridge," I said as he pulled me into an embrace that felt comforting and needed.

Twenty-Eight

Who Knew the M5 Was So Long…?

It was a wonderful feeling to come home on Sunday and telling the children that I'd found our new home. Their little faces lit up for the first time in months. Lexie was so excited to have a garden big enough for a proper slide and swing set – which I'd somehow promised, although I have no recollection of that promise! Louis couldn't wait to create his new bedroom, which I'd assured him would most definitely have a view of the sea, and plenty of room for his new-found love of LEGO (and my new-found dislike, especially when it was between my toes!)

We sat together on the sofa on Sunday evening and I showed them the many photos I'd taken of the house and the garden. Zak sent over the video he'd taken, with added commentary which had the kids in hysterics.

Packing the house was going to be hard, I knew that. But what I didn't anticipate was the sensory overload.

Most of Annie's clothes had now been sorted into the keeping pile, seven bin bags had gone to the local hospice charity shop, May,

Malc and Andrew had taken a few items and the rest we'd had to bin as no one wanted holey leggings!

I'd decided to keep some of her better-quality high heels, but boxed them up for storage in the new loft. When Lexie got older, she might have a love of posh shoes and she might love the idea of wearing her mum's.

Packing up and getting rid of stuff from Annie's dressing table was so hard. Whenever I moved anything, I got a waft of 'her', her perfume, her moisturiser…it was just all-consuming. I threw away most of the stuff. But I bagged up some make-up and her perfumes, again for Lexie, and some perfume for Louis, who loves to smell the 'fancy bottles'!

I hired a skip and got rid of loads of junk that we'd been keeping hold of for years! I even found the very first Christmas tree Annie and I bought when we moved in together. I couldn't part with it, so I promised the kids they could have it in the new kitchen. I sent bags and bags of baby clothes to the hospice charity shop as well, all except twelve baby-grows each. I sent those to my mum's best friend, who spends her spare time making memory quilts. The quilts came back looking absolutely stunning, and I planned to have them on the beds when the kids walked into their new rooms – kind of a surprise.

On Sunday night, our last night in the house, Lexie and Louis if we could make cakes, one last time, just like Momma used to do. So, the three of us stood one last time at the kitchen island and made chocolate crispy cakes, and then ate the lot!

Monday morning dawned with a beautifully clear sky and warmth that wasn't too hot, but still nice. The moving company arrived at 8am as promised (there was a tiny worry that they wouldn't show up!). The kids ideally would have been with May and Malc, having had a sleepover the previous night. However, once Louis cottoned onto the fact that a BIG truck was coming, there was no way he was not going to be there! I mean, it's got more than four wheels, mind!

The truck was more than big enough to eat up the contents of the house. I'd loaded the car with things I felt we'd need straight away

— a box of food, the kettle and drinks, toilet paper and a box of games to keep the kids entertained. A box of Beau bits. Plus, most importantly, Annie. I strapped her urn into the front seat. The kids squished together their car seats next to one another in the back, with the boxes in the footwell in front of and next to them, leaving the boot relatively free for Beau. Everything not breakable went into the roof box.

As I took one final look around the now-empty house, I couldn't help reliving all the events that the four walls had contained. The children coming home from the hospital for the first time. So many laughs, tears, Christmases, birthday parties. All in all, it had been a good house to us, and I should always remember it fondly. However, it was tainted. It was also the place where Annie took her final breath and, for that reason alone, I knew I couldn't remain within those walls. I will forever feel, however irrationally, that the house played its part in taking her from us.

I walked up the stairs and turned left and faced the now-empty master bedroom. The last room she saw. The room where I broke her heart. I had been such a naive fool. I will never allow that to ever happen again.

Moving from room to room, I checked cupboards to make sure we hadn't forgotten anything. Our worldly belongings were now packed inside a truck. Amazing really!

Walking out to the front porch, I locked the door for the final time, gently tapping the door to say goodbye and thank you.

I handed the keys over to Zak, who had kindly said he'd let the cleaning company in and then give the keys to the estate agents.

I was pleased to learn that a young couple who were expecting their first baby had bought the house; that somehow seemed fitting. Almost as if things had gone full circle.

I walked back to join Liv, May, Malc, Andy and Zak and joined in the BIG HUG Lexie insisted we all had. Tears began to flow after about the twentieth goodbye, with kisses being blown and, with promises of free holidays, we pulled off the drive for the final time.

May and Malc would be down to join us in a few days and my mum was already at the new house, having volunteered to stay and help me with the children, and be there to guide the removal company in. I knew our journey down would require more toilet stops than the van!

Thankfully, Zak had hooked up the iPad in the back of the car; he'd even loaded film after film, which did the trick of entertaining the kids for about forty minutes. Forty long minutes of peace.

"Daddy, I'm sad to leave our house. It feels like that's where Momma was." My grown-up girl. Always straight to the point, she's never been one to beat about the bush, definitely a trait she's inherited from her mum!

Concentrating on the merging traffic at Bristol, I fought back emotion.

"I miss my momma. I love her with all my hearts," Louis said, his voice was breaking. I looked in the rear-view mirror and saw Lexie reach across and take his hand.

"We're going to stop in a few minutes, guys, and how about we buy some food from the shop and have a picnic?"

Both nodded in agreement, but I could see the tears were ready to overflow.

Pulling into Avonmouth Services, the car park was busy, but not rammed – thankfully. After a mammoth toilet visit, we went into the shop and bought what appeared to be ALLLLL the food.

Retrieving Beau from the car, we walked her up on the dog walkers' area and then found a free picnic bench. I tied Beau's lead round the leg closest to me, and filled her travel bowl with ice cool water.

I unwrapped a handful of different sandwiches and the kids picked what they wanted, and ate them with big bags of sharing crisps. Now don't be mad at me, Annie – I made sure there was fruit as well! Beau enjoyed the scraps.

After we'd delved head first into the makeshift picnic, I watched the kids sharing out their food. They got on so well.

"Is it nice?" I asked. Both nodded enthusiastically. "You know I wanted to talk to both of you. I know exactly how you feel. Leaving our house, it feels like…like losing a link to Mommy, doesn't it?" Lexie nodded and Louis played with a single cheese puff. "Perhaps our new house won't have a link to Mommy? I miss her so much sometimes that my heart aches inside my chest." Both the kids were staring down at the table now. I knew they understood exactly what I was saying. "But we aren't leaving Momma behind. Do you know why?"

They both looked up in unison and stared at me, shaking their heads.

"Because we will always hold Momma here," I reached across the table and placed a hand on each of their chests, covering their hearts, "And, most importantly, we will always have our wonderful Momma memories. How lucky were we to have someone who brought sunshine into our lives? I wondered if now we've left the old house, perhaps you'd like to have some time every single day to revisit those Momma memories?"

"Oh Dadda, I'd love that! That way every single day we will have Momma time," smiled Lexie with glee.

"I'd like that too, Dadda," said Louis through a mouthful of cheese puff.

"Ok. Then it's a deal. Every day we will all sit down together and talk about a Momma memory, no matter where we are or what we're doing."

"I love you Daddy," said Lex as she continued devouring her picnic.

"I love you both so very much. Now, come on, eat up or I'll eat it all for you!"

Both giving a little squeal, they shovelled food into their mouths.

After coaxing Beau back into the car with the promise of her new squeaky toy, we were back on the road for the remainder of the journey.

We'd barely re-joined the motorway before the inevitable "are we there yet" began, and we were nowhere near Junction 27!

I somehow managed to survive the rest of the hour-and-a-half journey with my sanity intact! We twisted and turned our way down the valley into Combe Martin. The high street seemed to be buzzing with tourists, buckets in hands and sun hats on. Turning right off the main street, we started to climb the valley slope and up to our private drive.

The Wren's Nest came into view on the left-hand side and both kids were up at the window. Beau was up at her window too, and started barking, almost like she knew she was home.

Getting out of the car, I rounded the back door as my mum and Tess Jones came out of the front door.

"Nannnnnnnnnnnnnna!" shouted the kids, running across the drive and wrapping themselves around my mum's legs. "We didn't know you'd be here! Have you seen the sea?" shouted Lou.

"Yes pumpkin, and you know what? You were right, it's blue!" smiled Nanna at the apple of her eye!

The moving van was already here and the four men had obviously been working hard, as there was a lot of space in the back of the van.

"Welcome, Mr Lawson," said Tess Jones as she walked up the drive and shook my hand. "I hope you had a good journey?"

"Yes, not too bad given I was accompanied by two small bottles of pop and a yappy dog! Talking of which, let's release the hound!" I opened the boot and out shot Beau, running full pelt towards the gardens and orchard beyond. Thankfully the house had electric gates, so I knew the whole property was secure and 'Beau-proof'.

"They all look so happy," observed Tess.

"I think so Tess. I really think so!"

"Here you go, Mr Lawson". She handed me a Tupperware box full of keys. "The Wren's Nest is all yours."

"Thank you, for everything over the past few weeks. I really appreciate it." I genuinely did mean it. She had been a godsend, my lifeline to the south while I sorted everything out in the Midlands.

"You're welcome, it's been a pleasure. Also, a little message from Mr and Mrs Strawbridge. They said to say 'they hope it's ok to leave it?'" and with that she walked back to her car, climbed in and drove off.

Leave it? Leave what?

I walked over to the removal men to make sure everything was ok and to offer them a cup of tea once I'd dug the box with the kettle out of the car!

Moving to the front of the house, I turned to my left and took a big breath in and filled my lungs with salty sea air. The sun danced on the cresting waves below as they reached land at Combe Martin beach. I could hear Mum with the kids around the corner in the garden. It had definitely been the right choice to have Mum here when we arrived, freeing me up ever so slightly.

Pushing open the front door, I dropped Beau's lead where I stood and stared up at the full-height wall that encompassed the staircase. There it was, still hanging in pride of place

"Shine bright you beautiful one."

I cried. I cried and I cried, great howling sobs. Three months of anguish, frustration, worry, hurt, regret, anger, loneliness, sorrow, pain and confusion. I collapsed to my knees and allowed every ounce of it to leave my body. I didn't need to hold it together anymore. I didn't need to keep it inside.

I know that the removal men and my mum must have heard me, but no one came, and I'm glad. I needed to do this on my own. It needed to be a solitary act.

Finally, Beau came sniffing and headbutting me and, after discovering that I wasn't in fact dead, she trotted off to explore her new domain, obviously very pleased with herself. Lots of new things to sniff and claim!

Rising to my feet, I stood directly under the canvas and vowed: "Annie, I vow to you that I will ensure colour graces our lives every single day."

Twenty-Nine

The Teacup...

Our move coincided with the local primary school's fair that takes place during the summer holidays each year. It was a great way for the kids to mingle with their new classmates and become familiar with the school itself.

It was hard to believe that Lexie would be heading into Year 2 and Louis to Reception. The educational system was slightly different to what we'd been used to in the Midlands, as they operated a two-tier schooling programme, meaning that the kids would spend longer in the first school than they would have done in their old setting. This suited me, as I went through the two-tier system when I was growing up.

The fair was fantastic, and so well organised. When I introduced ourselves to the headmistress, who was greeting people on the gate, she instantly knew who we were, and welcomed both the kids by name. Then she walked us over to the tombola, where we were introduced to Lexie's new teacher, Miss Jarvis. It was a popular stall and Miss Jarvis was super busy, but she still managed to have a lovely chat with both the kids.

I, however, didn't fare quite so well and, upon returning to the car and checking my wallet, found that I'd been robbed blind by my own offspring, who were merrily examining their winnings in the back seat.

There were roughly two weeks of the summer holidays left by the time we moved, so lots of opportunities to explore our new surroundings. Nothing helps with exploring more than having a dog! After all, they do require lots of walking. Mum stayed down with us for a while, so I had the chance to go mooching up the very narrow coast paths, which were definitely walks for just me and Beau. I wouldn't trust Louis anywhere near a coast path!

Those first few weeks, walking and driving to new coastal towns and inlying villages, were perfect. We all recharged our batteries. Our days become softly structured, with exploring in the mornings and then home for lunch, followed by a few hours of unpacking and then reading, maths or construction in the back garden before tea.

I will confess (with pride) that my cooking improved dramatically!

Before we knew it, the first day of term had arrived. Louis's new Reception teacher, Miss Rodd, was fantastic and got Louis's number within a minute of meeting him – what a relief! I think it was, in some ways, easier for Louis to begin in a new school, because everyone else in his class was starting too.

Lexie, on the other hand, did not cope at all well. Meeting Miss Jarvis again at the door helped a bit, but I could see her little chin beginning to wobble. So, I pulled her to one side and allowed her classmates to go in.

"Sweetie, it's ok to be nervous. Everything is new – the school, the uniform, the teacher, even the dinner hall. But you know what isn't new?" She shook her head. "Mommy being here." I placed my hand just under her throat. "Remember, she's going to be with you every single step of the way. So, you won't be doing this alone." A smile spread across her face, the chin stopped wobbling and she hugged me and ran back over to Miss Jarvis (who Lexie insisted was called Miss Jelly for the first week she was there).

I'd met with Susie Jarvis the day before term started. I wanted to make sure that she had a good understanding of Lexie, and what our family had been through over the past few months. After the meeting, I came away feeling that she was exactly what Lexie needed, a strong independent female figure, who would enrich my daughter's life.

I felt a sense of accomplishment at knowing that both the kids were in school and I'd done that all by myself in our new home. Mum had returned home the day before, to allow us all to get ready in peace.

Driving back down the valley slope to the village, I headed up and out of Combe Martin on the coast road to my destination to meet the other estate agents I'd been dealing with for the past few months.

Dropping the car into second gear as the road descended from Berrynarbor into Watermouth, I couldn't help but smile as I passed the harbour; it was absolutely stunning. Navigating my way through the labyrinth of old ramshackle boats, boats in dry dock and tourists with their blow-up dinghies, I parked right at the front by the harbour wall.

Alex Cropley was waiting for me. After exchanging pleasantries, he simply handed me the keys and wished me all the best. Blimey, it couldn't have lasted more than two minutes. How very simple!

I climbed the steps, turned the old-looking key and pulled open the door. Beau instantly began barking at my heel. If there's one thing that dog can't stand, it's helium balloons. Doesn't matter what shape or size; apparently, they are all offensive! The interior appeared to be full of them – not a great start for my four-legged friend! All the balloons said "Good Luck" on them.

Pushing through, I found the counter and a card propped up.

Dear Mr Lawson

Wishing you every happiness as you embark upon this journey.

May The Teacup sail strong and true and hopefully the smoke detector isn't too temperamental.

She's been so kind to us, and we hope you will find eternal happiness and a spot of magic.

Jennie Hiller and family.

Moving back outside, I carried the card with me as I took in the majesty of the boat, my boat. My Teacup. My own café. I'd done it! I'd finally achieved a lifelong dream.

Now all that was left to do was work out exactly how one successfully runs a café! Shouldn't be too hard…?

I walked down the steps to the right of the door and sat in the built-in alcove, staring out through one of the portholes that faced out to sea across the harbour. I could smell coffee that had been brewed yesterday, cakes and, definitely, a hint of bacon. I loved it! Beau was beside herself, darting from my heel to those pesky balloons. Closing my eyes, I raised my head skywards and whispered, "I've done it, Ann. I've got our little café. Please watch over her, and give me the strength and courage to get it right. I miss you. I love you."

My first executive decision was to retain all the staff that the Hillers had employed. I'm not one for reinventing the wheel, and those guys knew exactly how The Teacup ran, and I'm not too proud to say that I learned every single thing I know about the old girl from Sandra, Bethan and weekend boy, Rory.

God, the hours I spent just getting my head around the logistics of how the business operated. It was much smaller than Morris and Co, but the weave was still complicated. Health and safety, food regulations, insurances, historic interest, on and on. All this, before I stepped anywhere near an apron.

My first official 'shift' could have gone better but, as Sandra pointed out, I'd never run a boat café before, so I needed to be kinder to myself.

I messed up the very first order for a cappuccino to take away and presented the very thirsty-looking fisherman with a mocha to drink in. Thankfully, I learned quite quickly that Old Bill, owner of the *Idle Times*, the forty-footer currently in dry dock next to the café, was a regular who really didn't care if his order was correct as long as he had something wet and warm to quench his thirst.

Moving myself to the safety of the kitchen, I gave myself a stern talking-to, and so began my baptism of fire in terms of improving my cooking ability! Ask me to whip up a bacon and egg butty for you, I can do it with my eyes shut. Move away from The Teacup's menu and I'll probably still struggle. But the point is, I can do it!

Over the weekends, I've even overcome my fear and started to learn to bake. The last time Mum came down, she brought all of my nan's old cake recipes, and I was so chuffed when I was able to bring the Tupperware boxes down and serve Nanny's shortbread and carrot cake at the café. I could feel it, I was growing in confidence with each passing day.

Never once have I regretted buying The Teacup; never a day goes by where it actually feels like work. The business has slotted well into our new family life. I drop the kids off at school while Sandra opens up. Bethan arrives for the lunchtime rush and stays while I collect the kids. We all come back to The Teacup after school, and snacks are eaten aboard, while I cash and lock up. Then we all head home for tea and walk Beau, not that she needs it, as she spends most of her days mooching around the harbour. Pete Duggins, the harbourmaster, has become a really good friend and has gladly said that Beau is free to wander.

Outside The Teacup, in pride of place, facing out across the harbour, is a beautiful maple wood bench with an engraving across the back,

ANNIE'S SPOT, BECAUSE SHE SIMPLY LOVED HERE.

Me, the kids and Beau are happy.

Thirty

The Anniversary...

The first anniversary of Annie's passing was extremely tough. We'd been living in North Devon for nine months, and I can honestly say it really felt like home. We'd been back up 'North' a few times to visit friends and family, but purposefully stayed well clear of Chestnut Grove. That place is a part of our history, not our future.

My Mum, May, Malc and Andy all came down for the weekend of the anniversary. Somehow, we all managed to squish into the house – Andy even brought his own blow-up bed! Unfortunately for him, Louis took a great interest in said bed, and Uncle Andy ended up sharing it with a rather wriggly little one.

We spent Saturday on the beach, having a picnic lovingly made by Lexie and her two nannies. There was a rather heated swing ball tournament and an epic rock pool excursion. However, the whole day was tinged with sadness.

I don't think anyone got a great night's sleep. Lexie crept into my bed at 1am and we pulled the curtains back and sat up in bed watching the sea lit by moonlight.

The children have soared since starting school. Louis is such an adaptable little chappie. I was never worried about him finding his feet.

Lexie, however, is a different story. She always has been, and always will be, Mommy's girl. She was Annie's shadow. Even from a young age, they were like peas in a pod. Annie's passing really shook my precious girl's soul. She struggled to find her place within the already established class. However, with perseverance and nurturing from her teacher, Susie Jarvis, Lexie has started to show signs of becoming a happier version of her new self.

I cannot find the words to express to Susie, and the school for that matter, how appreciative I am for the work and time they are giving to Lexie. When she struggles to express herself, or vocalise, they are patient with her. She has told me that she feels safe at school, and adores Susie.

When I chose to make the move from Bromsgrove, I couldn't have envisaged a better outcome for Lexie. She needed that external strong role model, and she's certainly found it.

Therefore, with the head teacher's permission, Susie had arranged to come and visit Lexie at home on the actual day of the anniversary.

Arriving at 2pm sharp, Susie Jarvis rang the doorbell and Lexie and Louis ran from the dining room through the kitchen, each grabbing one of my arms and dragging me to the front door.

"Misssssssssssssss Jarvis!" Lexie was visibly shocked. Later that night, she told me that she couldn't place her teacher anywhere other than in the classroom!

"WOW! Hi Miss!" smiled Louis. "Come in, I've got something amazing to show you outside." He grabbed her hand, released mine and guided her through the house. I just smiled at her bemused face.

We all sat on the patio overlooking the sloping garden down to Annie's Patch. The two nannies made a lovely spread of nibbles for everyone, while Malc and Andy battled to get the cricket stumps to stay in the ground,

After showing Susie "the MOST amazing" rock, Louis ran off chasing butterflies with Beau, leaving Lexie alone with me and Susie.

"Lexie, all of your classmates wanted to do something for you, to show you how much you mean to them." Susie pulled a big folder from the bag for life she'd been carrying. "So, we've made you this book. Everyone has written you a letter, or drawn you a picture telling you the best thing about having you in our class."

As she handed it over, Lex lost her voice as tears fell down her cheeks. She stared at the front cover emblazoned with rainbows and unicorns, her two favourite things at the moment!

"Thank you, Miss Jarvis. That is…wonderful. Isn't it lovely?" I looked down at her, and through the veil of her hair, for an instant I saw Annie, just a brief glimpse, and it took my breath away. I could see her chin wobbling as she tried to control her tears. She lost and the emotion overtook her. However, she didn't turn to me as I'd expected, or even to her grandparents or uncle. She stood up and ran to Susie, who held her and didn't let go until Lexie was ready. She pulled her up so she was sitting on her lap, and just held her.

"We love having you in our class, Lexie, and we love you. I'm not sure how we managed without you!"

We all laughed, and the tears subsided.

"Will you stay for tea, Miss Jarvis? Please? I'd like to show you some videos of my mommy."

"Oh yes, please stay!" echoed Louis, although he was halfway down the garden playing rock, paper, scissors with Andy.

"Well, thank you for the invite, both of you. It's so kind of you, but…" she made eye contact with me.

"We'd love for you to stay." I gestured to everyone.

"Absolutely," "More the merrier!" filled the air.

"Well, then, I'd love to join you all, but only if you and I can help prepare the food Lexie, once we've watched your video?"

"OOOOO yay!!!" Lexie smiled from ear to ear.

"Come on then kiddo, let's go and find your DVD."

The first Christmas without Annie was better than I'd envisaged. I think I'd built myself up for weeks and expected utter misery. In fact, it was warm, happy and full of laughter, mainly thanks to Annie (as always!)

As she'd promised, we each had Christmas presents to open from her, every one of us receiving a personalised DVD. Each one contained Annie's favourite pictures of us and her, little videos and audio of Annie talking about her favourite memories. It was absolutely perfect. For a while, the kids would watch their DVDs over and over again. I even had the sense to make copies of the originals, just in case anything happened to them. Now, however, they just tend to want to watch them of a Sunday afternoon, snuggled up on the sofa. It's not that they don't want to watch them more, it's just that they don't need to watch them. This, I believe, was Annie's plan all along. She knew just how much they needed her, and she never let them down.

Thirty-One

The Colour of Marriage…

Here we are then, we've reached today.

It's been just over two years since Annie left us – well, 745 days to be exact, and it's the biggest most nerve-racking day since the day we lost her.

Why?

Because I'm about to open my heart to colour again.

Because I'm about to ask another truly remarkable, wonderful, loving, kind, caring, considerate, thoughtful and compassionate woman to become my wife and my children's stepmother.

Was it a hard decision to ask her to marry me?

Honestly…?

Yes!

But only emotionally.

Knowing how wrong I'd got things with Annie, I wasn't sure I could even trust myself not to mess up again.

In those awful dark months after Annie left, I never EVER imagined that I'd embark on another relationship; it never entered my sphere of thought, ever. My axis shifted and my focus became totally on the children and ensuring that they were ok.

Thankfully, our move to North Devon was one of the right choices I made during those dark months. The kids – and I for that matter – have settled and we have all forged lifelong friendships.

Mum moved down here and now lives twenty minutes away in the beautiful village of Lynton. She has embraced village life, and has become an integral part of the community.

May and Malc have sold their house in Bewdley and have had an offer accepted on a bungalow with sea views in Ilfracombe. Every time the kids speak to their Uncle Andy, they badger him to move down here too. The poor bloke is systematically being worn down! What they don't know is that I've offered him a job as manager of The Teacup and he's accepted and found himself a lovely flat in Berrynarbor. Our whole family has been drawn to the sea.

The Teacup has gone from strength to strength and last spring I purchased another old boat and I am replicating the business in Ilfracombe harbour, hence the need for a manager. Even during the off-peak period, we still had a steady stream of loyal locals, so we didn't need to shut down.

The Wren's Nest has grown with us, and is exactly what we needed. Even Beau is happier down here. She loves the freedom that the open beach and waves offer her. Our lives have found a new way to seek out the colour in life.

Lexie and Louis were discharged from The Lavender Trust and we shall all always be so grateful for their help, support and advice during those early days. The children miss their mom terribly, but that sadness isn't raw anymore.

Sitting on the beach, a blanket wrapped around us, we watched Beau darting in and out of the surf. "Guys, I wanted to talk to you about something really important."

"Of course, Dad, is it about your hair?"

I stared at Lexie, shock etched across my face. "My…my… what's the matter with my hair?" I reached up to check it was indeed still perched on top of my head.

"Ohhhh, you know…it's just a bit less than what it was before!" Lexie didn't even look up from her sandcastle construction.

"Less…?" I began touching specific parts of my hair, shaking my head. I was getting side tracked. "Guys, how would you feel if I got married again?"

Silence…

Louis stopped constructing his sand fort and looked up, out to sea, out to the spot where we'd scattered Annie's ashes from a hired boat. Clearly, he was giving some thought to the question.

"Well," he said, "I think that's ok, Daddy. I think that Mommy would be ok with that too." That was it. He returned to stabilising his outer wall.

"Thanks, dude. Lex?"

She was patting the same patch of sand, over and over again. "I'm not sure, Daddy," she huffed out.

"Oh, ok. Can I ask why?"

"It's not that she's not perfect, because she is and I love her. It's just…"

"She's not Momma?" I asked.

Her big eyes rose up and met mine, tears forming, threatening to spill over. "No!"

"But sweetie, you know she doesn't want to be Momma, don't you? You know, both of you, that Momma is always with us, is part of our family? We'd just be growing our family?"

"She doesn't want to be Momma?"

"No darling." I pulled her onto my lap. "She'll be your friend, your guide, your support and an inspirational figure for you both, but no one, NO ONE will ever replace your momma." I held her tight to me.

"Well," she whispered from inside my jacket, "in that case I think it's the best idea you've had for a long time, Daddy. I love you."

"I love you, little Piggy."

"There is one condition though, Daddo!" Louis added.

Lexie and I turned and faced our grown-up little boy.

"I ain't losing my bedroom!"

We all laughed. He and Lexie are both so like Annie it's almost like she's with us still.

Beginning a new relationship shifted the axis again, and that scared, worried and confused me for a while. It wasn't what I intended to do, or even sought out. I would, I truly believe, have been happy to remain unattached for the rest of my life.

But along came, for want of a better phrase, an asteroid and smashed away all the walls I'd unknowingly built, stripped away the guilt that I'd covered myself in, and allowed me to see in colour once more.

Gosh, laughing, crying, talking, wondering, philosophical discussions, honest discussions, frank discussions and baring-of-soul discussions. All this and so much more helped me to realise that it had grown from something very simple into something lasting, and I know with every ounce of my being that I will never ever do anything to jeopardise it. Does saying I've learned my lesson with Annie make me sound like a bastard? I don't mean to, but it is the truth. Annie has shown me my faults, and my strengths.

Allowing love into my life again was so unexpected and so bloody wonderful. It is like starting over, but not. If that makes sense. Because I now know exactly how not to do things. Because of Annie, I now know what I've got to do:

- Recognise the value of the other person within a relationship

- Listen to them, always

- Always make dinner together

- Look at them, really look at them

- Love them unconditionally

- Never be late home from work

- Share the small and large things

- Laugh together

- Mock occasionally

- Always support them

- Allow them to sleep with a smile on their face

- Tell them I love them, wholeheartedly

- Cherish them always

So, this I vow to you, Susie Jarvis, as I ask you to marry me: I vow to give you all the Colours of Marriage, just as you deserve.

Now you have seen me at my worst, will you be with me at my best? Will you be my other wife?

Your Rob, Lexie, Louis, Beau and Annie xxx

Recipes

Unless otherwise stated, all recipes come from the author's recipe collection or head!

All recipes are aimed at four people.

Dinner One

Cottage Pie

Ingredients

3 tbsp vegetable oil • 500 gm mince beef • 1 onion, finely chopped •
2 carrots, chopped • 2 celery sticks, chopped •
1 garlic clove, finely chopped •3 tbsp gluten-free plain flour •
1 tbsp tomato puree • 500 ml beef stock • 2 tbsp Worcestershire sauce

Mash

3 large potatoes, chopped • 25 gm butter

Method

1. Heat the oil in a pan and fry mince until browned; set aside once cooked.
2. Put a little more oil in the pan and add veg (carrot, onion, celery) fry gently until soft, about 20 minutes.
3. Add garlic and plain flour along with tomato purée, increase the heat and cook out the flour for a few minutes.
4. Return the beef to the pan and mix it all together.
5. Add stock and reduce slightly, adding Worcestershire sauce.
6. Preheat oven to 220 C/200 C (fan)/gas mark 7.
7. Cook potatoes until tender, drain and add butter, mash until smooth.
8. Add meat and vegetables to an ovenproof dish, topping with mashed potato.
9. Place in the centre of the oven and bake for 20–30 minutes until the top is golden.
10. Dish up and enjoy.

Roast Lamb

Ingredients

Leg of lamb • Maris Piper potatoes, 4 large, halved • 3 carrots, chopped •
3 florets cauliflower • 4 frozen Yorkshire puddings • Gravy, instant

Method

1. Preheat oven to 220 C/200 C (fan)/gas mark 7.
2. Roast the lamb according to the instructions on the packet.
3. 1 hour prior to the lamb's end cooking time, add the potatoes to the same roasting tin.
4. 40 minutes prior to the lamb's end cooking time, add the carrots to the same roasting tin.
5. Place the cauliflower in a saucepan, cover with water and bring to the boil for around 15 minutes.
6. 5 minutes prior to the lamb's end cooking time, add the frozen Yorkshire puddings to the oven.
7. Prepare the gravy according to the instructions on the instant mix tub.
8. Once the lamb is cooked, allow it to rest under some tin foil (at least 10 minutes).
9. Dish up and enjoy.

Dinner Three

Louis's Winning Pizza

NB – Warning from Fi: having never actually made this combination of pizza I cannot in all honesty say if it works – so attempt at your own risk :-)

Ingredients

1 ready-made pizza base of your choosing per person • 2 tsp tomato paste • 2 tbsp canned tuna • ½ red pepper, chopped • 1 slice ham, chopped • 2 tsp sweet chilli sauce • ½ cup mozzarella

Method

1. Preheat oven according to cooking instructions on pizza base.
2. Spread tomato paste and sweet chilli sauce on the base evenly.
3. Top with tuna, sprinkle pepper and ham and then finish with cheese topping.
4. Cook as instructed.
5. Dish up and enjoy.

Spaghetti Bolognese, Dad's version

Ingredients

1 tsp oil • 500 g beef mince • 1 onion, finely chopped •
½ cup mushrooms, finely chopped • ½ cup carrots, finely chopped •
½ cup celery, finely chopped • 4 full adult measures dried spaghetti •
300 ml boiling water • 2 tsp tomato paste • 250 ml tomato passata •
1 tsp mixed herbs • 1 tsp Worcestershire sauce (optional)

Method

1. In a large saucepan warm the oil and add onions, celery and carrots. Sweat until tender.
2. Add mushrooms and sweat down.
3. Add beef mince and cook for around 3–5 minutes, until all mince is cooked.
4. Mix tomato purée, passata and herbs in a separate container and then add to pan with mince and veg.
5. Allow to simmer gently for at least 20 minutes, or until thickened.
6. In a separate pan, bring 300 ml of water to boil and add spaghetti, cooking until tender – 5–7 minutes.
7. Dish up and enjoy.

Dinner Five

Bangers and Mash

Ingredients

4 Maris Piper potatoes, chopped • 1 pack sausages • 1 red onion, sliced •
Gravy, instant • 1 tbsp butter • 2 tsp vegetable oil

Method

1. Preheat oven to gas mark 7.
2. Add chopped potatoes into boiling water, cook soft.
3. Once soft, drain water and add butter and mash.
4. In a frying pan, add 1 tsp vegetable oil, and gently fry off sausages.
5. Place oil and sliced onions in an ovenproof dish, then put sausages on the top.
6. Place in the pre heated oven for around 40 minutes or until cooked.
7. Make up gravy as instructed on packet.
8. Once sausages are cooked, add the cooked sliced onions into the gravy.
9. Dish up and enjoy.

Chicken Enchiladas

Ingredients

1 onion, chopped or sliced • 1 tbsp vegetable oil •
1 garlic clove, crushed (or cheat and use that tube stuff) •
1 tsp paprika • 1 tsp chilli powder • ½ tsp ground cumin •
500 g passata • 1 tbsp brown sugar • 1 tbsp cider vinegar

For enchiladas

2 onions, sliced (Fi likes them chopped!) • 1 yellow pepper, sliced •
3 tbsp oil • 2 garlic cloves, finely chopped (or a tube of garlic paste) •
1 red chilli, finely chopped • 4 chicken breasts, finely sliced •
400 g red kidney beans • 8 tortillas •
100 g grated Cheddar or whatever cheese you like

Method

1. Start by making the enchilada sauce. Put the onion into a medium saucepan with the olive oil and cook over a medium heat for 7–8 minutes, or until soft and just starting to brown at the edges.

2. Add the crushed garlic and cook for a further minute. Keep stirring, as garlic can burn really quickly. Add the smoked paprika, chilli powder and ground cumin, mix well and cook for a further 30 seconds. Add the passata, brown sugar and vinegar to the pan, season well with salt and freshly ground black pepper and cook over a low–medium heat for 10–15 minutes until thickened slightly.

3. Preheat oven to 190 C/170 C/gas mark 5.

4. For the enchiladas, heat half of the olive oil in a large frying pan, add

the sliced onions and peppers and cook over a medium heat for 2 minutes, or until just tender and starting to caramelise at the edges. Add the garlic and red chilli and cook for a further 30 seconds. Remove from the pan and set aside.

5. Heat the remaining oil in the frying pan, add the chicken and cook quickly over a medium heat until cooked through and golden brown, I always do the 'pink' check with chicken.

6. Return the onion and pepper mixture to the pan, add half of the enchilada sauce and drained kidney beans, season well and cook for a further minute.

7. Lay the flour tortillas on the work surface and divide the chicken mixture between them. Roll the flour tortillas around the filling into a cylinder and arrange neatly in an ovenproof dish. Spoon the remaining enchilada sauce over the top and put the cheese all over the top.

8. Bake for about 15–20 minutes, or until the filling is piping hot and the cheese bubbling. The bubbling cheese is vital!!!

9. Dish up and enjoy.

Roast Chicken Dinner

Ingredients

Large fresh chicken • 2 tbsp vegetable oil • 4 large potatoes, chopped •
2 large carrots, sliced • 4 leaves green cabbage, sliced •
1 packet ready-mix stuffing • Gravy, instant

Method

1. Preheat oven to 220 C/200 C (fan)/gas mark 7 and prepare the chicken as directed.
2. Put the oil in an ovenproof dish and add chicken.
3. Place the vegetables in water and bring to the boil and cook until tender, about 20 minutes.
4. Dish up and enjoy.

Jacket Potatoes and Salad

Ingredients

4 large King Edward potatoes • 2 tsp vegetable oil • 2 tomatoes •
½ cucumber • ½ red onion • ½ red pepper • ½ yellow pepper •
½ carrot • ½ lettuce • 1 tsp vegetable oil • 1 tsp lemon juice • Salt

Method

1. Preheat oven to 220 C/200 C (fan)/gas mark 7.
2. Scrub the potatoes and cut a cross into the tops of all, place in ovenproof dish and coat with vegetable oil.
3. Cook in oven for roughly 1 hr 30 mins.
4. Wash all ingredients for salad and allow to dry.
5. Cut all ingredients to desired size.
6. Add the dressing of vegetable oil, lemon juice and salt.
7. Dish up and enjoy.

Fish Pie

Ingredients

500g Maris Piper potatoes, chopped • 200 ml milk • 10 g butter •
10 g plain flour • 1 pack fish pie mix • Handful fresh chives •
Handful frozen sweetcorn • Handful frozen peas • Handful frozen carrots

Method

1. Boil potatoes until soft, drain and mash with half of the butter.
2. Put remaining butter in large frying pan and add flour. Heat gently, stirring regularly for 1–2 minutes.
3. Gradually whisk in milk, then bring to the boil, stirring to avoid lumps. Cook for 3–4 minutes.
4. Preheat oven to 220 C/200 C (fan)/gas mark 7.
5. Empty fish pie mix into saucepan and stir in.
6. Spoon mix into ovenproof dish and top with chives.
7. Top with mashed potatoes.
8. Bake for 20 minutes.
9. Dish up and enjoy.

Dinner Twelve

Chicken Kebabs

Ingredients

500 g chicken breast or pieces • 1 leek, sliced • 1 carrot, sliced •
1 red pepper, sliced • 1 yellow pepper, sliced • 1 vegetable stock cube •
2 tbsp water • Salad if desired

Method

1. Assemble kebabs using meat and chosen veg, sliding each onto a skewer.
2. Mix stock cube with a little water to make a paste.
3. Drizzle paste over kebabs and allow to marinate for 30 minutes.
4. Cook over grill for at least 10 minutes.
5. Dish up and enjoy.

Spaghetti Bolognese, Nan's version

Ingredients
50 g dried spaghetti • 2 tbsp water • 500 g minced beef •
1 red onion, chopped • 1 celery stick, chopped •
1 jar shop-brand Bolognese sauce

Method
1. Put 2 tbsp of water in a pan and allow it to simmer, adding red onion and celery. Allow to soften.
2. Add mince to vegetable mix and brown.
3. In separate saucepan add spaghetti and cover with water, bring to the boil and allow to cook for a further 5–7 minutes until soft.
4. When mince is cooked, pour over Bolognese sauce and allow to simmer for another 5–10 minutes.
5. Dish up and enjoy.

You've read Lawson's story…

Next, read Annie's.

Coming 2022.

Lightning Source UK Ltd.
Milton Keynes UK
UKHW040634261021
392861UK00001B/28